Tales from Portents

Other Books by Lou Paduano

Signs of Portents

Thank you for reading!
Lo Paduan

Tales from Portents

A Greystone Collection

Lou Paduano

Eleven Ten Publishing
BUFFALO, NEW YORK

Copyright © 2016 by Lou Paduano
All rights reserved. This book or any portion thereof may not be reproduced or used in any manner whatsoever without the express written permission of the publisher except for the use of brief quotations in a book review.

Eleven Ten Publishing
P.O. Box 1914
Buffalo, NY 14226

Publisher's note: This is a work of fiction. Names, characters, places, and incidents either are the product of the author's imagination or are used fictitiously. Any resemblance to actual events, locales, or persons, living or dead, is entirely coincidental.

Printed in the United States of America
Edited, formatted, and interior design by Kristen Corrects, Inc.
Cover art design by Kit Foster Design

First edition published 2017

Library of Congress Cataloguing in Publication Data
Paduano, Lou
Tales from Portents / Lou Paduano

LCCN: 2016920804
ISBN-13: 978-1-944965-02-0 (paperback)
ISBN-13: 978-1-944965-03-7 (eBook)

For my parents, who made all things possible.

TABLE OF CONTENTS

Resurrectionists	1
The Great Divide	93
Gremlins	135
View from Above	177
Eyes in the Storm	217
The Consultant	255

RESURRECTIONISTS

CHAPTER ONE

Kelli Andrews couldn't sleep. It was the same routine every night: an hour or two of deep sleep…and then the nightmares started. Work, the kids, bills, the never-ending holidays. Plenty to choose from but the best were the mix and match set that spanned childhood fears with the mundane nature of her life.

Emptiness greeted her rousing, the other half of the bed vacant. Marc was missing again. Kelli sat up, rubbing the dreariness out of her eyes. The clock beamed in bright red. Barely 5:00 in the morning, the sky still black. She wondered how long he had been away, if he even came to bed.

She thought this was over, that Marc worked through this. The late nights. The disconnect from everyone and everything. Sleepless nights of channel surfing and roaming the neighborhood. Almost daily since the death of his mother three months earlier.

Kelli persevered, although she had no choice in the matter. Two kids not even in double digits and a job to keep them in their modest yet suffocating mortgage. A breakdown was not in the offering for her, though she could have used a nice stretch in a padded cell, if only for a decent night's rest.

Death affected everyone differently. She hadn't shed a tear over the last few months, the loss a blessing after years of suffering from debilitating illnesses and physical pain. But her husband of twelve years took the passing hard.

Things changed a month ago. A reprieve, a return to normalcy—or so Kelli thought. Seeing the empty bed, she wondered if she was trying to convince herself more than anyone. Out of need. For the kids. For herself.

Her ankles popped as her feet connected with the soft carpet. Despite the nightmares, she was surprised how long she had slept without interruption. It showed, her back struggling to straighten, her balance precarious on her trek to the hallway. She preferred the idea of another two or three hours of rest but her bladder won out.

The door squealed upon opening and she held her breath. Waking the kids was not an option, especially with the chance of a little more sleep still in the cards even after a trip to the bathroom. And the hunt for Marc. She would check the couch first. He was most likely passed out, drool running down his chin. There was the chance he was still awake, teary-eyed and lost in memory, the television a distraction from the photo albums that had become a permanent staple of the coffee table lately.

Halfway across the hall, inching slowly like a covert operative, Kelli stopped. A figure stood at the end of the hall—a small shadow centered among the darkness. Matted brown hair and wearing Spider-Man pajamas, her son startled her with his presence.

"Grandma's here," he said, his seven-year-old voice booming in the early morning graveyard that was their home.

Kelli shook her head. "What? Quinn, baby, it's too early."

Quinn walked up to her. His hand slipped into hers and he pulled her down the hall. The bathroom faded from view, like the nightmares of the last few hours.

Kelli struggled to keep up with the boy's enthusiasm, her mind even slower to question their destination. They owned a small home, compact and single story. The hallway that led to their bedrooms and the single full bath (which would never be enough for all four of them) fed into the living room, which connected to the kitchen. The sound of movement from the latter caused her to hold back at the threshold of the former.

Quinn looked to her, puzzled, pulling harder. "Come on, Mommy."

Her confusion didn't subdue her senses. She recognized it: the sound of eggs frying on the stove and the smell of bacon sizzling on the griddle. It woke her up, the cloud of her deep sleep fading. Her smile returned.

Marc was back. *Really* back. For good this time. So ambitious, making up for lost time, he set to work making breakfast. A little early—by about two hours—but the effort behind it all bolstered her. Helping to keep her going after the burden of the last few months.

Her delusion ended quickly.

Lily, her four-year-old daughter, sat at the kitchen table. Quinn joined her, smiling and giggling, their plates full of food that would never be eaten. Next to her sat Marc, munching on a slice of bacon.

"What's all this?" Kelli asked, confused by the sound of cooking while everyone sat around the table.

The confusion ended with her arrival. A figure rounded the corner, stepping into the light, carrying two plates of eggs—over-easy and dabbled with enough pepper to clear your sinuses. A staple of only one person Kelli Andrews knew.

Her mother-in-law stopped, pointing at the empty table chair. "Take a seat, dear. You look pale. Have you been eating enough?"

Kelli froze, unable to think. Unable to speak. Her husband grinned, digging into his freshly prepared breakfast.

"Isn't it great, honey?"

His wife failed to agree. As she stared at the dead woman in her kitchen, she only had one response.

Kelli Andrews screamed.

CHAPTER TWO

Detective Greg Loren was late. As usual. The pattern that started by happenstance had grown into the man's custom. A habit, one more and more in his own control, yet completely out of reach. The same could be said of his personal grooming, to which the bare minimum was completed. A comb to his overgrown hair. No razor to his face. He opted for a ratty T-shirt from the laundry pile rather than make the trek to the Laundromat down the street. Thankfully most of the shirt was covered by the one suit jacket in his closet that didn't reek of old cigarettes, the reminder almost too powerful for the former smoker. Loren was a mess of a human, the fact more than obvious with a quick glance in the mirror—*if* he bothered to look at one.

He was late.

At least I remembered to brush my damn teeth this time.

The steps of the Caldwell Courthouse spanned half a block. Roman pillars of stark white separated the entrance, each one engraved with the famous speeches of the city's founders. From William Rath, the man who first named Portents back in the 1890s, to Wilbur Caldwell himself, the first judge, a man who built the law in the city from the ground up as structurally sound as the building. True men. Proud men. Men that stood for something more than themselves, making their stories captured and relayed for generations. What Loren stood for was lost in a gray cloud that had covered him for what felt like months.

Except today. Myron Jacobs, a scumbag of the worst degree, was due for his day in court. A day to put an end to his criminal career, thanks to the work of Loren. The detective was not going to let it slip away. Despite being unable to connect Jacobs to the homicide that Loren had tried to pin to him, Loren's investigation brought to light Jacobs' drug dealing operation. Loren needed the win, one way or the other. Even late to the show, this was his time to shine.

It ended quickly.

As he reached for the front door of the courthouse along Northern Boulevard, Loren was halted by a familiar face. The door opened before him and the tired eyes of Captain Alejo Ruiz greeted him.

"Hold up, Greg."

"Ruiz? I know I'm late but—"

Ruiz stopped him, pulling him away from incoming traffic. Loren caught a glimpse of District Attorney Sitwell and her colleagues glaring at him during their transition away from the doors. The pair stopped at a nearby bench, Ruiz's arms crossing his chest.

"You're always late."

Loren grinned, sitting at the bench. He fiddled with his tie, ironing out the massive wrinkles with his fingers. "So it's a fashionable thing then. Great."

"No." Ruiz sighed. "It's an annoying thing and not great. But today it doesn't matter. Or maybe it does. What the hell do I know anymore when it comes to you?"

Loren was surprised by the tone that hung on his every word—bitterness. Sadness. Concern. But worst of all, the thing Loren swore he never wanted to hear from those around him.

Pity.

The fault lay with him. He had not been an easy man to be around lately. Especially one to supervise, on or off the job. His anger ran hot, his moods soured on a dime. The reason—like the gray cloud around him, like the perpetual lateness for every event big and small—escaped him. In fact, the reason for *everything* seemed to escape him, including their pow-wow outside the courthouse instead of celebrating the conviction of a killer like Jacobs.

"What are you talking about, Ruiz?"

"Jacobs walked."

Loren flinched. "Bullshit."

"Greg—"

"Your sense of humor has always sucked, Ruiz, but I don't see what's funny about—"

"It's not a joke," Ruiz replied. He towered over the sitting detective, blocking the haze of the morning sun.

"I had him dead to rights," Loren snapped, hands clenched tight to his side. "The evidence was solid."

He spent weeks on the case, never able to connect him to the death of a young woman from the Knoll. It was an old girlfriend of Jacobs. No murder weapon. No witnesses. Loren was about to lose him. About to let a killer walk. Not an option for him.

So Loren had turned to Jacobs' other enterprise. Drugs. Tracking down the evidence, nailing down sources—all less than reputable, but with the right incentive they were willing to flip on Jacobs to reduce their own sentences. Most of it was circumstantial…but then Loren located Jacobs' stash—and his records. All came together to lock the arrest in place.

"The evidence is gone," Ruiz said, unable to look at the stunned detective. "Misplaced. Lost. Tucked under some rock never to be seen."

"It was in lockup. You saw it."

"I did."

"Then who the hell—?" Loren stopped, catching the concern on his friend's face. His head fell into his hands. "Dammit. They're blaming me."

Ruiz nodded. "They are."

"Did you—?"

Ruiz waved him down. "I defended you but that doesn't mean crap to these people. Sitwell is going over my head. She's been running her 'tough on drugs' platform and this looks to be a swift kick up her backside more than anyone else in terms of public profiles. She has to save face. And you…?"

"I get it," Loren muttered. "It flows downstream."

"They're talking about an internal review," Ruiz said. "Since this isn't the first case that's been blown."

Loren knew the implication: "the first case that hasn't been blown *by you*," Ruiz really meant. It was the second such instance in the last three months. Both connected to Jacobs and made appearances even worse.

Loren didn't care. He was focused on the review. "Mathers?"

"Will be there in his Sunday best," Ruiz said.

"Great."

Ruiz's look softened; he had the eyes of a father, not a superior. "I'll do what I can."

"Ruiz," Loren said, shaking his head.

The middle-aged Hispanic waved him down. "Stop. I will. But whatever this is lately—whatever is going on with you—it doesn't play well for you. You want to talk, you know where to find me, Greg. I hope you do."

Loren turned away. "I'm fine, Captain."

"Right."

Loren watched the worried captain depart, his head low and hands buried deep in his pockets. For as much as the DA might have lost face this morning with Jacobs, Ruiz was in worse shape. No surprise, with Mathers ready to jump all over him at the first opportunity.

Something needed to change. Loren needed answers, not only to what happened to the evidence in question, but also about his lack of direction of late. The depression. The anger. All of it.

"Detective?"

A shadow fell over Loren—tall and thin, stretching over the grizzled face of the melancholy detective. Loren peered up to see the man whose gray hair had predominantly replaced a thick head of brown. Assistant District Attorney Richard Crowne stared down at him with soft, blue eyes.

"I didn't mean to intrude."

"Not at all," Loren said, shifting to the side of the bench. Richard joined him, knees popping under his tightly pressed pants. "What can I do for you…?"

"Richard. Or Rich, even. The title gets a little overblown."

Loren smirked. "It is a mouthful."

"It is," the attorney agreed. "My business card barely fits my phone number because of it."

"Not that you need people calling you."

"Please."

Loren chuckled. The pair had played the same tune for years. Friends had that effect, though the term was almost foreign to the detective. They were not companions in the traditional sense. More like bound together through a shared experience. The one that seemed to link Loren to more people than he realized.

Loss.

Richard Crowne lost his wife, Jennifer, three years earlier. She took a bullet meant for her husband and he watched her die. Loren worked the case. The killer ended up with life and no chance in hell at parole. Their time together, going over suspects and finding the one that hated Crowne most of all, cemented their bond.

Loren knew friendship wasn't the reason behind the visit today.

"Is this about the case?"

"Is what?"

"You? Here right now? Is it—?"

Richard shook his head. "No. No way. Well, yes. But not the way you're thinking. Sorry."

"It's fine. Take your time."

Richard cleared his throat, setting his briefcase to the side of the bench. "I heard what happened in there and thought you might need a friend. Someone who understands sleepless nights and empty hallways. When I lost Jennifer—"

"I appreciate it, Richard," Loren shot back, stopping the man's sentiment. "I'm fine. Promise."

"I see," Richard said. His voice was soft, understanding immediately. Richard stood, reaching for his briefcase. "Greg. If you ever—"

"I don't."

"Right then. Detective." Richard nodded and started down the stairs, following Ruiz's route downtown toward the Central Precinct—where Loren needed to be next. To figure things out. The missing evidence. Jacobs.

This was supposed to be a good day.

Loren rubbed his eyes, his hands muffling the loud string of curses escaping his lips. He let the words settle in an attempt to find peace in them. Unsuccessful, Loren stood. The Caldwell Courthouse stood in the shadow of the hazy sun, tall and proud like the men behind its construction. Mocking Loren.

The frustrated detective left the steps of the courthouse, scanning the block on Northern Boulevard. Central was three blocks to the east along Evans. Central meant work. Responsibility. Loren turned west, spotting a hole-in-the-wall bar called McDuffie's.

Responsibility could wait.

CHAPTER THREE

Pine Woods Cemetery was not Soriya Greystone's usual stomping grounds. She preferred to stay away from the dead as often as possible. The concept of the end stirred up uncomfortable memories, a lack of control that she clung to desperately to maintain her confidence, her poise, her true power.

She had no choice in the matter, however. In typical fashion she screwed up and paid for her mistake. Running in the darkness of the graveyard that encompassed eight city blocks, she chased after her quarry. Young and much faster than she imagined, he carried a thin, wooden carving knife with an ornately crafted handle. Thick spirals dug into the wood in the shape of a crest.

It started with a murder. An older man found dead in his rat-infested apartment. Small puncture marks, tightly grouped, littered the corpse. Little blood spatter marked the scene or the body. And no blood left *in* the body.

Exsanguination. That put it firmly in Soriya's wheelhouse.

One other detail put her on the hunt for the young man racing through the cemetery: the knife. Out of all the puncture marks, one clear cut ran along the man's arm—*fresh*. Moments before his end. The old man, George Newborne, was targeted. It was personal.

That gave her a clear path, one that led her to Christian Fuller. Ten years ago his parents were killed, the murderer never caught. Or at least never jailed. Newborne was arrested for the crime but never went to trial. Insufficient evidence. Not to Fuller. Not to the lone survivor of such a horrific event.

Soriya cursed, scraping along headstones in the dark. Blood ran along her arm in a thin stream down her wrist. This should have been handled better. It would have too if Loren had shown up. They were supposed to confront Fuller together. But her calls to him went unanswered, right to voicemail. Loren didn't want to be bothered. Couldn't be bothered. It was starting to be a pattern with the man. Her so-called *partner*.

Still, she could have handled things. Fuller was a creature of habit. A stop at the local deli every Wednesday on his way home from work for the same overloaded sandwich. All she had to do was intercept him. She got cocky—she always got cocky. When he noticed her, he bolted down the block for the cemetery as the sun descended toward the horizon.

Idiot.

Fuller stopped, breathing hard. He leaned on a nearby tree, lurching forward as Soriya approached rapidly. The blade rose up in his hand, and the young woman skidded to a halt on the soft earth.

"Drop the blade," she yelled, hand inching for the pouch along her right hip. Pink ribbons skidded loose down her left side.

"I did what was right," Fuller said. Tears filled his eyes—the scared, lonely kid returning.

"You killed a man," Soriya replied, inching closer.

"He murdered my parents!"

"You don't know that."

Fuller shook his head, the blade just over his left arm. "I do. I've always known."

"Then you should have gone to the police."

"No. He was mine." The blade fell to his arm, Fuller's eyes wide.

"Don't!" Soriya called out.

Too late. Blood soaked the wooden blade, running down to the ornate handle.

"And so are you," Fuller finished. A spatter of blood fell to the ground. The earth shifted and moaned from the act, the sacrifice given to it. The blade might have made the cut on Newborne's body, but it didn't kill him. Something else did. The blade was just a summoning tool. The puncture marks made it clear for what.

Vampires.

The ground ripped open around Soriya. Fuller watched for only a second before fleeing the scene. Soriya noticed the blood dried to her skin down her right side.

"Great."

From out of the earth they came. Large red eyes and snapping jaws full of fangs. Their bodies the size of babies, their skin like porcelain, but deadly. And hungry for blood. Her blood.

Jenglot.

Some believed they were once human. Others believed the Jenglot were dolls brought to life through a summoning. Or through blood. To Soriya, the truth appeared to be a combination of the two theories. Not that this was a time for study—not by a long shot.

The Jenglot screamed, their voices high and shrill. Soriya ducked under the first, the ribbons from Kali swatting the next away. Fighting infants never made it on her bucket list and she sure as hell wasn't going to fall to them. One clomped down on her ankle, causing her to scream. She kicked the beast away, slamming it hard against a nearby tombstone.

"This is why I don't want kids," she muttered.

Fuller was a hundred feet away already—well on his way to an effective escape. With eyes locked on her target Soriya continued to fight through the mass of vampiric infants.

Smiling the whole time.

Fuller never saw the arm stretched out in front of him. He had been too busy looking back at his victim. By the time it came into focus it was too late. He slammed into the arm and fell back hard on the ground. The blade skittered away. Arthritic fingers snatched the wooden weapon before Fuller could recover.

"No!" the young man shouted.

Too little, too late. Mentor snapped the blade in half.

The shift came about instantly. The Jenglot, too numerous to defeat, shrank back away from the bleeding yet still swinging Soriya. Little mouths screeched in anger, their pint of blood denied them with the breaking of their link to the world. They crawled back through the open chasms in the ground surrounding her, the holes closing up behind the demons' retreat.

Soriya wiped her brow, staggering to greet her teacher. Mentor bent low, binding Fuller's hands tight behind his back.

"I had him," Soriya said. "You didn't have to—"

Mentor sighed. "Just say it, child. One time."

"Thank you," she said through gritted teeth.

He stood, a slight groan escaping him. His right leg was acting up again. "You're welcome."

Fuller glared up at her, eyes full of fury. She decked him across the cheek and he slumped to the ground, unconscious.

"I was fine, though," she said, shaking the aftershock from her knuckles.

"It looked that way to me."

"You heard what he—"

"Yes," Mentor said. He picked up the pieces of the broken blade, tucking them into his coat pocket. "Though how he came upon the blade is a mystery. I haven't seen one like it since the Luminaries left their library."

"You could ask him," she said with a grin, knowing the answer. "When he wakes up, that is."

Mentor shook his head. "I'll learn. In time. Someday you will regard patience over the thrill of the chase."

"Loren was supposed to…." She stopped, catching the glare. "I know."

"Yet you persist with the man."

"Tell me how you really feel."

Mentor shrugged then stopped. He bent low, hand resting on the headstone closest. "Strange."

"Mentor? What is it?"

His hand ran along the ground, pulling up dirt. Small grains of soil trailed between his fingers back to join its brethren. "This grave."

"One of many."

Mentor threw her a look and she yielded. "Years old, but look: fresh dirt. Recently seeded even."

"I don't understand. What does it mean?"

"I'm not sure," Mentor replied. He stood slowly, leaning hard against the stone. "I believe someone dug up this body and is trying to hide the fact."

Soriya glanced around nervously. She hated cemeteries. She hated being surrounded by the dead, reminded of the end to come. The everlasting stillness of eternity. But to disturb that peace? Who would do something like that?

She circled the stone, peering into the darkness surrounding them. The multitude of the dead. Her foot slid along the ground and felt an edge. Deeper shadows circled them.

"Mentor?"

He turned, following her gaze before joining her. They both looked into the open grave beside them then turned to four others littering the grounds nearby.

"Whatever they're doing," she said, "I don't think they're hiding it anymore."

CHAPTER FOUR

Everything was black.

He wanted to scream, to shout into the darkness that surrounded him, but he found no voice. He could not move, his eyes unable to adjust to the thick shade. He was lost.

A sound caught his ear. The darkness shifted, growing lighter, yet the cloud remained around him. A fog settled over him then lowered further and he could see objects. Out of focus like the scents surrounding him. Becoming clearer with each breath. Lilacs. Like the ones Beth kept in a window box off the front window. Her excuse to keep an eye on the city.

He was on the rooftop. Their rooftop. He had only been up there a few times, always at Beth's will. He never took to heights. Saying no to his wife was never an option, however. He hated to disappoint her.

Yet he did. In the end.

Obscure images sharpened, the world screaming into focus. She stood on the ledge, always on the ledge. A red sundress with yellow lilies along the trim, running up her curves. Her blonde hair shimmered in the light, resting on her shoulders.

Beth.

She turned and smiled, the smile that took her away from him.

"Greg."

Greg Loren woke with a start. Her voice rang in his ears and his hands fought to cover them, to block out the sound. It had been the same nightmare for weeks. Always ending the same—with his refusal to listen any further.

Afraid to listen further.

The couch groaned beneath him. His back followed suit, aching from the sag in the cushions. The wood frame of the ancient furniture begged for a reprieve that would never come. The television beamed soft light on his face. Another nameless comedy no one would remember in six months. Primetime television at its finest.

Loren rubbed his eyes, his hands scraping along his thickening beard. He needed a shave and a shower. He would settle for the latter. First, he went for the window, a stick of gum substituting his morning cigarette ritual. *Filthy habit.* Morning was a misnomer, though.

It was night.

He was late for work again, the afternoon spent at the bar across from the courthouse, another mistake piled on the rest. Like the Jacobs case. Like everything lately.

He didn't care.

Nor did he care about the four missed calls chiming on his cell phone, the buzzing echoing along the coffee table in the center of the room. Soriya. Late for work meant late for their planned meeting, one forgotten among the pitcher of beer and the sports talk blaring from six televisions suspended over the bar. He couldn't keep an appointment but knew every off-season move made by the Blackhawks over the last week. Priorities.

Soriya didn't need him. His role in her investigation was superfluous, the leads all stemming from her work, not his connections in the department. She was better off without him. The same with Ruiz.

Ruiz.

He needed to get to work. Needed to figure out where his head was at with the job. With everything. Loren shambled away from the window, not bothering to draw the curtain.

The bedroom sat at the back of the apartment, the shadows always staring at him during his trips to the toilet. Its use had become that of a giant closet, the floor taken over by laundry baskets of unwashed clothes. The bed remained made, had been for months, which was also the last time he decided to dry-clean the comforter and wash the unused sheets.

A monument to his former life.

He tried to sleep there once, tried to move beyond the loss of his wife. It didn't take, couldn't take. The couch was his refuge, but even that plagued him now, the nightmares still fresh in his mind.

"*Greg.*"

Beth called for him. Almost begging him...but for what?

He should have left it all behind. The apartment, the furniture, everything. Years ago. But he didn't, couldn't. Not with the chance of some link to his wife, some clue into what happened to her so long ago. Some sign that answered all his questions about her death.

Loren moved for the shower, throwing off his ratty T-shirt, knowing one would soon replace it from the laundry basket of unwashed clothes. The shower would be enough. Enough to drown out the sound of his wife's voice. For a little while at least. Never for long.

The past refused to abate.

Like his nightmares. And the angel caught in them.

CHAPTER FIVE

Richard Crowne missed his wife.
Their marriage was the bright spot in a troubled life of obligation and personal responsibility. Jennifer found a way to lighten the mood, to crack the right joke at the right time with the right people. No matter the situation, she found no discomfort. Nothing she would not do to help her husband thrive in his increasingly political position in the city.
A bullet ended that.
They were headed to dinner, a simple engagement, one planned for just the two of them. Unfortunately, there were hands to shake, questions to be asked, and the flow of favors to pocket for a later date.
But it started with dinner and catching up. She did most of the talking at these occasions. His preference. He loved being able to just listen to someone, rather than analyze their every word, monitor their posture, catch every inflection for nervous tics, for tells of a less than truthful nature.
Never with Jennifer.
Outside the restaurant, dinner was forgotten when the crashing sound of the bullet sliced through their laughter. It took him by surprise, the sharp pain in his right shoulder. He fell, reeling back, Jennifer falling with him, locked in his grip. She cried out for him, covering his body. More thunder ripped through the air, once, twice and a final third time.
He only saw her. Her brown eyes. Her ruby lips. The way her black hair sparkled under the starlight. She rubbed his cheek, the cold of her fingertips shocking him, dulling the pain in his shoulder. A single tear dripped down from wide orbs of light and then they closed.

He screamed her name. He shook her off and cradled her close. She had shielded him from the final assault. She saved him at the expense of her life.

He screamed for a long time.

Three years did little to change his feelings. The loss. The pain in his right shoulder when the weather turned bitter cold. He missed her, and nothing would ever change that.

Hands patted his back as he took his position in the closest pew of the church. Smiles from well-wishers, passing on messages of good luck with each nod and utterance. The church was busier than usual. It always was when they performed the ceremony.

The Andrews family sat across from him, a family reunited with a recent loss of their own. They were surrounded by others, patrons both recent and from the start of the project, all with a look of wonderment on their faces. Richard shared the same look.

It was time.

The altar was ready, the figure upon it covered by a white sheet. The room hummed, the great machines beneath the church whirring to life. It caused a slight vibration along the stone pillars stretching to the roof. Richard followed them to the ceiling. Ornate glass replaced masonry, allowing everyone to peer out into the night sky of Portents through tinted glass stained blood red.

A hand fell upon Richard's shoulder. He turned to see the hooded figure before him, only his thick, black beard noticeable under the dim lights. The Founder. The man who started the endeavor, the man who found Richard, and who saved him from the torment of his life without Jennifer.

They met at a fundraising gala downtown in passing, sharing stories of loss. From that first connection, Richard had come to know the Founder as a friend and more. It all led to this moment.

Richard's moment.

"It's time, Richard," the Founder said, and the world stopped. "Are you ready?"

Richard could not find the words. A simple nod escaped him, his eyes cast to the figure on the altar. The figure he waited three years to see again.

He was ready. He had been since the first crack of thunder. Since learning about the church from the Founder. Since he first witnessed the work being done by the Church of the Second Coming.

Since he first saw one of them *rise*.

He tried to move on, tried not to let his wife's death stop him from living. But he couldn't. He missed her too much. He needed her back.

It was time for her to return.

CHAPTER SIX

Greg Loren never dreamed of being a paper pusher. Never once in his thirty-five years of life did he feel the pull to the corporate world, the sit behind a desk and shuffle reports around to look busy sort of situation. Never. Yet as the stapler clanked under his tightened grip, he felt like nothing more than a corporate shill.

Paperwork was a necessary evil. Of course it was in a world piled high with accountability. The police, especially in the modern age, where every mistake found its way into the national spotlight, had to cover their asses as much as the next guy. Witness testimony stamped and approved next to arrest profiles, and situational reports left the exhausted detective feeling empty.

And hungry.

The malaise washing over Loren was the worst part. He dreamed of the job as a kid. Working the beat then getting his shield. Nothing could have been better. Saving lives. Catching killers. Better than any television show could depict. All completely real and made for him. Yet he failed to remember the name of the dead kid with the smear of cheddar cheese topping on his pants or the killer with the munchies. Gone. Lost. Like Loren. Another piece missing of the puzzle and the grizzled detective had no inkling why, or how to snap back into the world.

No one questioned him. Not even after manhandling the stapler for the last three minutes across from the break room. There were stares. There always were. Ever since Beth. Ever since he separated himself from the pack, a self-imposed social exile.

Another mistake. Another regret. Sometimes, anyway.

"Greg, old buddy," a voice called out, joined by a hand slapping his arm. The stapler fell to the table, scattering a pile of paperclips along the surface and to the floor below. Loren gritted his teeth, glaring at the appendage locked on his shirtsleeve.

"Standish?" he asked in a low growl. "The hand?"

Robert Standish sneered, his fangs showing. He was a beached whale with the grin of a shark. His gut protruded atop the tireless efforts of his belt, jiggling with his laughter.

"Always the same, Greg," Standish replied. He stirred a cup of coffee, the heat causing little beads of sweat along his brow.

Standish was Loren's former partner, their time together better left forgotten. They met under unusual circumstances, but his initial impression of the man never left.

He did not trust him, and he sure as hell did not like him.

Standish chuckled. "Except not quite the same from what I've heard. Trouble in paradise?"

He pointed to Ruiz's office at the end of the hall. For as long as Loren had been stationed at Central in the Detective Bureau, Ruiz's door remained open. Minus the occasional meeting or angry phone call, it was a policy with the man, an invitation to keep the lines of communication open at all times.

It was closed now and had been all shift, since their time at the courthouse that morning.

"A misunderstanding," Loren muttered with a shrug. "Your concern is touching."

Loren started for his office, pulled back by the man. "Hey now," Standish replied. "No one likes to see it happen."

Loren stopped, looking back at the man curiously. "And you have, haven't you, Standish?"

Standish went through a similar bout of missing evidence syndrome on three separate occasions. The review board found no evidence of wrongdoing on the overweight detective's part, and the case was dropped and forgotten by all except for Loren, who transferred away from the man as quickly as possible.

Loren's decision stung Standish at the time, the connotation of the man's guilt due to the request. Loren didn't care. The work came first, and being dragged down by the ineptitude of a partner with a shady history was not how he intended to spend his days.

Only now he was the inept one in the eyes of the department, wasn't he?

"Still standing though, ain't I?" Standish shrugged, throwing a friendly elbow. He leaned in closer, the smell of coffee sickening Loren almost as much as the man's grin. "How about you, Greg?"

Loren nodded, collecting his work. "I'd be lying if I said this has been fun, Standish."

"Greg," Standish said, reaching into his back pocket. He pulled out an open envelope. "You dropped this."

"What?" Loren snatched it from his hands. A letter from the sixth floor, which meant only one location: the commissioner's office.

"Two days isn't much time to figure things out, but with a friend like Ruiz there, I'm sure you don't need to worry. Not you."

Standish held the word *Ruiz* out when he spoke, as if even attempting the Hispanic's name gave him hives. It always bothered Loren, the man's ignorance toward everyone who didn't line up with his preferences. Racial. Gender. Everything. Loren's concern lay firmly on the letter in his hands. Two days until his review. He hadn't even thought of a defense, the need for one not even entering it. Two days to figure out how this happened to him again and why.

Including why Standish knew about it first.

Loren held the letter between them. "Stay the hell out of my mail, Standish."

Loren stomped down the hall, dropping his report in the bin outside Ruiz's office without looking. Standish's sneer drove him further and faster until he reached his office door. His head rested against the wooden frame, the letter tight between his fingers. It listed the commissioner and Mathers as heading up the inquiry. No help from Ruiz. Not a good sign.

The knob twisted lightly in his hand. He rubbed his eyes deeply. "Dammit. What else?"

When he opened his eyes there she was, sitting on his desk, feet dangling over the tiled floor. Soriya Greystone tilted her head, smiling all the same.

"Not the best way to start, but let's see where the night goes."

CHAPTER SEVEN

What are you doing here?

The same question repeated in his head as Loren turned the wheel of the cruiser into the parking lot outside Pine Woods Cemetery. He had cases. Quite a few, in fact, yet he had dumped them for an errand with Soriya. One out of his wheelhouse—not that he minded the switch from murderers. Homicide was a way of life but not the sum total.

Didn't mean he wanted to make a habit of chasing grave robbers either. After hearing Soriya's discovery, her interest in tracking down the culprits involved, Loren jumped at the escape from his own work. Swept up in her enthusiasm, the same way it had been for the last four years. Soriya's interest meant that there was something to it, something different, something unique. A balm from his crumbling life.

"You haven't said much," Soriya said. She sat impatiently in the passenger seat of the requisitioned patrol cruiser, her head almost completely out the window to feel the air. She hated driving around the city, so used to barreling along the streets, be it from the sewers below or the rooftops above. Out in the open air nonetheless. Loren hated feeling like an anchor around her, but he also lived in the real world. That meant cars, traffic, and road rage—the fundamentals of Portents.

He remained silent, looking around the parking lot. He spotted the security office at the far end and clicked off the headlights.

"Not that you have to," she continued, ducking inside as Loren rolled the window up. "But I have grown accustomed to your banter over time."

"Bad day," Loren replied. The engine went dead, the keys rattling against his palm. "And no, talking about it is not what I'm after."

"I figured that one out."

The night air was pungent, full-bodied. Rain was coming and soon. Not the place Loren wanted to be when it happened. Pine Woods filled the horizon in front of him, the light traffic rushing behind him. He had attended a number of services at the cemetery, mostly for work. He knew the layout, understood the manpower involved in keeping up with the grounds. The lapses in security were no surprise, not with the amount of land to cover and the lack of boots on the ground. No excuse, however, and he was grateful Beth rested comfortably four miles east at Black Rock.

Beth. His shoulders slumped with her name. He sighed, turning away from the dead. "Why bring this to me? I'm sure Mentor would have preferred—"

"Anything to keep me on the leash."

"True," Loren said, remembering the old man's penchant for controlling situations, including how he was addressed. *Mentor.* Like something from a damn comic book. "Not that you would listen."

"Exactly." She smirked.

"Not an answer though."

She stopped short of the door to the security office. "Questions need asking. You ask them nicer than me."

"Fair enough."

"Are you sure you're—?"

"I'm fine," he interrupted, pushing past her for the door. "Let's say hello."

It opened before his second knock. In the doorway stood a white-whiskered old man in full uniform, one hand hiking up his belt with each breath.

Loren cleared his throat, badge in hand. "Detective Loren and my associate." He shifted away from Soriya as he spoke, feeling her glare on his backside. "We have some questions."

The old man's face dropped, his cheeks jiggling as he spoke. "You know, don't you?"

"You might say the word is out."

He nodded, stepping aside. "Best come in then."

Loren and Soriya stepped in and the door closed. Cold air hit them like a wall, blowing from the fans set up in all four corners of the shed. Two computer stations sat in the center of the small office, camera feeds lining the back wall. A back room jutted off to the right, most likely a locker room for equipment, uniforms, and the occasional nap. Loren eyed the coffee maker then settled for a slice of gum with a roll of his baby browns. He missed smoking.

"The first one was about a week ago," the old man started. The name placard tacked to his chest read Sheppard. His eyes were sullen, his voice low, as if others might be listening. "Since then we've noticed older ones. Fresh soil over old bones."

"How many are we talking about here?"

Sheppard's eyes fell. "Eight."

"With no reports?" Loren asked loudly. Soriya remained silent, pacing the outskirts of the shed. "How is this not on the news?"

"We couldn't...." The old man stopped, shuffling to a seat in front of the security feeds. He continued the perpetual fight between his pants and gravity. "We notified the families and asked their permission to keep this internal. To try and flush out whoever could do such a horrible thing. To upset the community—"

"You mean your clientele, don't you?"

"Not mine," Sheppard answered, shaking his head. "I just work here."

"As security. Not likely if this keeps going on."

"But it is," Sheppard said. "And not just here."

Loren turned to the old man, eyes wide. "What?"

"I thought..." the security guard mumbled. He shuffled through a pile of reports by the computer, trying to avoid the detective's ire. "When you asked, I figured you knew already."

"I don't."

"We don't," Soriya joined in, and the old man jumped from his seat, away from her.

"Multiple cemeteries have been hit. Multiple times."

Loren and Soriya shared a glance. "How many are we talking about here?"

Sheppard wiped the sweat from his forehead. "Close to thirty last I heard."

Thirty. Thirty people dug up and extricated from their final resting places. How? And for what reason?

"Soriya?" Loren asked, knowing she too held the same set of questions. There was a reason she was interested. Lines drawn between what was acceptable in what she deemed *her* city. Murder was understood. Theft, a part of nature. Even with the unusual circumstances typically handled by the pair. But grave robbery? Unsettling the dead? A heinous act shared by the look on her face and in her clenched fists.

"I need names," Loren said, sensing her urgency. "For all of them."

"I only have our own," Sheppard said, moving back to his pile of papers, jostling the computer desks with his girth. "I'd have to make some calls."

Loren lifted the receiver and held it out to him. "Do it now. I need that list."

CHAPTER EIGHT

Riverfront bridged the pier and downtown. Residential neighborhoods rolled uphill, trees lining the roads. Modest homes ran in tight packs on narrow streets, growing more and more extravagant with each turn toward downtown.

Forbes Avenue ran the gap, Cape Cods interspersed with ranch-style domiciles. All well maintained, the community lush with greenery along the property lines. All uniform yet with unique flair. A garden walk-up for one, hanging baskets on the next, all accentuating the lighter side of Portents.

It took a full day to receive the list from Sheppard. A day lost to nightmares and aggravation. A phone call from three union reps about his upcoming review, something Loren still hadn't cared to put much thought into. He patiently declined their involvement, at least with the first two. By the time the third came in, he simply hung up. He knew those on the other end of the phone were protecting their own interests more than anything. The only one that could help Loren was himself and he couldn't be bothered.

Especially when the list arrived.

The count came to thirty-two. Sheppard was barely able to pass along the information let alone believe it. Loren was happy to leave the old man with that thought, hoping the internal investigation might actually become a priority in their eyes. Loren had his own thoughts on the matter, but they amounted to little. More questions than anything, part of the reason he made the trip to Riverfront with Soriya in tow.

Not that she was happy about it.

"How many is this?" she whined, her shoes squeaking around him, drowning out the sound of his own chewing. Watermelon flavor. *Filthy habit.* "I lost count an hour ago, Loren."

"Three."

She stopped outside the short white picket fence. "Liar."

He sighed. "Literally three."

The first two went nowhere. No surprise to Soriya who pointed it out with each step to the next stop. Loren *was* surprised though. People, although deceased, were missing. Their loved ones seemed detached from the news, unwilling or unable to discuss the matter. It didn't make sense. He thought for sure the father who lost his daughter in a car accident or the man down on Forbes whose mother passed three months earlier would have something to share. Even if only a minute of their time. Instead, he and Soriya met slamming doors and nothing but resistance. Hoping for some sign, some insight into the bizarre wave of crime afflicting the dead, they walked toward the next name on the list.

Much to Soriya's chagrin. She hated this part of the work. The *actual* work. When there wasn't some threat in front of her to punch and kick, some monster running around for her to sentence with the damn stone attached to her hip, she was a ball of tension. Always seeing the worst—always waiting for it, too. Sad part was she tended to be right.

Loren opened the fence and ushered her inside. "Try and suck it up, Soriya."

"But this is—"

He waved her off, noting the shadow in the front window watching their approach. "No more talking, Soriya."

A gentle knock was quickly answered by a short woman with thick glasses. She kept the door ajar only slightly.

"Yes?"

"Susan Barton? Detective Greg Loren and my associate—"

"Bodyguard."

Loren tossed the smug woman a look before returning to Susan with a disarming smile. "Colleague. We were hoping to ask you a few questions about your late husband? Thomas?"

"I don't see—"

"I understand his remains are missing," Loren continued, pressing closer to the slowly closing door. "Were you aware of this?"

Her eyes fell. "They called me. Yes."

"And you were fine with it?"

"They were looking for my Tommy," Susan said, fixing her glasses to the bridge of her nose. Her eyes remained low, away from the questioning detective. "Did they find him?"

"Not yet, I'm afraid," Loren said. He leaned on the frame beside the door, catching Soriya's wavering eyes, watching over the house curiously. "Could we step inside, ma'am? There are just a few more items to go over here."

"No."

Loren shook his head, surprised at the sudden chill in the air. "I'm sorry?"

"As well you should be," Susan replied sharply. "This is a private matter and should be handled as such."

"Mrs. Barton, please—"

The door slammed shut, and the lights flicked off. Their time was finished. Loren stepped back, hands on his hips.

"That went well."

"Want me to kick the door down?"

Loren sighed. "I have enough problems right now. Thanks."

Three strikes on the night and twenty-nine more potentials on the list. If the first three responded like Susan Barton, what chance did they have with the rest? And why shut him out at all? What was he missing?

"She's hiding something," Soriya said, leading them off the porch.

"You said that about the last two," Loren muttered, looking back at the closed door, wondering if he should knock again. He shook his head, leaving the porch for the stone walkway.

"Because it's true."

"It could be anything, Soriya. They could be hiding the fact that their home is a pigsty. Maybe hiding a lover they don't want mentioned in an official police investigation—which this is not by the way, because I don't handle grave robberies. Not yet, anyway. Or maybe, just maybe, these people are grieving and this whole thing opened up a ton of old wounds for them."

Soriya huffed, arms crossing her chest. "You don't believe that for a second. Any of it."

"I don't know what to think about this case. Come on."

She refused to budge, stamping her feet on the ground. "To the next one? How will that go any better?"

"What do you propose?"

"Anything but this," she yelled. Her arms swung out in exasperation. "Doing something to prevent another. Just doing something."

"This *is* doing something. You don't like it is all."

"Don't give me the line, Loren."

"This is the job, kid."

"Yeah. That one." Soriya turned away, the breeze catching her hair and whirling it around her like the ribbons down her left arm. Dancing in the dark. "Fine. You follow your list."

"And you?" Footsteps approached and he caught sight of a woman walking down the street.

"I'll let you know what I find out."

Loren turned back and Soriya was gone. Lost to the shadows, like always. "Great," he muttered. "Dammit, Soriya."

Frustrated and hungry, Loren shuffled down the stone pathway to the sidewalk and the white picket fence. So inviting, yet an illusion, like the answers he sought. The woman out for a stroll stood on the other side and he almost collided with her, lost in thought.

"Sorry."

"My fault," she said in little more than a whisper. Dried tears clung to her reddened cheeks. Her jacket sat opened, the shoelaces of her sneakers whipping around with each step. She left somewhere in a hurry.

"Ma'am? Can I—?"

"You spoke to my husband. Marc Andrews."

"I did but—"

"He wouldn't say anything, wouldn't tell you, but I will."

"Tell me what?" Loren asked.

"About the bodies," she said. She peered up and down the block nervously then leaned close to the detective, whispering, "They're bringing them back to life."

CHAPTER NINE

Loren smiled to the brunette behind the counter, then dropped a fiver in the empty tip jar. A mumble of thanks left her lips before she went back to cleaning the spotless counter. The exhausted detective took a sip from his steaming cup of darkness, letting it burn all the way down. Then he grabbed the cup next to his and carried both to the booth on the far side of the diner and his waiting companion.

Kelli Andrews. The wife of Marc Andrews, the man he had interviewed earlier that evening. He said he had lost his mother for the second time in the last three months—but he hadn't, according to the distraught woman in the window booth.

He placed the cup in front of Kelli, sliding across from her, the bench squealing under his weight. "Don't ask me if they got it right. I had enough trouble trying to pronounce it."

Kelli smiled. It was a sad smile that aged her in the bright lights of the diner. Her hands cupped the half coffee, half who-knows-what mixture—how they came up with these drinks was beyond the dated detective. She took a long sip. Loren watched her closely while dumping three packets of sugar in his small beverage.

"Thank you, detective," Kelli said, sliding the cup back to the center of the table.

"It's Greg. And you're welcome."

Her shoes tapped a beat under the table, her eyes unable to peel away from the clock on the far wall for more than ten seconds at a stretch. Kelli Andrews wasn't supposed to be here. The more time allowed to lapse meant more time for her to realize that fact. More time to fall in line with the rest of Loren's evening.

"Kelli, I know—"

She waved him off. "I know how it sounds."

They're bringing them back to life. Loren tried to hide his own feelings on the matter, but failed miserably. "Bringing people back from the dead? Only one way it sounds, unfortunately."

"I've seen it," she pleaded, begging to be believed.

"Your mother-in-law, right?"

She nodded. "Three months ago. She went in her sleep. Peaceful. She had been in such pain that her death was a blessing. Not to my husband, though. He became detached. Got lost for a bit. Little to no sleep. Long walks in the dark. I worried about him."

With good reason. Portents wasn't safe after the sun went down, though most didn't realize the true reason why. Loren stirred his coffee absentmindedly. "Something changed?"

"I didn't know what at first. He was just back and I was so thankful for it. The kids were too. Laughing and playing. He met someone down our street, he said."

"You're talking about Susan Barton?"

"Yes," Kelli said after another satisfying sip. "But nothing scandalous, which I hate to admit was my first thought."

"In this day and age—"

"I know," she interrupted. "She lost her husband a year ago. Heart attack. Talking with her helped him. I thought it did, anyway. There were still the long walks, the sleepless nights, but it was different now. Like he had a purpose. If I had known...."

She trailed off, staring out into the darkness. Loren joined her, giving her the time, enjoying the silence. Few cars sped by outside. One sat parked on the far side of the street. A beat-up Chevy. It looked familiar. Loren took a long sip of liquid fuel, shaking off the lack of sleep. The last thing he needed was to start feeling paranoid, even with the connections Kelli made.

"Kelli."

She shook her head, tears in her eyes. "I saw her. In my kitchen. He brought her back with these people he's met. They are bringing them all back. But that's impossible...isn't it?"

Loren's hand reached for hers. "Let me take you home. I can ask your husband a few questions. Straighten the whole thing out."

"That won't be necessary, Greg."

A shadow grew along the table. Both turned to see Richard Crowne approach, followed by two large men in trench coats. Another pair took up position at the entrance of the diner.

"Richard? What are you—?"

Kelli's eyes flared. *"You."*

"Kelli?" Loren asked, eyes shifting between her and the newcomer, his suit worth more than the detective made in six months. "You know this man?"

"He's one of them," she spat, pulling back to the wall. "One of the people with my husband. At their church."

Richard grinned, his hands out and waiting for the woman in the booth. "Mrs. Andrews, you're distraught. Please come with us. Your family misses you."

Despite her silent refusal, her head shaking frantically, one of the men behind Richard moved for her. He snatched her wrist, clutching it tight, and pulled her out of the booth.

"Richard, what the hell are you doing?" Loren tried to stand, Kelli's terror filled eyes stabbing at him. A hand fell on his shoulder, forcing him back on the bench of the booth, the other silent member of Richard's crew keeping him in place.

"Sit, Greg," Richard said, calmly joining him at the table. "This doesn't concern you."

"Detective, please…" Kelli begged while being pulled across the restaurant. One of the men by the door joined the first to assist. No one else budged in the restaurant. The staff looked the other way. The tip jar was overflowing.

"You're not well, Mrs. Andrews," Richard called out, trying to calm the frantic woman. "We want to help."

Kelli kicked and screamed, her cries echoing even through the closed door once outside. The final member of Richard's crew joined he and Loren at the table, leaning close to their ringleader.

"Take her home," Richard whispered. "I'll be there soon."

The man nodded, joining his silent brethren outside in the parking lot. Kelli's screams faded. Lost in the darkness. Loren felt the pressure on his shoulders. He wasn't going anywhere. Not yet.

"I apologize, Greg. Not what I wanted you to see."

"Too late for that," Loren snapped. "What's to stop me from carting your ass down to Central? You and your goons?"

Richard smiled. The woman behind the counter walked up and delivered a cup of coffee. The attorney's eyes never left Loren as he pulled the cup close for a long sip. "An offer."

"Pass."

"You'll want to hear me out, Greg. You of all people."

Loren gritted his teeth. "You're part of this. Digging up corpses."

Richard shrugged. "A crude act, but necessary. For the work."

"What work?"

"The work of God, Greg," Richard replied, leaning close, his eyes shining under the lights of the diner. "The work of miracles. Miracles like you've never seen."

Loren said nothing, fighting the urge to reach across the table and grab his so-called friend. He needed answers. It was why he was in the diner in the first place. But this? Miracles of God? Did he even know the real Richard Crowne?

"I know that look," Richard said, reading his face. "I shared that look for awhile but then I realized the truth. It saved me, Greg. It can save you too. Will you let me save you, Greg?"

"What the hell are you talking about, Richard?"

"I can show you."

Richard nodded slowly, and Loren felt the pressure on his shoulder dissipate. The silent man stepped away from the table, his brisk steps carrying him out the door to their waiting car. When he returned he stopped at the entrance, holding the door for someone.

A woman stepped inside, a thin coat around her slender frame. Her heels clicked with each step along the tile floor of the diner. Catching sight of her at once, Loren peered back to Richard in confusion then back to the woman. His mouth fell open, and Richard's smile grew wide.

"Impossible," Loren muttered.

The woman slid into the booth. Her fingers slid between Richard's and he pulled her close. "You remember my wife, Jennifer?"

CHAPTER TEN

The squealing sound echoing through the street outside the diner was not the late night traffic skirting up the Knoll for the Expressway. Nor was it the pedestrians hooting and hollering at their freedom under the bright moonlight, lashing out against curfews and rules. It was the sound of Robert Standish's head slamming against his steering wheel.

He had been following Loren all night. After reading the review letter, it was an easy choice to make: follow the man and see if he had any fight left in him. Everyone saw the changes over the last few months—hell, probably the last few years. Loren always had a short fuse, ever since the loss of his wife, but the way he systematically wrote off every friend in the department—with the exception of that damn captain—Standish knew a winning bet when he saw one.

His bookies told him so all the time.

Loren was a man lost, one deserving to be knocked down further. From their very first meeting, one that ended with an unconscious Standish on the floor of the Second Precinct, payback was in the cards. Their partnership served as little more than his first opportunity but Loren always managed to skirt away from conflict. Again, the influence of Ruiz. Protection from above. But now?

It was Loren's turn to play the fool. The lout. The loser.

Standish followed his target nonetheless. *Insurance.* Whatever case Loren managed to snag with the help of the harlot that was there the night the two officers first met—giving Standish a welt on his cheek, one never forgotten—it kept Loren moving, distracted.

Good. Or so Standish thought.

Until the diner.

Loren's first guest—a woman, attractive but plump along the thighs and a bigger rump than Standish preferred—made him curious. They appeared to share a heated discussion, but were interrupted by another player. Standish stared at him, then banged his head against the steering wheel in frustration.

Richard Crowne. Assistant District Attorney Crowne.

A mouthful, but one that resonated with the officer. What was he doing there? Meeting Loren secretly in the middle of the night off the beaten path? Why?

"What the hell are you two talking about, Greg, old buddy?"

Did he know? Could he have figured it out? Standish cursed his enthusiasm at finding the review letter, at confronting Loren just to dig the knife deeper into the man's gut. The idiot.

Standish started the car. He needed to move, to think. Jacobs still owed him for the save at the courthouse. Standish wanted his money, and closing accounts seemed to be the best play. Especially if Loren figured things out.

Loren was not supposed to be engaged. He was supposed to be distant, detached and lost. He needed him that way. He needed him seen by the department as a man at the edge, the hairpin trigger about to explode.

It was time for Loren to fall.

Standish put the car in drive and shifted into the light traffic up the Knoll. Inside the diner, the district attorney and Loren were lost in conversation. Planning and plotting. Standish sneered.

It was time to make a few plans of his own.

CHAPTER ELEVEN

Soriya Greystone hoped Loren enjoyed her performance. The drama behind it, the over-the-top yelling in the dead of night so everyone heard, especially the woman in the small Cape Cod in the Riverfront district. Mostly, though, the young woman tucked behind a thick row of bushes hoped Loren saw through it all.

Susan Barton was hiding something. After three poorly received interviews, Soriya was convinced of the fact. She needed answers, and the right track to get them ignored Loren's procedures. *This is the job* only went so far. Even Loren could have told her that, but instead he half-assed the work. The way he had for weeks, if not months. They were going to have to talk about that. Eventually.

At the moment, however, Soriya had better things to do. Loren's departure with a strange woman gave Soriya the time necessary to double back on the house and curl up in the shadows. After hours of waiting her body ached for release, joints stiff from the lack of any movement. Mentor asked for patience. She gave him patience.

It paid off. In spades.

Susan Barton slipped out into the night, a light shawl covering her shoulders and neck. Another figure joined her, tall and lanky, his back to the snooping woman in the bushes. He wore a wide-brimmed hat and heavy coat, escorting her up the walkway and down the street.

"I knew someone was in there," Soriya said, inching out of the bushes. "But why hide him?"

Was Loren right? Was she simply ashamed about moving on with her life after the loss of her husband? Were the rest the same? Their loved ones forgotten to the past, allowing them to reclaim their own lives?

She kept her distance, always close enough to keep the pair of midnight strollers in sight. Another mistake like the Christian Fuller case was the last thing Soriya needed. *I can be patient, Mentor. I've got patience coming out of my ass on this one.*

They stopped seven blocks away at an unimpressive corner lot home to a modestly built church. It appeared run down from the front, its use limited in terms of services. Yet Mrs. Barton and her companion were not alone in their approach to the holy place. Dozens of others gathered, arm in arm with loved ones. They greeted each other with smiles and open hands, guiding others to the double-door entrance.

Soriya remained outside, letting the worshipers enter. She climbed to the roof of the small coffee shop across the street, getting the lay of the land. Despite appearances, the church was more involved than Soriya imagined from the ground. The roof opened up, shielded by glass stained in a deep crimson red with black grids throughout. Work had been done to the place recently. New stone archways. Elaborate carvings along the towers to the rear.

"It's a little late for a church service, isn't it?" Soriya asked. "Midnight Bingo league?"

She left the safety of the roof, sneaking quietly over to the church. Soriya ducked along the side of the structure, opposite the small parking lot, and found a side entrance. It had been chained shut, bolted with a large lock. She grinned. Her finger grazed the stone at her hip, the light beaming from its surface.

ᚾ

Strength rippled up her arm. The lock snapped in her hand. The chain loosened and the door opened gently to avoid the loud wrenching noises.

After ducking inside, Soriya found herself on a lower level to the church. The dull hum of machines, their fans whirring to remove excess heat from the room, drowned out all other noise. Soriya turned away from the noise, passing a lavatory on the left before coming to a stairwell. Chatter from the patrons gathered above, little more than murmurs. She followed the sounds, sticking close to the wall.

Susan Barton stood at the top of the stairs, her companion close to her side. They held hands, squeezing each other.

"Tommy, I missed you so much."

"I know," the man replied, his face still shadowed from Soriya.

Susan smiled, pulling him toward the main hall of the church.

"Don't ever leave me again."

"Never."

They kissed before entering the church proper. Everyone else waited inside. The doors closed behind her, engulfing Soriya in darkness. She inched to the glass dividing the entrance with the nave of the church. She stayed low, afraid of interruptions from both sides.

"Tommy?" she muttered, scanning the pews. "Her husband's name was Thomas."

Soriya's eyes flared, everything coming into focus. Marc Andrews, the man that had stonewalled them prior to Susan Barton. He stood with his two children and an older woman. Not his wife. He had lost someone too—his mother, Loren had said.

Beyond them, upon the vestibule, was an altar. The stone resting upon it appeared scarred from age. Ancient. Out of place from the rest of the room, imported from somewhere else. Behind it, carvings littered the wall, all indiscernible from the rest except for one in the center. A dove. Rising from the ground.

Rising.

"Oh, no," Soriya said, falling back for the stairs. She needed to get out of there. She wanted answers but never had she imagined what secrets they were hiding.

"What are you people doing?"

CHAPTER TWELVE

The review ended early. Ruiz assumed any meeting with Mathers and the commissioner included a catered lunch and possibly dinner—all this mixed in with off-color humor not fit for print and the occasional circle jerk. Only after this would they actually work. With Loren's involvement, however, Mathers was all business. He hated the detective, one of the few to earn his ire, if for no other reason than he was Ruiz's friend.

It went as expected. For the most part. Ruiz did what he could, said what he could, pushed back when he could, but it wouldn't be enough. Mathers preached until his face looked like a cherry, quoting Bible passages as if they had a clear bearing on events. Ruiz hoped the lecture played as horribly as it looked but knew it would be enough to win the attention of their superiors. What didn't help matters, what surprised Ruiz more than anything, was Loren's silence.

The beaten captain watched his friend depart the proceedings and stop at the closest drinking fountain. Loren looked terrible, as if sleep decided to take a vacation from his schedule with no return date in sight. Personal grooming joined the strike, the man's beard uneven and itchy just from the look of it. His hair dangled over his face as he drank from the lukewarm dispenser. He splashed water on his cheeks, rubbing his eyes deeply. He settled on the wall adjacent, popping a stick of gum between his lips.

Ruiz rolled his eyes, stomping over to Loren. He pointed down the hall. "My office. Now."

Loren followed slowly, and Ruiz held the door open for him before slamming the thin oak shut. The silent detective crashed on the couch to the right. Ruiz paced maniacally around the enclosed space. Each pass unsettled the piles of paperwork on his desk, files falling to the floor in a heap.

"That pompous ass," Ruiz muttered, hands behind his back. "That wasn't a hearing, it was a damn execution. Mathers. If I could wrap my hands around his throat...."

Loren snapped the gum between his teeth. Ruiz hated the sound, and cringed with each pop. The detective kept his head low, between his knees, hands clasped in front of him. His eyes were distant. Lost.

"We'll fight this, Greg," Ruiz continued, his pace slowing. "I'll dispute it until I'm blue in the face. Something goes missing on his watch and we're to blame? Bull. Commissioner can have my badge before I roll over for that prick."

Still nothing from his friend. Ruiz let out a long sigh, circling the desk. He pulled his chair around, settling on the deflated cushion that caused more pain than comfort most days.

"Where are you right now, Greg?"

Loren stopped snapping his gum. "What do you mean?"

His eyes were an abyss. Dark as night. His friend was falling and there wasn't a damn thing Ruiz could do.

"You just took it," Ruiz replied. "You. No patented snark. No sarcasm. Not a damn word."

Loren settled deeper into the couch. "There wasn't anything to say."

"Are you kidding me? There was *everything* to say!" Ruiz shouted. "They want to railroad you out of here. Put a giant sign on you that says, 'Here's the problem in the department but it's all good now. We fixed it.' Evidence be damned."

Loren shrugged, turning to the window. Gray skies settled into the area overnight. The first drops of rain greeted them. The storm arrived, building with each passing cloud.

"Still nothing?" Ruiz asked, astonished at the lack of fight in his friend.

Loren stood, reaching for the door. "Ruiz."

"Sit down," Ruiz commanded. "Ass on the damn couch."

Loren's hand fell away. He sat, chewing his gum. He wasn't pleased. Ruiz failed to care at the moment.

"Out with it," Ruiz said.

Loren shook his head, hands running the length of his thighs. He kept his eyes everywhere else, refusing to make contact with the man in the center of the room. He spoke with a distant voice. "Do you…do you think people can come back, Ruiz?"

"Come back? Greg, what are you—?"

"From the dead, Ruiz," Loren said, finally looking at the captain. "With everything we've seen in this damn city over the years, I mean…is it possible?"

"What?" Ruiz straightened in his chair. His previous concern was quickly turning to fear. "Greg, I don't know what you've been—"

"I saw something," he said. "Someone. She couldn't have been there but she was. I don't…. How is it possible?"

"It isn't, Greg. It can't happen."

"I know," Loren said. He stood, hands wringing before him as he settled by the window, looking out at the gloom covering the city. "You're the church-goer. My faith couldn't fill a thimble, but you? All their talk about resurrection?"

"Those are stories," Ruiz said. "I know, God strike me down. The idea of the Second Coming? Just a story."

Loren turned back to him. "That's where you draw the line? Heaven and Hell work for you but the Day of Judgment is a fantasy? How do you get to pick and choose?"

Day of Judgment? This wasn't only a curiosity to Loren. This was studied, which meant this was more than a question keeping the detective from sleep. This was real. To him, anyway. To Ruiz, though, it was a clear sign talking things out wasn't going to be enough. His friend needed help.

"My faith, my choice. So watch it, Greg," Ruiz started. "What I believe comes next is for me and me only. Just like your faith is your own. That white light? That better place with old friends, family, and loved ones? I know it's there."

Loren's hand spread along the window. He stared into the gloom. "And if it's not?"

"It is," Ruiz answered. "No doubt. But people coming back? Not possible. Dead is dead."

Loren turned away, lost in the rain.

"Are you listening to me, Greg?"

He turned back, head low. "Yeah. I'm listening."

Ruiz stood joining him at the window. "I know what something like that would mean to you."

"To anyone."

"You're pushing too hard again. When was the last time you slept?"

"I'm—"

"Fine. I know. You're always fine."

Loren nodded, his grin false. He started for the door. "I should go."

"We'll fight Mathers on this, Greg," Ruiz called, his friend turning away once more, his sad look lost in the shadows of the day. The gloom was more a reflection of Loren than the rain outside. The door closed behind him, soft steps carrying him down the hall. "If you have any fight left."

CHAPTER THIRTEEN

"It can't be real."

The muttering continued for hours with Soriya Greystone rummaging through the myriad of texts laid around the Bypass chamber. Grabbing a stack from Mentor's bedroom, the young woman nervously paged through each one in the larger room, the dull hum of the floating orb failing to soothe her.

After finishing with one, Soriya dropped the book on the pile, a term used loosely as each slid from the top, creating a dumping ground. Each failed to provide her the comfort she sought. The answers to explain what she had seen the night before.

"It's not possible. It can't be."

Another text dropped with a crash. Useless. Empty. She tried to catch her breath, her heart pounding in her chest. There had to be an answer, some insight she had failed to glean from her time in the church, surrounded by those people. And their loved ones.

The dead.

"It can't—"

"Soriya?"

Mentor stood in the door to his bedroom, hand rubbing his stiff right leg. She tried to keep quiet at first, noticing the old man resting uncomfortably on his cot in the corner. The search took priority and his presence was forgotten. She needed it to remain that way, his look of concern frustrating her further.

She turned back to the texts. Religious tomes, architectural studies on the city, anything that might clue her in on the process behind the church, on the raising of the dead—something impossible.

"It can't be real!" she screamed. The book in her hands, ratty from years of use, flew through the air in a fit of anger. It soared toward the waking man, a fastball cutting through the dim light of the chamber. Mentor deftly caught the projectile with a resounding snap of his fingers, flipping to the cover.

"Feel any better?"

"I don't," Soriya started, catching the anger in her voice. She kicked over the remaining pile of books, letting them join their brethren in the growing heap. She sighed, her hands running the length of her dark hair. She crouched down, collecting the treasures accumulated by the man watching her closely. She started to pull them up one by one, returning a handful at a time to the bedroom. "I'm fine."

Mentor stood silently, letting her continue. One pile after the other, the lone book caught in his grasp, the title still drawing him in. When she finished, there was a brief pause, then she moved for the stairs and the world above.

"Where are you going?"

"To work," she snapped, the lack of sleep showing. Her head fell low and she stopped short of the stairs. Mentor's hand squeezed her shoulder lightly.

"What is it?"

There were tears in her eyes and she quickly wiped them away. "You told me. You said it wasn't possible."

"What?"

She pointed to the book in his hand, at the image of Christ's tomb at the Church of the Holy Sepulchre. "To bring someone back."

"Is that...?" Mentor tried to ask, surprised by the question. She pulled away from him, heading back to the center of the chamber and the orb of green light. "Soriya?"

"Did you lie to me?" she asked, her eyes sharp. "Because I was a kid? To make me stronger? To make me forget them?"

Her parents. Her family. Hell, her entire former life. All lost the day of the car accident, her memories shattered to a blank slate. She always wondered, always wished, for some glimpse, some snapshot of remembrance. Some way to know who she really was, who she was supposed to be.

Mentor moved close, his voice soft. "I would never—"

"Because I didn't," she spat, the angry tears of a child struggling to tear themselves from her eyes. "I never did. Never will. My parents—"

She stopped and wiped her eyes. The Bypass stood before her and she stepped closer, her hand grazing the rift. Mentor had told her about it so many times, how the floating orb linked to every where and every when. How it linked everyone in a thousand different ways. All possibilities. The past and the future.

Where we all end.

When she was a child she spent hours pondering their fate—her family, her parents, more than anyone else. Where they went in the end. How they were doing. If they ever thought of her like she did them. So many questions wrapped in the mind of a child. Wishing for answers.

"If I could see them, Mentor," she whispered, turning away from the possibilities tucked under the veil of the Bypass, "just once."

He smiled, his thin gray eyes tired. He pulled her close. "You will, Soriya. Someday. But to bring someone back…."

She turned away. "It's not impossible. I saw it."

"The graves."

Soriya nodded. "Loren and I—"

His eyes widened. "Does the detective know as well? What is being done?"

"I don't think so. Why?"

His glare answered the question.

"You think—"

Mentor shook his head. "I think loss affects all of us differently, my child."

"You think he'll bring her back." She turned to the Bypass once more, watching the thin shadows flit along its surface. Dreaming the dreams of a child. "You think I'll help him do it."

"For the right reasons."

Soriya nodded, remembering the lesson. "The kid in the cemetery. Fuller. You said the same thing."

Mentor held out the book for her when she faced him, the page opened and folded over for her to see. Her eyes widened at the image of the dove adorning the sepulcher and at the rock wall beneath. It bore the same markings, the same look and age as the altar at the church she had seen the night before.

"You have a choice to make, Soriya," Mentor said. "Not for yourself or Loren. For everyone. Can you do that, no matter the cost?"

Soriya took the book from him and the answer within, wishing she had one for the question asked. Hoping she would when the time came.

CHAPTER FOURTEEN

Richard Crowne was content. Even with the chill of the night air biting his exposed skin, even with the ache in his right arm from holding the lantern steady for close to an hour, his smile remained. He was joyful at the work at hand...but more than that, he was thankful at the fact that he did not have to do that work.

Two men shoveled dirt in a large mound, covering the ground on either side of him. They worked without pause, without the banter of camaraderie. The earth gave way under their merciless digging, their purpose outweighing the lateness of the hour.

Richard kept watch, scanning the cemetery grounds. The lantern in his hand stayed low to offer as much light as possible. The rain dripped on them, the clouds overhead rolling in quicker, getting darker with each new wave. The storm would arrive soon. They would be gone by then, as long as they remained unseen.

The payouts helped at first. Security guards were never well compensated, and had to take multiple jobs to afford a decent living in the city. An extra thousand here and there to look the other way was always appreciated. You simply had to ask. Payouts, however, only went so far. Pressure to end the string of robberies throughout the cemetery network of Portents meant the risk was too great to continue greasing the wheels.

Speed and efficiency came next, distracting the staff with other members of their congregation. The bereaved were unable to be consoled without assistance. Two such individuals stood at the entrance, keeping guards facing a different direction.

It wouldn't always be like that. Richard knew it better than most, his excitement at stepping out of the shadows palpable. The need to hide their miracles drew to a close. The world would soon understand what they could offer.

Richard couldn't wait for the unveiling. Soon everyone would see the gift of the church, the power of their altar, and what it offered those lost. No one needed to suffer or be alone anymore. They would all witness the miracle, as he did.

First, there was someone else who needed it. Their gift, the power behind their faith. A friend in need, Richard considered him. A true friend thanks to their shared loss. He had been given a glimpse of their work. Even though he ran from Richard's explanations and the sight of his wife in the diner, questions plagued his friend—questions that demanded answers.

It took some convincing for the Founder to agree. But he knew Richard was right. Richard had been right to follow the nameless, hooded figure to the church all those months earlier. Faith and trust all leading to the truth.

To the miracle of resurrection.

Richard heard the sound of a shovel hitting metal, the clang drawing the hands of the men to tremble, hoping to avoid any further noise. They peered up to the assistant district attorney, who nodded. No more time need be wasted.

Richard looked around the grounds of Black Rock Cemetery, stepping to the head of the plot. He crouched low, his hand grazing the tombstone, fresh as the day it was installed. His fingers settled into the grooves of the lettering, feeling each turn. He needed her to prove to Greg Loren, his true friend, the power they could share with the world.

Richard smiled. Soon Greg would see. Soon everything would be right with his world.

As soon as he had Bethany Loren next to him.

CHAPTER FIFTEEN

Another sleepless night. He needed to be at work. He needed to help Soriya track down leads, or at least share the ones that had popped up in her absence. Instead, Greg Loren sat at the edge of his couch, the light of the television keeping him transfixed. Zoning.

No, not exactly zoning. More like obsessing. Richard's intervention at the diner screwed him up more than he admitted. What it meant, the return of Richard's wife, how her presence impacted Loren and everyone else? The image of her was too much for him to process with any speed or clarity. He needed time. Time to figure everything out, to figure out the church that had brought back Kelli Andrews' mother-in-law as easily as Richard Crowne's murdered wife of three years. Everything circled back to one thing. The same thing it always did when it came to Loren.

Beth. Always Beth.

Loren slammed the power button on the remote, dropping the living room into darkness. He shuffled to the window in the front of the apartment, ignoring his dismal appearance in the mirror over the mantel. It was raining, a fierce, blowing rain, pounding against the side of the apartment building. The rhythmic patter drowned out his neighbors, the noise of the city, leaving him in solitude.

Was it truly possible? Could she come back? Could he ask her to do that? To give up the afterlife for him? To make him whole again? Would she even be enough at this point? He had fallen so far over the last four years. Even work was threatened now by his own apathy, his own inability to fight. To put in any effort. Like nothing mattered or had since he lost his wife.

Not lost. *Taken.* Beth was taken. Couldn't he have her back? Was that too much to ask?

His head settled against the window, feeling the cold right through the thin pane of glass separating them. He needed another beer. More than that, he needed a cigarette. A pack of them. A trip to the corner store wouldn't be too extreme.

Loren scanned the block and stopped at a car parked across the street. His brow furrowed.

I've seen that car. At the diner last night. But—

A man stood beside the Chevy, staring up at the second-floor apartment and the shadow of Greg Loren. He tried to look casual, checking his watch, but the rain took that out of the equation. No one would want to be out in this weather. Especially with their car right there. Loren recognized the man's balding head and burgeoning gut. He had seen him enough at the station.

"Standish?"

Robert Standish checked his watch once more then started up the block, slowly. He tucked his coat tighter to impede the rain. Loren waited a short moment, then raced to the front door, slipping on his jacket.

By the time he made it to the sidewalk in front of his apartment building, Standish was a block over. He was still in sight, walking with a slight shuffle. Loren followed, double-checking his six at every opportunity.

He maintained his distance, tracking his former partner down the Knoll and away from the expressway. Not the best part of town—the residential neighborhoods giving way to mom and pop stores long since closed for the night. Deep alleys and more shadows forced Loren to slow his pace, marking each movement in the dark.

Why didn't I bring my gun?

They traveled like this for eight blocks, Loren curious why Standish didn't drive, and instead chose to fight through the rain. Caution? Or something else?

Standish cut across the street at Fourth for an alley next to a recently shuttered salon.

Loren peered around the corner, tucking close to a dumpster, most likely used to clear out what remained from the defunct shop. Standish held his back to the mouth of the alley but his companion was in full view of the peeking detective.

Myron Jacobs.

"Son of a bitch," Loren muttered. The scumbag that walked two days earlier, thanks to evidence that suddenly decided to pull a Houdini.

"Did you bring it?" the tall black man with the thick sideburns asked. His voice loud, carried over the rain. He was always yelling. A point of pride for him.

"This isn't some corner deal, Jacobs."

Loren inched to the edge of the dumpster, fighting to hear Standish through the rain.

"And I ain't playing with you, cop. Did you bring it?"

Jacobs stepped closer to Standish, hoping to intimidate the older, out-of-shape officer. He was greeted with a gut shot that sent him reeling to the floor of the alley. Standish, though not known for his fitness, carried enough muscle under his bulk for the job at hand.

"Who saved whose ass from jail time, pal?" Standish asked. Loren heard the grin behind the man's words. "Say it."

Jacobs struggled to his feet, nursing his stomach. "You did."

"Damn right. Show some respect."

Jacobs laughed, spitting hard at his companion, barely missing his shoes. "To a cop on the hook to half the bookies in town? Tough sell."

"You stupid son of a—"

Standish wound up once again, and Jacobs fell back a step.

"All right, all right!"

"The money," Standish shouted. "Now."

Jacobs fell back in the alley, reaching beneath a pile of old placards and billboards tossed aside like refuse. He came back with a black bag. "Here. What about my—?"

Standish reached into his coat, pulling out a large envelope. He tossed it on the ground beside Jacobs. "You'll find the evidence in a locker at the Southside terminal. Information and the key are inside. And a bonus."

"What are you talking about?"

Standish slung the black bag over his shoulder. "Leave town tonight. Ticket's inside."

Jacobs retrieved the envelope. "And if I don't?"

When he looked up Standish was holding his gun. Jacobs stepped back once more, hands up yet clutched tight to the envelope drowning in the rain.

"Then I show you the other prize you've won. No one'll even blink at a dead junkie in the street."

Jacobs nodded. The message was clear.

"Pleasure doing business with you, Jacobs." Standish turned for the mouth of the alley. Loren tucked close to the ground, sliding deeper into the darkness.

"Go to hell, Standish," Jacobs yelled over the storm.

Standish laughed, pulling the black bag tighter to his back. "Like I'm not already there."

The cop shuffled away from the alley on the other side of the dumpster before heading back up the Knoll to his waiting car. Loren shifted toward the abandoned building, part of the shadows. Jacobs followed soon after, hugging tight to the small locker key.

Loren wished he had his badge and his gun, but mostly his gun. Something to take the man down, to give Jacobs the justice he deserved. Instead, he watched the man slip into the night once more, free and probably hightailing it from town if he was smart enough to heed Standish's warning.

Loren did have one thing, though: anger. And finally someone to focus every ounce of it on.

CHAPTER SIXTEEN

Greg Loren was hunting.

Eyes shifting like a cat in the jungle, Loren stalked slowly through the second floor of the Central Precinct. Stares flowed his way like water, the leftover gloom from the rain a memory with the new day. Worried looks. Glances from people who had become little more than strangers over the last few years.

They didn't care about him. No one truly did anymore. They didn't rush to his defense at the idea of evidence going missing. No one stepped up to the plate to bat accusations away from Mathers and the commissioner. If they had actually tried to understand Loren and the pain covering him like a second skin, they would have seen the truth. They would have seen everything as clearly as he did now.

Standish. It was Standish all along.

He studied Loren, tracked him like an animal, monitoring his every move, his every mood. He knew about the review, and he needed Loren to worry about it, to focus every thought on the upcoming meeting rather than the truth behind the missing evidence.

He was the man behind everything.

Finally he caught his quarry. Standish stood, circled by his brethren, outside of Ruiz's office. They carried their coffees like their conversation: loose and light. A distraction from the job, laughing and living, while Loren was circling the drain. Because of Standish, all because of Standish.

Loren rushed over to him, forgetting everything else. He pushed through the crowd, cries ringing out over spilled beverages and soaring paperwork. All failed to pull him from his target.

Standish's eyes widened for a moment, right as Loren snagged the man's collar and forced him against the wall.

"How long, Standish?" Loren screamed.

"Greg?" Standish uttered, eyes flaring with concern. "What are you—?"

Loren pulled him close then shoved him back into the wall, a grunt escaping the man's lips. "How long have you been in his pocket?"

"Who?"

Loren's right hand dropped from Standish's collar. He pulled back hard and fast then shot forward, the punch leveled against the man's gut. Standish fell, cursing through spit. Loren reached down and pulled him back to the wall.

"Jacobs," Loren snapped. "You know damn well you are."

Standish's eyes flitted around the room to see a dozen officer's eyes staring back at him, watching the show but refusing to intervene.

"You're wrong," Standish said, wincing from the shot to his side.

"Lying piece of shit."

Another punch, this one connecting with the side of Standish's face. The force of the blow spun him around, his bulky frame threatening to topple over. Loren kept him upright. He took a deep breath before driving Standish's body to the ground while maintaining a grip on his left arm. He twisted it hard, pulling it up, feeling the resistance tighten.

"What are you—?"

"Say it," Loren yelled. "Tell them about what you've done!"

Standish was sweating, shaking his head. "I don't—"

Loren screamed, pulling on the man's arm until it snapped. Standish was smiling and Loren didn't know why. But then Standish's screams of pain joined Loren's shouts of anger, the older man's left arm dangling uselessly by his side as Loren pulled him back up.

"SAY IT!"

Blood covered the man's lip and he spat crimson to the floor. He leaned close to Loren, a smile on his face. "You'll burn for this, Greg," he whispered. "All I did was light the match."

Loren dropped Standish, falling back on his heels.

The meeting with Jacobs, waiting until he was seen outside the apartment. It was all a set up—all for this, for the only reaction Loren could give. This one. In public. Surrounded by the only people he had left in the world.

"You son of a bitch."

Loren grabbed Standish's collar once more, squeezing tight. Frustrated, he threw him aside like garbage, the beaten and bloodied officer staggering through the bullpen. Standish tried to catch himself, his left arm throwing off his center of gravity. His right shot up in time, but could not stop the impact as the overweight officer smashed through the glass of Ruiz's office door.

"No," Loren muttered, rushing over to the man. *What did I do?* Hands wrapped around his arms, pulling him back.

"Detective!" Pratchett screamed, the tall officer struggling to restrain him. Another pair raced to Standish, pulling him free from the glass, shuffling shards off exposed skin. They helped him to a nearby desk.

Ruiz rushed out of his office. "What the hell is going on?"

There were no answers, only the broken aftermath of the chaos. Wayward glances and mumbling, all pointing toward the restrained Loren. Ruiz turned away, catching sight of Standish, dazed and bleeding in the middle of the bullpen. "Well? Call a damn ambulance already!"

The spectators extricated themselves from the equation before Ruiz had the chance to remove them. Loren could only see Standish's sneer until Ruiz broke the connection, stepping between them.

"Ruiz—"

"Go home, Greg."

"Captain," Loren pleaded, pointing toward Standish.

Ruiz refused to look. "You're done. Get out."

Loren felt his heart stop. His throat closed up. It was over.

Ruiz looked at him with dead eyes. "Pratchett, escort him from my building. Now."

CHAPTER SEVENTEEN

Soriya Greystone watched it all unfold. The fight, the screams and the rantings of one man—Greg Loren.

It wasn't possible. Listening to his anger, seeing the fists fly without provocation. Loren, even at his lowest moments, maintained some civility with the world. Even drowning in grief, lost as easily as his wife had been, Soriya knew him to be a good man who did the right thing over all other desires.

Tucked behind the ajar door to his office, Soriya hoped to pull him back to their case, to share her findings about the church she found and the work being done there, to motivate him to help.

Doubt always plagued Loren. The loss of his wife was his greatest motivator but also his greatest weakness. The anchor wrapped around his ankle, dragging him into the murky depths. Soriya truly and totally believed their time together changed him—for the better, so the past might melt away.

There were bad times inherent in any relationship. An anniversary remembered, a memory sparked by a location—all triggers of the guilt in Loren's heart. She knew he didn't feel guilty for his wife's death, but in not being there for her until he was too late, in not being able to solve the mystery behind her fall. She knew the open case was a gaping hole in his heart.

Seeing him fall before her, dragged toward the elevator by two officers, his eyes wide with horror, his screams echoing along the tiles. There was nothing left of him.

He couldn't help her now. Maybe not ever again.

Soriya closed the door, moving for the window. She ducked out on the ledge and slid shut the window behind her.

"Dammit, Loren," she muttered, more angry with herself than with the man she respected. Her friend. Her partner.

She needed him but that was off the table. The church, the flock of resurrection-crazed people in her city, needed her attention now. More than Loren.

They needed to be stopped. No matter the cost.

CHAPTER EIGHTEEN

It was cold but Loren felt nothing. He paced the grounds outside the Central Precinct, lost in the shadow of William Rath's fifteen-foot statue in the circle that separated the precinct from Heaven's Gate Park. Pratchett remained by the doors, his eyes heavy with concern. It was a look Loren thought was lost to the past, one he never wanted to see again from his colleagues, from people he called friends. Yet it was one that had shown up much too often of late.

Pity.

He blew it. He had the chance to make things right but his anger won out. Each footfall as he stomped along the puddles from the night before attempted to shake the rage from him, but it circled back. Standish played him. Out of all the circumstances imagined, the scenarios of what might happen to him during his malaise, he never believed it possible. Standish, of all people, beat him.

He recalled his appearance outside his apartment the night before, standing in the rain, begging to be seen; he recalled the slow walk down the Knoll to meet with Jacobs. Even the meeting spot, which gave Loren a perfect view and close enough to listen to every word. Baiting him, knowing how off his game he truly was. Standish used him perfectly; all it cost him was a broken arm and a few bruises.

Loren couldn't believe it. He screamed, hands balled up in fists against his side before he collapsed on a nearby bench. He was exiled from work, his final refuge to forget the past. It was the only life he had left and he had lost it, letting revenge and rage trump everything learned over the course of his career. Using his fists instead of his brain. Like his old man.

"What the hell are you doing, Greg?" He pulled hard on the thick strands of overgrown hair. "What the hell did you just do?"

The constant concern over losing his job, mostly due to his lackluster performance from the last few months, brought him to this moment. Rather than fix the problem—to turn Standish in using the evidence at hand, Jacobs for one and the payoff for the other—he screwed up. So worried about keeping his job yet he did more to ensure its loss in the last few minutes than any review panel or missing evidence could have.

"Greg?"

Loren didn't look up at first. The voice was distant and it took a second for him to realize it was coming from someone else and not his own inner musings. When he did, Richard Crowne stood before him, tall and proud, satisfaction on his face.

"Oh, I don't need this," Loren said. His hair fell away from his face, his hand moving for the bridge of his nose. Richard, refusing to take the hint, joined him on the bench.

"Everything all right? Are you—?"

Loren stood, turning away from the man. The brief glimpse of his grin was too much. On top of their conversation the other night, on top of Standish and everything related to his review in the precinct, he didn't need any more.

"I'm fine," Loren snapped. "Going home."

"I wanted to—"

"No." Loren interrupted, then stopped. It crept back, rippling under the skin—the anger. So much confusion from the last few days. "Not now, Richard. Maybe not ever. I don't want to hear about it."

He exhaled slowly, stepping out of the shadow of the monument to the past. His steps quickened, pressed by the wind, a shrill breeze that carried the message from Richard Crowne all the easier.

"I have your wife."

Loren turned, eyes bloodshot and wide. "What?"

Richard stood in front of the bench, hands outstretched. Calm and collected. Loren felt nothing of the sort. He rushed to the man, fingers wrapping tight around his collar to pull him close.

"What did you just say?"

Richard's smile remained. "Beth. I have her."

The grave robberies. Richard admitted to them at the diner. Why hadn't Loren stopped him then—slapped the cuffs on him and carted his crazy ass away? Out of friendship? An unspoken loyalty for the loss they shared? Or something more? After seeing Jennifer standing beside the table, there had been nothing but doubt. Why hadn't he done more?

"What did you do? Where is she?"

Richard cleared his throat, patient. Loren squeezed tighter, his knuckles white. Then he let go, stepping back. The attorney nodded his appreciation, straightening his jacket.

"I'll take you to her, of course. That's why I came. You should be there for her." Richard Crowne smiled. "When she wakes up."

CHAPTER NINETEEN

He called it the Church of the Second Coming. Loren asked him to stop talking after that. It was enough to hear, that and the fact that they were holding his wife…hostage? Was that the right word? Or was it leverage? For what? Loren had yet to file a report or get a warrant to investigate Richard Crowne and his so-called "Resurrectionists" further.

Still, he followed Richard to the church. Men, women, and children gathered quietly, flowing like the tide to the front doors of the great hall. They smiled and shook hands, a true community tucked away beneath the shadow of the city. The congregation left the lobby for the nave, hopeful eyes watching the exhausted and overwhelmed detective carefully.

Loren stopped just inside the front doors. Security blocked him on all sides but maintained their distance. A gift from Richard— one of the many offered, it seemed. Having someone in the district attorney's office on your side definitely helped in their efforts to steal the dead from their places of rest. Thirty-two at last count. No, thirty-three now.

"I want to see her," Loren said. The altar at the far end of the hall was empty. A white sheet covered it from view, but Loren was still able to make out the stonework at its base. It looked old, out of place with the rest of the materials used in the church, like it had been brought in from somewhere else. The carvings, ornate and decorative, covered the pulpit though Loren had no clue what they represented including the large dove on the back wall rising from the ground. The moon showered the congregation in light, blood red from the stained glass.

Richard's hand pulled him back. "You can't. Not yet."

Loren grabbed the man's hand and twisted, forcing Richard to the wall. Security rushed them but the calm attorney shook his head.

"This is a delicate procedure," Richard continued. "We take painstaking steps to ensure everything goes well for the ceremony. Now, please. Greg."

Loren let go. "If you're lying—"

"I'm not," Richard said, brushing off his suit.

Security remained, anxious, waiting for the newcomer's reaction. Loren knew the score. "Not like I have much choice in the matter, do I, Richard?"

"Of course you do. We're the same, Greg."

He was pointing to the main hall and the woman in black near the altar. It was Jennifer, Richard Crowne's wife, smiling and waving at them like she hadn't been dead and buried the last three years.

"Without Jennifer I was so lost. Having her back is a blessing."

"One you're forced to hide," Loren said. He walked over to the glass separating them from the rest of the assemblage, hands pressed hard against the cool surface. He felt the hum of machines, coming from below, running the length of the church, getting louder, more steady with every passing second.

"For now," Richard said, joining him. "Not forever. This place is a gift for the world. We are witnesses to the Second Coming."

"I don't see any messiahs."

"Seeing is not necessary to believe," Richard said, arms outstretched. "How else could we do this? Science only takes us so far. Rebuilding the body. Preparing for the ceremony. But this place? Our faith? All of it carries us the rest of the way. By God's will. How else can it be explained?"

"How did you find out about this place, Richard?"

His hand fell on Loren's shoulder. "A man approached me in my time of need. A complete stranger, yet he offered me a hand in the dark. He found this place. Built all this. A beacon to the heavens. He called to us one by one, healing our wounded hearts, ending our grief, asking nothing in return but our faith. And our trust, in him and the work."

It was right in front of Loren. The smiles and joy on the face of the congregation, waiting patiently to welcome a new member.

They were no longer the lost and the grieving. They were rebuilt as much as those returned.

"It's unbelievable, Richard," Loren whispered. He wiped the tears from his tired eyes. "If I hadn't seen it. Seen her...."

Jennifer stepped through the doors, joining them in the dimly lit vestibule. She took her husband's hand.

"But you have," Richard said. "How could I not share this with you?"

Loren turned away, leaning hard on the wall.

"Greg?"

He nodded. "I need a minute. Could I—?"

"Of course," Richard replied, ushering him to the stairs near the entrance that led to the lower level. "There's a washroom down the stairs. Greg—"

"I know," Loren said. Security eyed him cautiously. "Just a minute. Please."

Richard nodded. The four large men monitoring their conversation backed off slowly. "Take your time. We'll be ready soon."

The echo of the steps carried him to the lower level. The humming was louder, the sound of movement joining it at the far end of the hall behind a series of closed doors. Loren ignored them, rushing into the restroom. He turned the handle over the sink, a torrent of water streaming into his cupped hands. He splashed it over his face, fighting back the tears and the exhaustion. The confusion and the choice being offered. A choice he didn't know how to make. Beth was with him, here in the church. She could come back as easily as Jennifer had. She could be there for him again, building him up, bringing him back.

Saving him.

"What are you doing here, Greg?" he asked the shadow in the mirror.

"That's my line."

Loren spun around to the stall in the corner. Soriya Greystone stepped out, a smile on her face. "How?"

"Doesn't matter," she replied, checking the door. "This place is swarming with security. We don't have much time. Come on."

She pulled him away from the mirror and into the hall. He stepped away, his voice low. The shadows of security littered the stairwell behind him.

"Soriya? Where?"

She pointed down the hall to the humming sound. "The altar seems to be connected to a lab below. I was heading there when I heard you coming."

"That must be where they prepare the bodies."

Soriya nodded. "Sever the connection and no more resurrections. Or whatever they think this is."

"Just like that?" he asked, unable to move. Of all the things they had seen in the last few years working together, doubt never crept into her voice. She believed in everything, had seen everything there was to see in the city. Her city. She doubted *this* of all things.

He didn't.

"Loren?"

He shook his head, stepping back for the stairs. "Think about the good it could do, Soriya."

"It isn't right, Loren. You know that. Now let's—"

"No." Loren pulled out his sidearm, taking aim at her.

"Loren, what are you doing?"

Security rushed down the stairs, following the sound of their argument. They hesitated behind the armed detective.

"Stopping you," Loren answered. He took another step back and the guards took over, rushing the young woman from all sides.

"Loren," she cried out. "Don't do this!"

Loren simply watched, tucking his gun away. The guards were effective, their number in the confined space overwhelming the brutal attacks of the young woman. She managed to take out the first two quickly, but by then the second pair were on top of her. They restrained her, her flailing limbs subdued. Her eyes pleaded for an answer, some explanation from him. For his betrayal.

"I'm sorry, Soriya," he said. "I have to do this. I have to save Beth."

CHAPTER TWENTY

"You did the right thing, Greg."

Loren wasn't as sure, slowly climbing the stairs. Security dragged a solemn Soriya Greystone behind him, her eyes begging for his help, before being pulled away. Her wrists were bound and she shuffled along with their prodding until they were out of sight.

Richard's hand fell on Loren's shoulder. "Greg?"

"I never thanked you, Richard." Loren turned to his friend. "That was wrong of me."

"You don't—"

Loren shook his head. "You're a good friend."

Richard smiled. The pair turned for the double glass doors and the entrance to the nave of the church. All eyes were on them. "Are you ready?"

He had been ready since her death. Since he lost every connection with the world. Beth kept him grounded but also lifted him up, letting him soar higher and higher. She made him better. He needed to feel that again. He needed to feel her again. No matter the cost.

They walked up the center aisle. Each step brought them closer to the altar. On both sides Loren was met with congratulations from well-wishers. Smiles from complete strangers yet not strangers at all. Bound together through their common experience. Their grief, their loss, and their reborn hope.

Inching closer to the first pew beneath the altar, Loren noticed the change. The white sheet continued to cover the ancient stone in its center but now a figure could be seen beneath it. The shape of a body.

"Is that—?"

"That's her," Richard said, proudly.

"Can I?"

"After the ceremony. You'll have eternity."

Loren nodded, quietly ushered into the pew. He thought of praying but couldn't find the words. He didn't know who to ask in the first place. Was this God's will or the will of the people? He didn't know the first thing about what was happening, only that it was necessary. It was all that mattered to him—his girl back in his arms, forever.

"He's wrong, Loren," Soriya whispered. She sat, restrained in the pew behind them, fighting through the guards' grip to get closer to her friend—the man he was supposed to be, anyway.

"Why is she here?" Loren asked Richard.

"I asked them to bring her. To see for herself the miracle. To be a witness."

Loren shook his head. "I don't—"

"We have nothing to hide," Richard said with a sincere smile.

"You have everything to hide," Soriya snapped. Audible gasps filtered through the crowd. "Loren, you have to listen to me."

"No," he snapped, refusing to look at her. "I have to do this. I have to save her."

"You are *damning* her," Soriya said. "Not saving her. Look around you. Look at the so-called saved."

He kept his eyes on the altar, the figure beneath the sheet. "I don't—"

"Look at them, Loren. Really see them."

He did. In each of their faces he saw their happiness, their joy. Being back, being with the ones who missed them so much, truly content.

"They're happy, Soriya."

"They have to be," Soriya yelled, pulled back by the guards. "Have you heard them say a bad word? Share a negative thought? Argue? They aren't whole. No one comes back whole. You want to save Beth? What would *she* want? Have you even asked yourself that? You have to stop this, Loren. Please."

He looked again. This was his friend, the woman that had carried him along for the last few years. She saved him at his lowest point and he returned the favor by betraying her. But she was wrong. She had to be wrong.

Except he could see it. In their eyes, tinted black under the dark red shadow of the moon above. They were not the same as the men, women, and children that grieved for them. They were not connected to them. Not the same.

"That's enough," Richard said, standing. "Get her out of here. We're starting, Greg. You'll have your wife back soon and everything will make sense again. I promise."

The guards pulled Soriya down the pew, her cries to Loren chilling him. A cloaked figure moved over the covered form of Beth. The Founder, Richard had called him. He was the man who built this place, who funded the machines humming beneath their feet. Science and faith as one.

Loren turned to Richard, the man's smile saddened by the words of Soriya. He gripped the hand of his wife tighter, needing it more and more as a crutch. The past was unable to fade, to give room for a future. Jennifer said nothing in her defense. She simply smiled beside her husband, without a thought or a care as to the three years she spent buried. Dead and gone from the world.

"No," Loren muttered.

"What?" Richard asked.

Loren stood, rushing for the center aisle.

"Greg, what are you doing?" Richard called after him. The cloaked man on the altar paused, the machines buzzing louder and louder.

"Loren?" Soriya asked, the guards pulling her away. Loren's sidearm was in his hand. He said nothing, letting the weapon throw out his demand, to which the pair of guards acquiesced, falling away from the bound woman. He turned Soriya around. His pocketknife sliced through the bindings.

"Loren, what are—?"

"Do what you have to," Loren said.

Soriya nodded. The guards rushed them, and Soriya knocked them back with a stiff roundhouse kick. She flew down the aisle for the altar. Richard tried to stop her, eyes wide with panic, the same panic that kept the crowd locked in their seats, unsure and unable to act. Loren shook his head at the attorney, gun raised.

"Greg? Why?"

"Because she's right, Richard," Loren said sadly. "This is wrong."

"We can bring her back."

Loren shook his head. "That's not my choice. I won't be selfish like that. No matter how much I want to be."

Soriya leaped up toward the covered sheet, forcing the Founder back with the swat of her hand. He fell back then pounced at her, hands up in a rage. He bore a thick beard and dark eyes, the only things visible within the darkness of his hood.

Soriya didn't flinch; she was fearless, just as Loren knew her to be. She waited for his assault, dodging his blow then swept her fist up, catching his chin. The force drove him back, his hood flying off and his head slamming into the image of the dove. He slid down and did not stand again. Soriya moved for the body covered in the white sheet.

"Loren!" she yelled down to him.

Richard charged Loren, grabbing at the detective's shirt desperately. "Tell her to stop, Greg. We can make this right. Just stop her. Please."

"I need you to say it, Loren," Soriya said, "I…I won't do this if you tell me to stop."

Richard's grip on his collar tightened. Loren heard the pleas of those surrounding them. The desperate, holding onto the grief of their losses. They were miserable, unable to live—like him.

"Do it," Loren said. "Please. Just do it already."

Soriya nodded. She stood back, the stone locked in her grip. Light beamed along its surface, filling the great hall of the church.

$$\text{Þ}$$

The humming of the machines sputtered and wheezed, sparks flying in all directions. Fire erupted from beneath them; the building rocked as if from an explosion. The hum of the machines ended, destroyed, but the fire continued, spreading further and faster all around them.

The patrons of the Church of the Second Coming raced for their lives, rushing down the aisles to the exit. Richard stayed behind, no longer pleading with Loren, his hands falling to his sides, his eyes full of terror.

"No."

Soriya lifted Beth's covered body from the altar, before it was consumed by flames. The Founder shuffled down the pulpit, joining his flock in their panic. The dove rising from the earth disappeared behind a wall of flames.

In that instant, with the altar enflamed, everything changed. The returned fumbled and faded. It hit Jennifer first, the closest to the fire. Her smile went crooked, her eyes closing before she collapsed to the ground.

"Jennifer!" Richard choked.

The others fell quickly, littering the church with bodies. More kindling to burn. Richard ran to grab his wife, pulled back by Loren. The detective forced him down the aisle, kicking open the doors for the others to flee from the growing cloud of smoke. By the time they made it to the street, Loren realized Soriya was gone.

So was the Founder.

Richard collapsed in the center of the road, the cries of the grieving congregation louder than the approaching sirens. Loren crouched beside his friend, the man who had attempted to save his life. His hand fell on his shoulder, tears joining the others on his cheeks as the two men watched their world burn.

"I'm sorry, Richard," he said softly. "I'm so sorry."

CHAPTER TWENTY-ONE

Loren waited for the end to come.

Three days passed since the fall of the Church of the Second Coming. Three days of arrests, interviews, and a mountain of questions asked on both sides of the table. The perpetrators became the victims, their hope and happiness lost in the fire that consumed the church. Most had nothing to offer the police; their thoughts were turned to their losses. Their grief, much like Loren's, returned in full.

Most were released quickly. They played no part in the mass robbery scandal making its way through the major news organizations. Stories of the dead returning, of loved ones long since passed walking among the rest of the city, were squashed early even by the most fervent followers. A secret kept between them. *Who would believe it anyway?*

All record of the church was buried deeper than the mechanism that brought their loved ones back to life. The machine, their faith, whatever it might have been. Loren still didn't know.

When all was said and done, the Founder, though still in the wind, was the one to take the fall. His name unknown, his stories denied even by the members of his church in the aftermath of the fire, the Founder became the bogeyman the city needed for the crime of stealing loved ones from their place of rest. A sketch showed a white man with a thick black beard, and it littered the walls of every precinct in the city, displayed on every newscast for days—all without resolution.

Out of all the congregation, Loren remained concerned about only one in their flock, but even Richard Crowne escaped unscathed—in the eyes of the law at least. Professionally, Richard quietly tendered his resignation from the district attorney's office. Loren went to visit him at his home only to find a For Sale sign on the front lawn. Loren wanted to search for him. To try and help him understand things even the tired detective failed to fully grasp.

Unfortunately, he had bigger concerns.

Sitting patiently, hands folded between his knees, Loren stared at the floor. Black loafers shifted from right to left, a slow pace around the confined space of the office. Ruiz's office. The captain called him in early for his shift, his first official one since the incident that left Robert Standish in the hospital with a broken arm and a concussion. The glass on the door had been boarded up with cardboard and a roll of duct tape. Ruiz, his friend for so many years, looked at him with sadness in his gray eyes.

"I don't have a choice," he finally said, his hand resting on the letter on top of his desk. "Not after Standish, after everything. You're to be suspended immediately."

It felt like a hot poker slipped between Loren's ribs at the sound of the word. *Suspended*. His work life had met his home life in one unavoidable collision of mistakes. It was his own fault—the path he had chosen months earlier. His anger, his malaise, and the errors in judgment that came with the pair.

Ruiz sat, hand to his brow, unable to glance at him directly. The same way things started at the courthouse only a week earlier. "A panel met to review your conduct over the last few months. I'm sure you're not surprised to hear that. I had a few choice words over it but with what they came back with…let's just say I couldn't say much. They've recommended leave and therapy—something you've needed for a long time."

Loren heard it in his friend's voice: the disappointment, the never-ending pity.

"You agreed with them."

"I did," Ruiz said with a nod. He leaned forward, hands drawn and open. "Of course I did, Greg. They wanted you gone. For good. No matter what Internal Affairs has found on Standish, which it turns out is quite a lot. Jacobs was hauled in trying to board a plane, more than happy to flip on his so-called savior. Doesn't matter here, though. This is about you, Greg. You need help. Professional help." He scoffed. "Not that you'll take it."

Loren stood and walked to the window. The sun slowly sunk behind the obsidian tower at the center of the city. Sunsets were few and far between lately. It was once always a priority, when Beth was alive. They made it a point to watch pink and purple hues dancing across the sky, which bound them together before he left for work. Even after he lost her, he tried to catch it, thinking for an instant she was with him, holding his hand, smiling at sharing the moment. There were so many they never had the chance to share.

"I will," he whispered.

"What?" Ruiz asked, surprised.

Loren turned to his friend, nodding. "It's the right call, Ruiz."

Of course it was. After everything? All the mistakes? After turning on Soriya, the one person who had stuck with him through and through, all for his own selfish needs? Part of him would have let her die rather than lose Beth all over again. If not for her being there, for being his strength for so long, Loren would have been lost to the world years ago. But after the anger and the distance shown on the job and off? To all those around him, including Ruiz?

It was the right call.

Loren unclasped his holster and removed his sidearm. His badge and weapon slid between his fingers. He placed the items on Ruiz's desk, patting them lightly before letting them go. "I'll be back for these. When I'm ready."

Ruiz stood, leaning hard on the desk. "This isn't what I wanted, Greg."

"It's what I deserve," Loren replied.

The door to the office pulled open, the sound of the bureau quieting at the sight of him. Soft stares, quiet looks of contempt rushed over him. He turned back to Ruiz, saddened.

"This and a lot more, Ruiz. A lot more."

CHAPTER TWENTY-TWO

They should have been celebrating. The church was destroyed. Everything was back in its place. It sounded to Soriya Greystone like the perfect excuse for a night off and some fun. Instead, a chill beyond the strong gusts of wind ran through her.

Atop the Rath Building, she watched him depart. Sullen and broken, Greg Loren cast a long shadow over the quad, longer than the great statue at its heart. He walked slowly, head down and hands deep in his pockets, lost in thought.

She wanted to call out to him, to pull him back from his grief, to comfort him. To do *something*.

A hand stopped her.

"Don't."

She didn't turn to face Mentor; her eyes locked on her partner and friend.

"I have to," she said quietly. "He needs me."

Mentor shook his head, his hand unyielding. "You need him."

Her eyes fell away. The shadow of Loren faded from her view as he approached Heaven's Gate Park before disappearing beyond its borders. She bent low, picking at the stray stones littering the roof's ledge.

"He lost everything, Mentor," Soriya said, clutching a small pebble between her fingers. She flicked it away, watching the stone tumble to the street below, the sound of its end muted against the rush of humanity. "When someone finally gave him some hope, a future to hold, I pulled it away. I took it from him."

Mentor sat beside her at the edge of the roof, staring out at the city before them. "It was the right thing to do—the only thing to do. And it was his choice."

"It doesn't feel that way."

Mentor smiled, taking her hand in his own. "In time."

The shadow was gone now, Loren lost to the night. Soriya wondered if she would ever see him again. Would they ever share a joke or break a case together again?

She wished she could hold onto the way things were for just a little longer.

"And Loren?"

Mentor said nothing to this, letting out a soft sigh before standing. He helped her up, the strain visible on his aging face. He didn't need to answer.

It was the same.

Time. All they needed was time.

CHAPTER TWENTY-THREE

Greg Loren set his badge next to his gun and closed the center drawer of the desk. His fingers stayed on the knob, lingering in thought and motion, until they fell away. The chair slid back into place, blocking the drawer.

It was time to leave.

The decision took months—months of intense therapy, group and one on one sessions with a number of professionals. Ruiz was right. He needed to talk things out, reevaluate, grow. It centered him, refocused his world, or the lack thereof. To a point.

One more step remained, however. Even after being cleared to return to work, despite Mathers' objections and the loss of all respect from his fellow officers, something remained out of place. He earned back the gun and badge, Ruiz happily turning them over as well as his old office. A gift from his captain and his friend. The familiar routine of everything, falling back into place.

Except it was different.

Loren was different.

Or needed to be, anyway. After falling so hard, after making an almost fatal mistake at the Church of the Second Coming, Loren knew that change was necessary. Coming back was not the answer. Staying hadn't been the answer for almost four years.

It was time to leave.

Ruiz took the news poorly. Words were spoken in anger, mostly out of a renewed concern for the other. Both sides tried to persuade their counterpart and both failed. But the decision remained Loren's alone.

Chicago waited for him. A job, though similar to his current standing in the department, brought a change of scenery and with it a chance at something new. New friends. New relationships. And his family as well.

A chance to start over.

Loren dropped the last of his files in a single box on the desk. The box consisted of almost a decade of his life. A lone file remained loose. He took it in his hands, thumbing through the thick dossier carefully. His wife's file.

Four years had passed without resolution. He agonized over the details every day. The case became his life and now it sat in his hands, the anchor around his ankle pulling him back into the deep. Loren set the file down and closed the box. He patted the cardboard lightly, running his hand along the edges. Then he turned and headed for the door.

He didn't need it. The box was Portents, through and through. His mistakes and his regrets, the guilt over his wife. The pain he dulled with work, with Soriya Greystone and the world she introduced to him, and more. A lot more that he exorcised with therapy over the last six months. There was no need to revisit it.

Not for his new start, not in Chicago.

His hand reached for the door, but he was unable to turn the handle. He bit his lower lip, wishing for a piece of gum to distract him. He looked to the box on the desk and started back. Opening the flap, he removed the single file on top, his wife's name and a case number adorning the tab. He tucked it under his arm and headed to the door, the handle turning easily in his hand.

On the desk, the lid of the box remained open. As it always would for Greg Loren.

THE GREAT DIVIDE

CHAPTER ONE

Another death. The news came over the radio an hour into his shift.

Rushing to the scene, Officer Alejo Ruiz quickly locked it down with the help of a dozen other "uni's" and a bit of luck. The dropping temperatures of autumn kept the streets quiet—not that the city ever needed the help.

With Portents, few risked the streets at night.

Cordons in place gave Ruiz a breather, one interrupted by a call from the scene itself. He hoped for the call, one to help his career. A career he loved and one he was damn good at. Four years at Central, snatched by the top precinct right from the academy. A commendation under his belt and another one on the horizon thanks to a high profile bust along King's Lane—almost where he stood now.

The Knoll bled into King's Lane, the traffic a maze through downtown. Ruiz knew the area well, had patrolled it regularly since landing at Central. Portents was his home. Always had been. He understood the city, a requirement for his job. What came with each turn, with every sunrise and sunset.

And his ever-important career. The young man inching toward thirty looked to advance in the department. He envisioned a detective's shield in the coming year. The exam that loomed over him was worse than any shadow the city could create. A captain's desk in five years…and after that? The sixth floor of the Rath would be calling before his fortieth.

He had ambition.

Some saw it in his eyes; some recognized it immediately, while others mistook it for arrogance, a feeling Ruiz never allowed. He had goals, larger ones since his wife Michelle gave him the news, but he remained content with the job at hand.

Do the job and do it well. A lesson from his mother—one of many he carried with him since her passing.

Ruiz slipped under the rope line, a spring in his step, past the forensics team working the scene. The center of the intersection at King's Lane and Cross was vacant of vehicles, traffic diverted two blocks out by a number of officers. Foot traffic remained and many scurried back and forth from the affair to their waiting squad car or van for equipment or to update Central.

The body in the center of the intersection demanded attention, especially from the detective assigned the case, Julian Harvey. A seasoned vet, still punching the clock daily. Harvey (never call him Julian) was the picture of dedication. And the picture of a man long in the tooth, wondering when sixty passed by only to realize he tracked time by case numbers.

Harvey surveyed the scene, pacing slowly—the only speed available. Ruiz watched him closely, studying him the way the old man studied the body. He noted every look, every grimace of pain from his left side—indigestion, most likely—and every wide glare of revelation, wondering what came with it. So focused on the man, Ruiz failed to notice his lack of movement and the shift toward him.

"Ruiz," Harvey said, deep and low.

Ruiz stiffened up and joined him. "Line has been pushed up a block. Traffic diverted up the Knoll, at least two blocks out. Four uniforms in every direction. I can call in for more if you need them but it will take time."

"Won't matter," Harvey replied, turning back to the body. "Press will find a way through long before then. The good ol' boys will anyway, not the bottom feeders pulling from other sources. Lazy asses."

"Detective?" Ruiz asked, a slight grin on his face. Harvey was known for his rants, his "informed opinions," as he called them. Few were on the positive side.

Harvey shook his head. "I didn't ask you here for an update."

"You didn't?" The question held hope behind it.

The old man smirked at the inflection, continuing his slow pace around the body in the middle of the intersection. "Exam is coming up."

"It is." Two weeks until the detective exam. His chance to advance in the department, a necessity and a desire all wrapped in one test.

"Getting the nervous sweats?" Harvey asked. "Sleepless nights?"

Ruiz hesitated, unsure how to answer. They weren't close, not enough for the truth. About his insomnia, going over everything in his mind like a giant Ferris wheel, over and over again. But Harvey asked just the same, and lying to a detective was never a good place to start a conversation. If that was what they were having.

"Some."

Harvey nodded. "Good. You should. Shield means something still. To some of us."

Ruiz scanned the faces in the crowd. "Where is Detective McCullough, sir?"

Harvey smiled. It was the right question to ask. "On leave. Indefinitely."

"Poor guy."

Harvey shook his head. "Tell that to my mounting caseload. Job affects us all differently. You have to accept it. Live with it and grow with it. Fight the damn thing and it rolls on you worse than a jalapeno burrito at El Mexicana." He held his gut. "Trust me on that one."

"A wonderful image to share."

The old man crooked a finger. "About as pleasant as this schlub."

Ruiz followed the finger to the waiting body. He had made a point to ignore the corpse in the center of the intersection. It wasn't his place. It sure as hell wasn't his case and Ruiz always made a point of adhering to strict protocol—the good boy in him, the one that needed that promotion sooner rather than later. The bad boy tended to let curiosity reign.

"Well?"

Ruiz turned to the detective, confused. "Sir?"

"Make it Harvey and move on," he said. "You want the rank, kid. You've got the chops for it. Show 'em off."

"That's not procedure. There are—"

Harvey waved him down. "Indulge me."

The body came into focus for the first time. Young. Twenty to twenty-five. Caucasian. Skinny, almost gaunt in his face, at least from what was left of his face. The extremely low weight pointed toward certain predilections but they would be assumptions, not fact, at this point.

The body lay in a crumpled heap. His legs were shattered with bone protruding. His arms were tucked under behind his back, snapped at the elbows. The right side of his face was sheared of skin, caked to the pavement. His left eye lay open, the iris tinted yellow.

Ruiz held his breath for a moment, Harvey watching his every move. Then he turned to the seasoned vet. "It looks like he fell."

Harvey smirked, nodding his confirmation. "Care to guess from where?"

Both men peered into the cloudless night sky. The moon, along with the streetlamps on all four sides of the intersection, illuminated the setting. The closest rooftop was no less than thirty feet away and none stood higher than three stories. Nowhere near high enough to inflict the damage seen on the young man.

"No idea," Ruiz answered.

"Same here." Harvey crouched low next to the body, picking up something small between his fingers.

"Sir? Harvey?"

The old man turned, slipping the object into a small evidence bag then sealed it. It joined others inside. He held the bag out to Ruiz.

"While you're figuring out that little chestnut, try this one for size."

"What is...?" Ruiz stopped, holding the bag up. Black as night, the objects, numbering in the dozens if not hundreds, appeared to be—"Feathers?"

Harvey shook his head and patted the young officer's shoulder. "Going to be one of those cases, kid."

CHAPTER TWO

St. Sebastian's Church had been a second home to Ruiz in his younger years. Between thrice-weekly visits with his mother and community events, Ruiz spent more time wandering the grounds surrounding the place than he did his own backyard. He served as an altar boy for three years, worked with the food pantry connected to the church for six, and made friends that lasted a lifetime.

So when Sunday rolled around, he knew where he would be spending his morning. It was the same place he'd been every Sunday since he was old enough to walk. He was married in the church, bringing his wife, Michelle, into the tradition—one happily shared.

They sat near the back of the nave, the third pew in and far to the left, away from the throng of people spilling out of the front half of the church. The long sermon continued, the addition of a missionary from their efforts in Africa taking his turn at the microphone to discuss the work being done overseas and the money necessary to continue, of course.

Ruiz shifted closer to his wife, his hand settling into hers. His gaze followed the act, running up her thin legs, covered by black pants. She smiled, his attention shifting north for the dark skin of her arms and her thick lips.

Eighteen months of marriage had not dulled their relationship. On most days they still referred to themselves as newlyweds, acting accordingly as often as possible. They occupied the same space in the world, sharing everything between them. A profound experience in Ruiz's mind, to want to know someone so completely. To be totally focused on their well-being. Forever and always.

His hand left hers, landing lightly along her thigh. He squeezed it slightly, muscle rippling under the surface. Then his fingers inched up and in, his grin widening.

Michelle retook his hand, leaning close. "Keep it rated G, mister. At least until the car."

"Promises, promises."

She smiled, patting his arm. "God's watching, you know."

Ruiz looked around, making sure no one else joined in the big man's fun. "He always is. Damn voyeur."

"That will cost you a Hail Mary or ten."

"I'll make it up to Him."

Her eyes caught his. Green like emeralds and twice as valuable.

"Eventually," he said.

The missionary finished his plea at the vestibule and stepped aside for the pastor, a man Ruiz had known little. He was not the pastors of his youth—vibrant, angry men who cast down God's wrath on the sinful. No, the current crop—all short-lived of late—spouted compassion and tolerance over all. The soft approach, Ruiz called it. Sometimes the people needed a good verbal spanking to put them back on the right path.

Ruiz and Michelle settled in for another such speech, this one echoing the missionary's own plea for assistance. Both did what they could for the church, monetarily. The weeks of multiple visits and volunteer work long since passed for Ruiz, his schedule tight enough for an hour service once a week. Still, the pleas were plentiful enough and did not need to be set on repeat mode for the largely elderly crowd.

He turned to his wife, just as she leaned closer.

"Did I tell you—?"

"I never—"

They stopped, a soft chuckle shared between them. Ruiz rolled his finger, giving her the floor.

"Go ahead."

"You sure?" she asked quietly.

"Definitely," Ruiz said. He loved hearing about her work, the mundane trappings of her everyday job. It made him feel normal. Genuinely interested in it, Ruiz enjoyed getting involved in the conversation. From work, to family, to friends, the house and everything in between, the pair shared everything—a change from how he was raised. While church may have been the ultimate sanctuary for his mother, there were reasons behind it. Reasons that made the dinner table in the Ruiz home a sullen place, a void for discussion. It made him all the more grateful for Michelle.

"Nancy sent the e-mail Friday night."

Ruiz rolled his eyes. "An observation?"

"Tomorrow."

"Monday morning?"

"After a vacation," she reminded him unnecessarily. She had been home for the long holiday weekend without him. Work had taken up twelve hours over each of his last six days, never once abating for a late-night rendezvous with the missus.

"You are a lucky one."

"A doomed one, you mean."

"Lesson set?" Ruiz asked, while the baskets passed by. He dropped their envelope in face down. He disliked the look the parishioners gave when they read the amount within, even if the contribution was more than generous.

Michelle shook her head. "For two weeks, thanks to the woman's constant rescheduling at the last minute. Not going to matter."

"No, it doesn't."

She sighed, slouching in the pew. "Retirement at thirty sounds good."

"Better than dismissal at thirty."

"I'll drop dead before I teach for a test that doesn't mean anything for the students," she snapped, drawing a look from a man two rows in front of them. She covered her mouth, eyes immediately taking to the floor.

"Dead?"

She leaned closer. "Dead."

He grinned. "Retirement it is."

She wiped her hands in the air. "Griping over. Your turn."

He held off, waiting for the end of the service. As the final hymn filled the room, mostly from the microphone of the pianist and not the fleeing crowd of parishioners, Ruiz shook his head.

"It's nothing." He meant it too. Talking about work was a thrill for him. Before Michelle, he spent so much time internalizing everything on the job, even with the occasional gabfest with his colleagues, of which there were few. Now, he loved the back and forth with his wife. He had seen what holding back had done to his own folks. And the great divide built from it.

"The murder?" she asked, nodding to some neighbors from up the block as they headed for the door.

"If it was," Ruiz muttered.

She held tight to his arm. "Feathers?"

"So glad to have leaks in the department," he said, rolling his eyes.

"Sounds bizarre."

He sat, helping her back to the pew. The church emptied slowly. "It is."

"That detective has you involved? Harvey?"

He nodded.

"He going to help come exam time too?"

Ruiz turned away from her glare. "I'm not going to ask him to do that."

"You should."

"But I won't."

"Stubborn." She crossed her arms over her chest. Her green eyes flitted around the room before settling back on him. "He's coming."

Ruiz nodded, taking her hand. He squeezed it. "I can hang out with him later. Promises were made."

She patted his hand. "Promises will be kept. Later. Go see your boyfriend."

Ruiz stood. "You mean my future pastor, don't you?"

"He's not serious about that," she said with a laugh. "Is he? I mean, Edgar? Seminary?"

"Edgar Rusch is not one for serious talk," Ruiz replied, waving to the approaching man—a connection made with the church in Ruiz's youth. One that outlasted the thrice-weekly visits of his family. Rusch was a neighborhood kid, a friend above all others, even when the academy took Ruiz away from things for a few years. Edgar Rusch stayed with him, held tight to their relationship. He may not have been the most stand-up individual, or the most committed—especially when it came to work or even dating for that matter—but his loyalty to Ruiz knew no bounds. Ruiz always appreciated that.

Ruiz started for the end of the pew then turned back. "Do I tell him?"

She stared blankly for a moment. "The news?"

"What else?"

Michelle nodded. "Tell him. He's going to know soon enough anyway, and you're bursting from hiding it."

"Am not."

She laughed, pushing him. "Literally bursting."

"I love you." Ruiz crouched beside her. His hand grazed her stomach. "Both of you."

"You better," Michelle said. "Now go. Play."

He grinned, rushing to tell his childhood friend the news.

CHAPTER THREE

Central Precinct buzzed around him. Sunday, filled with the ramblings of friendship and the sharing of way too much to drink, bled into Monday and Ruiz worked diligently through a headache and the reports that had accumulated on his desk over the last week. Typical procedural paperwork kept him from clocking out on time regularly but not tonight.

No, the case had gotten to him. Tethered to him tighter than any hook, reeling him into the muck and mud. The dead kid with the feathers—how it was being passed around the station, how disc jockeys were peddling the death on late night talk shows.

There were hundreds of feathers surrounding the victim. What could they mean? How did the kid fall? Too many questions that demanded answers from the intrigued officer. He closed the report and sat back in his chair.

The first floor of Central was a bullpen style nightmare landscape, populated by duty officers and the daily traffic that infested the area. Desks faced every which way and never remained stationary, constantly being shifted and co-opted for the work of the day.

Chaos ruled.

Ruiz enjoyed it, appreciating his time at Central more and more. He arrived early, left late, and always threw a friendly grin to anyone that passed by. Even if his smile wasn't returned.

"Surprise, surprise," Brian Walters crooned, hand slapping hard on the corner of Ruiz's desk to jolt him from his thoughts. The officer of ten years was joined by his usual cohorts Mikel Petrovich and Christian Burke—Ruiz's partner on the beat. "Look who's pulling a double without being asked."

"I heard Ruiz has volunteered to cook and clean for the squad too. He's that efficient with his time," Mikel chuckled, his accent dulled by the city after so many years, not that he didn't try to break it out for effect periodically. For the ladies, of course.

"No way would he do that for us lowly grunts," Brian said. "Now the detectives upstairs?"

Burke nodded. "Can't wait for that exam, can you, Al-ey-ho?"

Ruiz smirked. Fifteen months with Burke had brought new meaning to the term *ignorant redneck*. "I'll miss you too, Burke."

Burke scoffed. "He thinks he's got it made already."

Brian spun Ruiz's chair. He towered over the sitting officer, finger poking his chest. "Don't expect us to shine your shoes. You're more grunt than any of us. You'll see."

A throat cleared and the finger fell away. All four men turned to face the new spectator.

"Ruiz," Detective Harvey said, plainly.

Ruiz stood. "Detective?"

"If you have a minute?" Harvey asked, pointing down the hall.

"I think I can manage," Ruiz nodded. He grinned at his cowering colleagues. "If that's all right with you, gentlemen?"

They said nothing, scattering throughout the bullpen. Ruiz watched them depart, joining Harvey.

"Let's take a walk."

They traveled in silence, Harvey's staggered step slow and patient, eyes ever forward. Ruiz noted the quiet nervously, unsure and uncomfortable.

"They mean well," he finally admitted.

"Seemed that way," Harvey replied, dismissively. They both knew the score in the department. And that was before the race card came into play. "Not that you should care."

"No?"

"Hell, no," Harvey said. "Guys like them are a dime a dozen. They lack forethought. Ambition, you see? Most of the grunts here remind me of my good-for-nothing nephew. Happy to sit and zone than think for himself. He's actually thinking about applying to the academy but I'll be damned if I see a Pratchett in this department in my lifetime."

Ruiz looked away, unsure what to say.

Harvey smiled. "Never mind, kid."

They stopped in front of the elevator. Harvey hit the down arrow repeatedly, even with the sound of the car approaching.

"Where are we going?"

"Coroner's."

"This about the feathers?"

The doors opened and Harvey stepped inside, holding it for his companion. "Hopefully."

"Why me, sir?" Ruiz asked without moving.

"It's Harvey, remember? I need a second pair of eyes. You're elected."

Still, the young officer hesitated. Curiosity was one thing, but this went above and beyond. "I shouldn't. This isn't—"

Harvey sighed. "I can ask or put in the reassignment for you. This is the job, kid. You want it or not?"

Ruiz nodded, and stepped into the elevator with the old man.

"Good. I hate suffering alone."

The doors closed and the elevator shifted, making the drop to the lower level. Ruiz immediately covered his mouth and nose. "The smell."

"Gets worse," Harvey said with a laugh. "Keep hoping they relocate but anything with a dollar sign in front of it is off limits. Election year."

The doors opened with a clang at the sub-basement. The coroner's office had been a staple of the building since the Central Precinct's inception decades earlier. An independent entrance to the rear kept the department separate from the traffic to the rest of the building. It also kept the stench contained, except for the elevator system running at the end of the hall.

Ruiz had stayed away from visits to the dungeon-like setting as much as possible. It just wasn't his beat. The stories were enough—horror tales enthusiastically shared by his partner, Burke—not that they were necessary. Ruiz had a friend on the inside.

"Hady," Ruiz muttered when the pair rounded the corner to the central examination room. Tables lined the space, two abreast, staggered every few feet in the center of the room from one end to the other. Most remained empty. The one closest to the small staircase from the hallway was occupied, though blocked from view by a stumpy woman with thready black locks over her shoulders.

Hady Ronne served as assistant coroner, a position held for the last three years. She served as Ruiz's friend since their childhood days, running around the streets of Portents with Edgar Rusch and the other kids in the neighborhood. They had been fast friends; she even had a crush on him in their awkward prepubescent years.

She had so much energy then. They called it pep. Something changed during high school, though. She changed. She put on weight. Her hair darkened and thinned. Her social graces faded faster than her looks. She transformed from beauty to beast and she was treated as such.

Except by Ruiz. Friends they remained but even he saw the change, though he never questioned it. Everyone changes, don't they? They accept it, as Harvey himself stated two nights earlier, or they fight it and lock themselves away from the truth.

"You're acquainted?" Harvey asked curiously.

"Grew up together."

"Saves me the trouble then. Doctor Ronne?"

Hady didn't turn, lost on the body before her. That was how it was with her. Her work took priority over everything else, and at the expense of everything else.

"Doctor?" His hand grazed her shoulder and she turned suddenly. Her eyes flared, almost in anger, pupils expanding. Then they lightened, a calm but emotionless look returning.

"I didn't hear you."

Harvey rolled his eyes to Ruiz. "Of course. This our stiff?"

"Yes."

Ruiz moved for the chart, reading the scribbled notes. "David Connelly."

The boy's body stretched out across the table, broken bones settling beside the remnants of his torso. The right side of his face looked like a pulped orange but the left looked at peace. Whatever that meant for him, Ruiz could not be sure.

"How did he die, doc?"

Hady's eyes stayed low. "A fall."

Harvey huffed. "We ruled that out."

"Doesn't mean it isn't true."

"Sorta does, doc."

"He was dropped somewhere else?" Ruiz said, trying to start the conversation. "Then moved?"

"No," Hady said without pause. "He died at that intersection."

"Dropped from what?" Harvey asked. "A damn plane? Come on."

"Not my department," Hady answered, moving for her equipment beside the table.

Ruiz settled next to the body of the young man. The mystery of his death circled them, though it seemed to impact Hady less. She preferred the dead to the living. It was another change he never questioned. The boy's arms had no hair on them, like they had been shaved clean or plucked out like the feathers found at the scene. There were markings on the inside of his elbows.

"Hady?" Ruiz called, pulling her back to them. "Are these track marks?"

"They are," she said. "I found markings between his toes as well."

Harvey whistled. "Sounds like Mr. Connelly here was growing into quite the addict."

"Did you find anything in his system?"

"I did. And on his person." Hady grabbed a small vial from the table and handed it to Harvey. He twisted the lid off, taking a short whiff. He pulled back, closing his eyes.

"What is it?"

Her reply was terse. "No idea."

"Hady," Ruiz intoned.

The woman sighed and shrugged. "I've never seen anything like it. But his system was full of it. If the fall hadn't killed him, this would have. Very soon."

Harvey handed back the vial. "Great. Come for answers and get more questions."

Ruiz felt the same and asked the same question right before Harvey did, the old man turning to him with tired eyes.

"You sure you want this job?"

CHAPTER FOUR

He cut out early. Four hours into the night shift at Central and Ruiz was unfocused and detached, living in another world. Another case, as it were. The usual patrol, the typical banter with Burke and the crowd did little to distract him. Three domestic calls, one involving an old woman and a parrot—don't ask—did nothing to detract from the case of the fallen man and the bag full of feathers.

Harvey called it the itch, and it fit—the notion of something digging beneath the surface of the skin that could not be appeased until scratched. Repeatedly. Forcefully.

Ruiz had the itch. Bad.

Especially after their visit with Hady. The composition may have been a mystery to the bleary-eyed assistant coroner but the label was clear enough. A drug was in Connelly's system, one that threatened to end his life as easily as the swan dive that did the job.

A drug meant a supplier, a distribution chain. It meant other players in the game. It was a lead, at least, the only one so far.

Harvey had the case covered. Of course he did. He was a detective with hundreds of cases under his belt, if not thousands. He had been doing the job when Ruiz was in diapers, belching out his alphabet after a stiff bottle of milk. Harvey could handle the murder without a doubt. But he asked for Ruiz's input, his eyes on the scene. He wanted him to run with it, didn't he?

After bailing on his shift, to which Burke had more than a few things to say, Ruiz decided to proceed with his one and only lead. He turned to contacts, men and women scattered throughout the city of Portents. Some he had employed from time to time to keep an ear out. They served as boots on the ground. Ex-cons, ex-junkies, or at least so they claimed when in his company.

He knew better. Most of the time.

Snitches were necessary for the job. A little slack on a low-level skel meant scoring the bigger fish later on. The law of averages, or so it was justified, even by a rules-and-procedures officer like Ruiz.

His first three attempts at insight into the drug that flooded David Connelly's body came up empty. They were wastes of time. But the fourth? The fourth led him close to the scene of the crime, west of the Knoll, into the waiting maw of the strip east of the Maple—a known drug haven and one heavily patrolled when manpower allowed.

Dante Jenkins wasn't a crook, or at least not one that required jail time. He was a hood looking to find his own version of "easy street." One Ruiz provided occasionally to glean the latest news from the streets when working the job.

When Ruiz parked his rusted-out sedan off Evans, Dante stood in front of a closed convenience store with a young woman. Girl was more apt and Asian to boot. Ruiz plodded slowly behind the snitch, the man's attentions elsewhere.

"I'm talking surround sound, baby," Dante cooed into the girl's ear. She ran her hand along his chest, the other through his hair, drawing him closer. "Blow your clothes right off. I mean, if you're wearing any, know what I'm..."

His laughter died at her widening eyes. She backed off, hands dropping to her side. She spun on her heels, rushing down the street, leaving behind a confused and disappointed Dante.

"What's wrong with you?" he yelled after her. "Naked! I was saying be naked! Where are you—?"

"Dante."

His head fell to his chest, turning to face the waiting Ruiz. His eyes rolled. "Aw, come on, cop. You know how long it took me to get with her?"

"Five minutes and $100 an hour?"

"You think I need to pay with *this*?" Dante lifted his shirt and shook his hips.

Ruiz turned away. "If I show up more often? Yes. Whatever *this* is. And don't do that dance ever again."

"What do—?" Dante's eyes flared at the approaching Ruiz, who pressed the young black man against the wall of the convenience store. "Hey!"

Ruiz spun him around, pinning his hands to the brick, then spread his legs. Hands patted Dante's muscular frame, stopping at his waist.

"I think I've done pretty good for you, Dante," Ruiz said behind his back. "No jail time, even with the stash I found at your place. Not to mention this little affair."

Ruiz stepped away and Dante left the wall. Ruiz held tight to a Glock he found tucked in the man's pants. Dante's hands ran through his thick hair.

"I was holding that for a friend."

Ruiz grinned, securing the safety on the weapon. "And I thank you for it. Friend might be a stretch, though. Guess we'll see what you've got for me."

Dante slid down the wall, head tucked between his knees. "Dammit. What you need?"

Ruiz tucked the Glock away with a smile. His fingers slipped into his right pocket and removed the single image within. He held out the photograph and Dante snatched it from him. "Local boy. Landed hard on the street. Probably heard about it?"

"Yeah," Dante said with a shrug. "Crazy crap. What else is new?"

"Some drug was found in his system. Something new. I need a name."

Dante jumped to his feet. "Whoa. Out of my comfort zone, cop. You know me."

He did. Very well, in fact. Had his rap sheet memorized. Knew his associates too. Dante may have walked the streets solo, he may have kept to himself in his life of crime, but he also paid attention to the world around him. He paid close attention with a keener eye than any legal means would provide.

"I do know you, Dante," Ruiz said. "That's why I'm here. Who is it, Dante? A name is all I need. Or do we take a walk to Central to explain my new favorite backup piece?"

"But—"

"Dante."

His head sank. "Damn."

Once he started talking, there was no stopping him. Most of the information shared was gibberish, hearsay that amounted to little in the way of a workable lead. He did not have a supplier name. He did, however, have the true address of David Connelly, one that had been attracting attention over the last few weeks. And not by the nicest of clienteles.

Ruiz made it his next stop. A halfway house north of the port, a low-income district bordering on tenements. Ruiz left the badge hidden beneath a light coat. His sidearm remained fixed, tucked away from view. A ball cap hid his features from the few people wandering the streets at the late hour.

He asked a delirious woman on the stoop for Connelly's room number. After a lecture on the fading colors of the world and the demon that was Walt Disney, she gave the number.

The door laid ajar, the first of the vultures already having departed the dead man's domicile. Ruiz shuffled through ratty mattresses strewn across the floor and the upended shelves that once lined the far wall of the room. Albums from bands older than Ruiz, worn-out paperbacks, and the rare DVD joined the wreckage once called the floor. None of it mattered.

Something caught the officer's eye. Trapped in the shelf of the broken wall unit was a business card. Ruiz plucked it clear. A single address was scribbled along the back.

A scream cut through the hall, joined by a dozen more seconds later—worse than a prison cellblock. Ruiz's heart pounded. He checked his watch. Only four minutes had passed. It was long enough. He slipped the card into his pocket and raced for the door, leaving behind the mess that remained of David Connelly's life.

He stopped short in the hallway, looking down to the front door of the halfway house. Five men waited for him; the other occupants of the home crawled into the shadows away from them. The man blocking the front door smiled upon seeing him, pointing up. The others rushed forward, blood in their eyes.

Company had caught up. And they were none too happy to see him.

CHAPTER FIVE

Run, you idiot, run!

The clatter of footsteps racing up the stairs to the second floor of the halfway house joined the thumping in his chest. Ruiz raced for the end of the hall, trying to find an exit. Derelicts and tenants alike threw curious stares but quickly tucked into the corners as the lone officer crashed through the warped and splintered emergency exit.

Ruiz's feet swung out from under him, his body crashing down the long flight of stairs before coming to a halt at the bottom in front of the waiting door. His body ached, his back on fire, but he jumped to his feet, the handle out of reach. He turned back to the stairs and saw them.

Five of them. They hooted and hollered, their cries increasing, echoing into the night air. His car was in the other direction. His turn south was more instinct than actual thought.

Two of the men, hooded in oversized sweatshirts, flanked him on the right. Another pair was on the left. They snapped at him, mimicking animals more than men, their eyes and teeth glints of light in the dark. The fifth stayed behind, still caught in the hunt, but subdued. Ruiz turned, cursing the act immediately, but he had to see for himself.

The fifth was free of his hood, scraggly locks of white hair running down to his shoulders. Scars ran down his cheeks, red on pale skin. But the eyes spoke to Ruiz most. Yellow with black pupils wide and engrossing. Pulling the fleeing officer in with their depth.

"Little bird, little bird," the fifth man cooed. His voice was thick and deep, a booming microphone compared to the snaps of his companions. "Fly away home."

They were catching up. There was no doubt and no way to outrun them all. Ruiz was fit, exercised regularly, and stayed away from the trappings of the job, donuts and all. But these five had the edge. A drug. A manic behavior that echoed their hollering through the night. They were going to catch him.

And then?

He knew the answer. No goodbye to Michelle, no way to contact her to tell him how sorry he was for what he did. What he should have done. As a husband. As a father. Dammit. No chance to witness the birth of his child. His son. (Of course he was going to have a son.) He even had the name picked out—Diego, after his father. A stupid thing to hold on to in the end.

Air left him—a jolt from the left. A lucky shot from the kid closest to him. Ruiz fell hard, rolling with the blow as kicks flew his way from the others. Hard kicks, which lined his ribs with future bruises. Bruises he would be lucky to see from the way things were going.

The roll helped. It kept him moving and threw off his pursuers. They backed off from each other, unsure who should proceed first. The act was gentlemanly, allowing the others to have a crack at the cop in their midst. It gave him breathing room. It gave him a moment.

All he needed.

Ruiz let the roll continue. He brought his feet under him and launched up toward the pair of men on his right. Shocked looks met his scream; his arms were spread wide to tackle both. All three fell to the ground in a heap, the clatter of footsteps rushing from behind. Ruiz elbowed the two downed men hard, falling back into the approaching pair. He slipped between them, grabbing tight to their arms, one left and one right, before pulling them into each other. Their momentum swung them hard into a collision and they staggered back.

A grin slipped from the officer's lips. The fifth man held back. His yellow eyes burrowed into Ruiz, giving him pause. The four men, groaning and cursing, regrouped slowly.

His moment was up.

Construction was rampant on the east end, capital flooding the area from major industries to give it a new lease on life. Ruiz ran, taking the fence of the site at Clemson and Willis with effort, falling hard against the asphalt within. The four hoods followed suit, mere steps behind him. Their leader held tight to the fence, eyes wide with anticipation.

"Faster, little bird," he called into the night. "Faster."

It filled his head, the words of the man with the bleached hair and the yellow eyes. Less than human, cawing after him while his flock surrounded him. Sweat dripped in Ruiz's eyes, blurring his vision. He swatted it away, pumping his legs harder and faster, feeling less and less momentum.

Move your ass, dammit.

Encouraging words that fell flat. Fell hard, just as easily as Ruiz did at the turn from the heavy equipment trucks blocking the far exit of the site. A slip against the loose gravel littering the ground surrounding the new office building being constructed. His left leg gave out, and his hands hit the ground first.

Jagged stone pierced through his pants. Blood ran down his legs. His chest ached, his back flared in pain from his fall down the stairs. Even their kicks were starting to take hold. His body fought him on every front at the worst possible time.

They surrounded him with excitement in their eyes. Yellow eyes locked on him like an owl on the hunt. His flock gathered around him for feeding time. A few licked their lips; the others cracked knuckles and necks to prepare for a struggle their prey had little to give.

I'm so sorry, Michelle.

It was better than a prayer for Ruiz. It was the only thought that mattered when the shadows scurried closer and closer over him.

Until they stopped.

It came from out of nowhere. A stiff breeze ran along his backside, through his thick black mane of hair, then rushed away from him. From that initial breeze it picked up speed, growing exponentially in a matter of seconds. Ruiz tucked low to the ground, hair rushing over his eyes. He fought it back, locked on the surprised look of the five men surrounding him.

Right before the wind blew them off their feet, their chanting and hollering turned to screams. The gale force carried them across the construction site, bodies flailing out of control, lost to the mercy of the elements. They crashed hard against the metal beams supporting the structure in the center of the lot, the wind holding tight to them for seconds before dropping them to the earth with a crash.

Groans filled the air as the men fought their way to their feet. The wind remained, a reminder of their pain. The four men looked to the yellow-eyed center who kept his grin fixed, despite the snarl of his lips.

"Be safe, little bird," he yelled over the wind. The others fell back into the night, leaving Ruiz with their final warning. "Or we'll find you."

Ruiz blinked hard. The wind faded as quickly as his attackers. He spun around hard, looking for some explanation, some reason why he was still breathing.

He found it in the form of a man, heavily shrouded by the shadows of the construction site. In a blink, the figure was gone and Ruiz was alone. But not before he caught sight of something in his hand. Something that appeared to glow brighter than the stars above for a brief moment before falling dark.

A stone.

CHAPTER SIX

Ruiz struggled with his shirt. His gauze-padded hand was useless to assist, leaving him with the left to work the buttons into place. It was slow. It was damn well aggravating but not as much as the hospital surrounding him.

Hospitals made him physically and mentally ill, just by standing in one. The first time occurred as a kid. A car accident landed him in the emergency room, where he had to stay overnight for observation. Away from his family. Away from his life. If ever death decided to stop by for a chat, it was that night.

How little things had changed.

"I'm leaving," he announced to the nurse. He fumbled with the second button from the top, the most crucial of all buttons if he remembered correctly, cursing under his breath while undermining the lithe woman's effort at her thankless job.

"Sir, if you would—"

"I said I'm leaving." He hopped down from the bed, shuffling away from her. The frustrated nurse huffed loudly, then departed. He wondered how many people she would bring with her next time, hoping his damn shirt would be buttoned by then so he could rush out without another round of prodding.

And questions.

He had enough of those. The man with the stone. Whatever that was. And the yellow eyes of the thug that chased him. The yellow eyes that refused to leave Ruiz when he shut his own.

Morning had yet to break, and was inching closer and closer with each tick of the clock. It certainly was a night to remember. He had deep scratches and sore ribs—bruised, not cracked—which needed cleaning and bandaging. He hated hospitals but recognized their necessity, at least on some level. Stepping away from the window slowly, Ruiz heard steps clacking along the threshold of the room.

"How many times—?" Ruiz stopped at the sight of Detective Julian Harvey in the doorway, fedora in his hands and anger in his eyes. "Oh."

"Yeah," Harvey muttered through gritted teeth. "Oh."

Ruiz's eyes fell. "Detective, listen—"

"Shut it, Ruiz," Harvey snapped, dropping his hat in the chair beside him before he sat. "Just shut it. What the hell were you thinking?"

"I—"

"What part of shut it don't you understand? Oh, I know you want to spin me a tale, give me the heroic version of the *accidental* incident that landed you here, but we both know better."

Ruiz waited a moment. When silence filled the room, he took a deep breath, hands before him. "Listen, there was—"

"Not done yet," Harvey continued with a sneer. He was playing with the officer, Ruiz realized, watching the way the man's eyes grazed over his wounds, noticing the tenderness. "You do this again, Ruiz, what do you think happens? You think being young means indestructible, but it doesn't. You want to skirt procedure? Want to be a cowboy out there? Guys like that don't have long careers and we both know you ain't them. You have a future. Live to see it."

Ruiz bit back the urge to speak. He had held the same argument, the same reasons as well, in his head. Curiosity won out, exactly what both expected would happen.

"Done?" Ruiz finally asked.

Harvey padded his knees, sinking deeper into the chair. "Hear any of it?"

"Some."

Harvey tsked. "Doubtful."

"Someone was there," Ruiz said, trying to move on.

"From the looks of you, I'd say five or six someones."

"Not them," Ruiz said, pacing the room before turning back to the man. "And it was five."

"This time. With the boys at the station, though?"

"At least ten." Both grinned, laughing off the severity of the night. For a moment. Ruiz continued his pacing. "But listen. I'm talking about someone else. Some guy. Couldn't really see him but he did something to them. Like he summoned a damn hurricane to blow them away from me."

Harvey's eyes flared. "A hurricane?"

Ruiz shook his head. "I know how it sounds. He had this thing in his hands. A stone or something."

"A stone."

It crept out softly. No question about it. There was a sign of recognition in the old man's eyes. He wasn't surprised by the tale.

"You—"

"Alejo."

The question left him before being asked. Michelle rushed into the room, ignoring the grizzled detective in the corner for the standing officer.

"Michelle?"

Her arms slipped around him, pulling him close. "Hey. Easy there."

She held him tight. "Suck it up, Officer."

"Good to see you too."

Michelle pulled back, her hands running down his arms. "What the hell were you thinking?"

"Good question."

She turned, ignoring Ruiz's disarming smirk, toward the man in the corner of the room. The bandaged man slipped between the pair, sighing. "Michelle, this is Detective Julian Harvey."

"Harvey is fine," the detective replied. He stood, hand extended. "Ma'am."

She shook it. "Michelle."

"I wouldn't go too hard on him." Harvey let the shake end, collecting his fedora from the chair. He puffed it back into position, letting the brim run across his fingers in a slow rhythmic motion. "Let his body handle that part."

"I'm fine," Ruiz said, attracting glares from both of his visitors. "Leaving, in fact."

"Are you crazy?" Michelle asked. "You just—"

"I'm bandaged," Ruiz interrupted, lifting his scraped right arm. "I have a bed at home."

"Then I suggest you use it," Harvey said. He fixed his hat over his thinning hair. "Take a couple days. Your exam is coming up. Focus on that."

Ruiz nodded, shaking the man's hand. "Detective."

They shared a look, Harvey's thin baby blues acknowledging every word left unsaid—from both sides of the conversation. Behind them was a warning. *Do what I'm asking, kid. For your own good.*

The look faded quickly, a smile showering Ruiz's wife. "Congratulations, Michelle. I never had the pleasure but I always wanted a bundle of rugrats."

Her mouth fell open and she turned to her husband. "I didn't know you shared."

"I didn't." Ruiz shrugged.

"Take the time, Ruiz," Harvey said, inching for the door. "Listen to your wife."

"Handsome and smart."

"Oh, I like her." Harvey's cheeks flushed. "See you at the office."

They waited, watching the man's shadow shrink against the long hallway of the hospital. Once alone, Michelle settled beside her husband, looking him over closely for the first time. Always the protector of the family.

"How bad?"

"I'm fine," he said, puffing his chest. Her hand grazed his ribs and he felt searing pain run down his side. "I'll be fine."

"Alejo—"

"Let's go home."

She stopped, gnawing lightly on her lower lip. There was no changing his mind. She nodded and fixed the mismatched buttons on his shirt, careful not to upset his ribs further. They started for the door.

On the slow trek to the car, Ruiz thought about the case, about David Connelly and the feathers. About yellow eyes and his four followers.

Be safe, little bird. Or we'll find you.

Ruiz bit back the fear. *Not if I find you first.*

CHAPTER SEVEN

He couldn't leave it alone. During the fitful sleep that carried him from morning to late afternoon, nothing else occupied his thoughts. There was no distraction to keep him sated until his body healed. He did his best to wait, to hold off, hoping—almost praying—for a call to come through with word that the Donnelly case had been closed.

That those damn yellow eyes would never bother anyone again.

Not that he knew definitively that the two men connected in any way, shape, or form. But he did, didn't he? It was there, right in his eyes, in the taunts echoing through his exhausted mind, chasing him as effectively as the group of five had the previous night.

Be safe, little bird. Or we'll find you.

By the time the sun set, Ruiz couldn't handle it any longer: Michelle's hovering, the silence of the phone, even the background noise of the television...everything grated him the wrong way.

So he left.

A quick explanation, one that tore out his heart, with each lie slipping from his tongue to his adorably concerned wife. He blamed work, his inability to rest. He would go to the office and finish some reports. Nothing taxing, nothing vital. He wouldn't even pull out the uniform. It was just a little paperwork and nothing more.

He took his gun, though. He couldn't very well leave without that. He was already doing the dumbest thing possible, against all good reason. *Best not tempt fate any further.*

The card was where he left it in the driver's side door, collecting dust with the spare change stuck underneath. He freed it.

374 Ness.

The Corridor.

It took him forty-five minutes with the evening traffic to reach Ness. Once there, all signs of life vanished. The Corridor was having a tough time of late. Some called the experiment to mix business and residential neighborhoods a failure after only a few years. Some say it was doomed from the start, a curse upon the area from powers beyond. The properties built—and built quickly at that—were staggered blocks of emptiness. Windows shattered by kids, the vacant lots more graffiti playgrounds than homes.

Ruiz parked two blocks over from Ness, his sneakers silent against the pavement as he walked. He removed the gauze running up his right arm, the pain a dull ache. He scurried, keeping low despite the pain of his bruised ribs, sticking close to the defunct lots on the business side of the experiment.

The home in question was dark throughout. Broken windows adorned the front and sides with cracked and torn siding frayed along the edges like a well-worn book. Ruiz pulled his coat in tighter, the cool wind ripping through him. He waited.

Would it always be like this with Michelle? Nights and days away from her and the kids? *Kids*, like he had plans on the second before the first even screamed hello to the world. Ruiz, the master planner, at work again—setting the schedule with his perfect world and his perfect life, having it all make sense with the flick of a switch.

Thirty minutes into his chilled stakeout, Ruiz made a dash for the home. He sprinted, hopping the chain link fence outlining the property, and tucked low near the side of the single floor bungalow. No movement within. No noise. Good enough for him.

Ruiz slipped into the home, and tripped on the sill. A quick curse escaped his lips, his feet stomping on the hardwood floor for stability. His bruised ribs begged for a reprieve but he ignored them. His gun was in place, stinging the open cuts on his palm. The sidearm led him through the home.

He entered at the outskirt of the kitchen. Cupboard doors were opened, boxes of goods threatening to collapse the shelves. Dishes filled the sink, the smell forcing Ruiz back a step. Scratches embedded in the floor ran the length of the room, like someone dragged knives along it.

The bedrooms fared no better. Mattresses settled in each corner. No frames were necessary. No furnishings, either. No lamps, desks, or even pillows. No clothes in the closets.

And no drug lab.

A bunch of squatters and most likely the crew that ambushed him the night before but nothing to suggest their connection to Donnelly.

Ruiz stepped into the living room, frustrated. He was so sure the evidence would be here. In its place was a flophouse, a party home in the middle of nowhere for a bunch of kids. Kicking angrily at the torn-up couch, Ruiz's foot slipped and he fell forward. Steadying himself, Ruiz bent low, reaching for the obstacle threatening to knock him over. It settled between his fingers, a foot in length and soft to the touch.

A feather.

Dozens of them littered the floor, tucked in the couch cushions, covering the vents and piled high in each corner. Ruiz followed each pile, lifting one up to confirm it matched the last—all black like Donnelly's keepsakes—until he reached the edge of the living room. The feather seemed stuck in place, fighting him. He followed it to its root and discovered more feathers, rising higher and higher until he realized the truth—

They were attached to a body.

"Boo."

Ruiz fell back, landing hard against the ground. Yellow eyes popped open, surrounding him.

The tenants had come home.

Ruiz fought to keep his gun steady, spinning to greet each of them in turn, hoping that his nerve showed better than it felt.

It was them. The men from the previous night. Only different. *Changed.* Feathers were locked in place along their arms like immense black wings. Their eyes, wide and misshapen, glared at him. Even with the matching sets he could tell the leader among them, stepping out from behind his brothers.

His feathers were white.

"Welcome to our nest, little bird."

They laughed at him, the sound a cry from their long, beak-shaped noses. One turned to a cough, growing more and more intense until he fell forward, gripping tight to his chest. Feathers flew from his body, his bony arms reasserting themselves.

The white-haired leader stepped forward, a smile ever present. He reached into his belt and retrieved a small vial. Ruiz recognized the thick, black liquid as the drug Hady found on the victim, David Connelly.

The convulsing junkie took the vial and eagerly downed the liquid inside. Immediately the cough faded and the change returned. Feathers, thicker and brighter in their darkness, spread wide down his arms. His eyes roared with a yellow hue. His wings carried him from the floor, allowing him to float in the air.

Until the next hit was needed—a hit Connelly never received. *That* was why he seemed to fall out of the sky. Because he did.

"What the hell are you?" Ruiz yelled over their laughter.

Yellow eyes moved closer but the leader held them back. "You should have flown away while you had the chance."

"Don't move," Ruiz bellowed. He jumped to his feet, gun threatening to slip from the sweat collecting against his palms. He backed up, the hallway to the kitchen free from their presence. "I...I called it in. Backup will be—"

"Too late, little bird," the leader cooed. He could read Ruiz's fear like a book. "Far too late."

Ruiz's finger slipped from the trigger, fear freezing him in place. He watched the black feathers dancing in front of him edge closer and closer with each flap. Soon darkness would be all he had left.

Until a hand landed on his shoulder. Ruiz felt a cool breath against him.

"Run."

The shadow from the previous night, the man with the stone, leapt over Ruiz into the fray. His final act pushed Ruiz back and the frightened officer fell to the ground, unable to act.

Only able to watch.

The man sported a thin beard against his cheeks and fire in his eyes. His trench coat was black, blending with the shadows of the room. He wore sneakers and jeans but when he moved they bled together like fluid color. He pounded into the packed room, each step decisive and confident. He slammed back the first two assailants, quickly diving to avoid the assault of the two behind him. They soon joined the first pair on the ground, reeling from their attacker. Only the white-feathered leader stood. And alone, Ruiz finally saw something in his eyes other than excitement at the kill.

Fear.

Taking the opportunity, Ruiz reeled backward and away from the fight, trying to get his footing and failing. His hand slid from the wall and knocked into the adjacent door. It shook from its frame, not completely clasped from its last use. Stairs within led to the basement.

Curious or not, Ruiz wanted to get clear of the home. He wanted to forget the night ever occurred, beg for his wife's forgiveness and then take the week off. Hell, maybe the month. He earned it.

But curiosity was a bitch of a thing, one that crept into a man's veins and clung tighter than any drug the five beaten men in the living room could ever handle. And Ruiz was only human.

He took the stairs slowly, the gun in his hand steadier now. Work lights sat positioned throughout the room and Ruiz clicked the one closest to the bottom of the stairwell. He stopped, unable to move.

A table sat in the center of the room. A woman was strapped to its surface. Tubes ran from her wiry frame to machines beside the table. They connected to a series of beakers and test tubes on adjacent workstations that stretched across the basement.

The drug lab. But the drug itself?

She was unconscious, the tubes running black from her chest and throat. Ruiz inched closer to the woman. But *woman* was the wrong word for her. Her bottom half agreed with the assessment, thin legs and slight feet matching the definition of the fairer sex. Feathers stretched up her arms and coated her torso. Her face did not carry the eyes, nose, and lips of a woman but the great beak of a bird and the oversized eyes of one as well.

"Wh-what?" Ruiz stuttered, stopping next to the creature. "What are you?"

"A harpy."

Ruiz spun at the sound of the voice, finger ready to pull the trigger. The man from upstairs stood at the base of the staircase, hands open before him. His light gray eyes echoed his own, but they appeared older—much older.

"She is a harpy."

"Stay there," Ruiz said, hoping his voice didn't sound as weak as he imagined. "Stay right there."

"I will," the man replied.

"Who is she?"

"I don't know."

Ruiz's eyes flared. "You just said—"

"*What* she is. Not *who* she is." The man looked around the room. "Or how she came to be in this place, though I'll be sure to ask."

The man stepped into the room and Ruiz shook his sidearm, inching back into the beakers of the lab. "I said don't move."

"Officer—"

"No," Ruiz snapped. "I've heard enough tonight."

"Not quite."

The voice came from the top of the stairs, and echoed in the basement. It stopped the two men, who were locked in a stalemate of stares from across the table where the woman was strapped tight. Steps joined the voice, inching closer to the room. Ruiz refused to look, refused to let the man before him come any closer. He had seen the damage he'd wrought, his responses adding nothing to his credibility.

But the voice, now present in the room, knew him well enough. A hand patted the stranger's shoulder and the nod of his head inched him away from the table and the waiting gun of the overwhelmed Ruiz. Detective Julian Harvey smiled at him with open hands.

"We should talk, kid."

CHAPTER EIGHT

Ruiz sat on the front porch steps of the abandoned home, looking out over the Corridor. Nothing looked right in the darkness. Nothing felt right. The world waited to swallow him whole and spit him out. Everything was different now.

Cries of pain slipped from the windows and the open door, whipping with the blowing wind. The five men within—boys really, and looking more like them with each passing moment—screamed for relief. Their highs were ending, the hormone forcibly removed from their captive, fading from their systems. The feathers floated softly to the ground between their roiling frames—the pain of the act hopefully lasting for hours, if not days, if Ruiz had anything to say about it.

Not that he did. He couldn't find the words. Men (boys) high on a drug that allowed them to soar over the city like birds. The drug offered the ultimate high and the ultimate comedown. How did it come to this? Why was this possible?

Four years in the department and the numerous incidents seen during that time expanded his worldview. It changed him, but fell within the purview of the job. The job and the city he called home his entire life.

Portents.

He knew the city so well. They complemented each other as much as he and Michelle did on some level. His experience within Portents was an open book, one he explored for the last thirty years, only to find he was still stuck on the title page.

The door settled into the frame, soft steps creaking along long, swollen boards. Detective Julian Harvey reached for the banister, gripped it tight to sit beside the ruminating officer.

Ruiz remained silent, afraid to speak, afraid to understand anything that had happened. Why it happened, what it meant for him.

Harvey took a deep breath, hands on swollen knees. "He calls himself Greystone."

The man with the stone. He took out five hoodlums in the living room of the abandoned house as if they were no obstacle at all. Something Ruiz's bruised ribs and scraped body knew differently. *Greystone.*

Harvey shook his head before the question came out. "No idea if it's his actual name or what. No first name, or at least he's never thrown it my way. I've run into him a few times. Some bad times. Like tonight."

"The department—?"

"Doesn't know. Or doesn't want to know," Harvey said. "But they should."

A vigilante prowling the streets? Another change, one under his nose for how long? "And that thing? That thing he took out of here? That you let him take out of here?"

"What did you want me to do, kid?"

Ruiz ran his hands through his hair. "What was it?"

Harvey stared out to the street, the flashing lights of their backup approaching but still blocks away. "A harpy. His word, but it sounds better than bird lady. Something that decided to come out of the myth closet and have a peek around town."

A thin glare met the detective.

"Don't give me that look," Harvey said. "I know how it all sounds."

"Bullshit," Ruiz snapped. He stood, clomping down the groaning steps of the porch for the front walkway. He jammed his hands into his pockets, the wind cutting through him—the cold chilling him to his core.

"Ronne ran tests on the feathers," Harvey continued. "They weren't from any known species of bird."

Ruiz turned back to him, eyes flaring. "Do you even hear yourself?"

Harvey shrugged. "This is how the city works, kid. Really works. We do what we can but there has always been something more out there. Something most of us never see."

"It isn't real," Ruiz replied, shaking his finger at the man. "It can't be."

"It is," Harvey said. He pointed back to the house and the dull cries of pain within. "This crap here? The Greystone? The damn harpy? It's real and it's all been here a lot longer than we have. Accept it."

"I don't."

Ruiz squeezed the badge in his pocket and took it out. The gold glinted under the streetlight. He was so sure of things, and of his role in them, his future with them. Detective at thirty, captain at thirty-five. A family man bringing the light back to the city.

All a lie, the truth underneath ugly. Damn ugly.

"Ruiz," Harvey called. "Sit down."

He turned back to the old man on the porch. Harvey kept the secret of the city and now asked Ruiz to do the same. Not just keep it but also understand it. Live with it. Ruiz shook his head.

"No," he answered. "I can't do that. I can't believe it. Won't. I've lived here my entire life."

"So have they."

Ruiz turned away, the shield clutched tight in his hand. It felt wrong suddenly. Something he never thought possible. The badge had lost its shimmer. But he needed it. Now more than ever—not only for his own stability but also for his growing family.

Harvey stood, joining Ruiz. His hand rested on the young man's shoulder. "Go home, kid. Be with your wife. The city will be here tomorrow. It will always be here. Will you?"

Ruiz didn't answer. Couldn't answer. Not without time. Instead, he simply left. Deserted Harvey to the crime scene and the approaching backup and started for his car.

He took his time going home, lost in the myriad twists and turns of downtown, before joining the expressway north for Venture Cove and his small, innocuous domicile. No sign penetrated him, no prolific answer visited him during his musings along the dark streets of Portents. Nothing grabbed at and shook him from the cloud infecting his being. Emptiness consumed him.

The feeling stayed with him even as the rusted-out sedan came to a halt in his driveway. He stepped out into the night air and noticed the light on inside. It was late, much later than he had intended when he snuck out earlier. Michelle should have been resting.

Ruiz raced inside, fear of yellow eyes hidden in every shadow forcing him into a run. His sidearm slipped into his grip.

The kitchen was empty, the light running from the bedroom at the far end of the hall. The nursery. Ruiz briskly padded along the thin carpet along the center of the floor, eyes on the ajar door.

He nudged the four-panel cherry door open, his hand along its edge to keep it from rubbing along the carpet. Then he stopped and stared at her. Michelle. She hummed a low tune, unpacking boxes and smiling at each onesie purchased over the last three months in preparation. Even the Darth Vader one Ruiz picked out, announcing to the world prematurely that a son was on the way.

She looked beautiful, radiant, and everything in between. He was lost in her presence. Lost everywhere. Except with her. Working so hard to put together the room for their child, put their lives together, as she always had. Ruiz tucked the sidearm away and thumbed the badge in his pocket. She was his protector. He needed to be hers. And their child's.

Even from the truth.

"You're home," Michelle finally said, surprised at his silent gaze. "I didn't hear you come in."

He didn't reply, letting her enthusiasm rise, her bare feet rushing her to the recently opened package in the center of the room.

"Look what I found after you left," she beamed. "I know. More shopping. But I thought it would look good on the wall above the crib. For our little monkey. What do you—?" She stopped, the enthusiasm melting to concern. "What's wrong?"

He fought for a smirk, sighing. "Nothing. Tired is all."

"You should have taken the day like Harvey said. How was work?"

He hesitated, hearing the question for the first time. The details slipped from his tongue and he swallowed hard. His silence split the room—the great divide forming between them. There was no sharing everything, not anymore.

"Fine," Ruiz said. "Just another day."

He smiled, taking the monkey image into his hands. He headed for the wall to get started on decorating the nursery. Preparing for the future.

GREMLINS

CHAPTER ONE

It was his day off. He never made that distinction before. Work days and days off bled into each other, his caseload never truly leaving him, his thoughts never straying from the pile of paperwork littering his desk or the red on the large board in the middle of the bullpen.

Then Beth died.

Days off meant something different to Detective Greg Loren. They meant searching, endlessly looking for the answers that led to his wife's fall. An angel, a beacon of light in his life, Beth parted the seas, tucked away the darkness, and sang a melody like no one's business. All for him. He needed her like no other, and when she died, he lost himself in the city of her birth. It was not his city, never his city.

The fall from their apartment building's roof led the initial reports to read *suicide*. Loren refused to accept that, an impossibility in his eyes. Murder was the alternative. His colleagues at Central did what they could, Ruiz more than anyone. They kept the case open, interviewing tirelessly. Dozens were brought in, questioned about their whereabouts. Ex-cons, men and women with a grudge against the stalwart officer of the Portents Police Department. All had an alibi. It was nothing but dead ends. In a blink, six months of searching led to nothing. Six long months of chasing shadows with Loren obsessing over the affair. It had to stop. *He* had to stop.

He couldn't.

He knew the truth. That truth kept him going, gave him new purpose on his time away from the precinct.

Like tonight.

Loren stayed close to the man, following him through a local supermarket, tracking him to the Laundromat at the end of his block and then to his apartment. Ronnie Phillips. Ex-con. The gaunt figure from the past earned a six-year stint upstate for assault and battery, released a year earlier for good behavior. Plenty of time to plan some payback.

He was the one. Loren was sure of it.

Pacing the stoop, Loren watched Phillips' shadow run across the window of his second floor apartment in Lowtown, a ghetto district south of the Knoll. The man displaced from the world by five years fit the bill. Bitter over his arrest, he fought the charges his entire time in court. Loren went so far as to knock down his first attempt at parole. The man could have easily tracked him down during his time in lockup. He had the anger—his conviction proved that. Phillips could have arranged for Beth's fall—her murder.

Questions needed asking. He reached for the handle, his sidearm drawn but tucked close and out of sight. Answers would be given, one way or another.

Then his phone rang.

The infernal device echoed in the street and the thin shadow on the second floor shifted for the window, forcing Loren to leave the comfort of the stoop. He headed north, fleeing from the open window, answering the call and cursing the caller in one breath.

Ronnie Phillips had to wait.

Midnight slipped away by the time he made it to the Second Precinct just outside the northern coves. The building looked old, older than even the Rath, which had been around for almost a century. The masonry was cracked. Graffiti lined the walls leading to the parking garage. Loren was out of his element but walked to the double doors at the top of the stairs. He wanted this over fast. There was real work to be done.

In the small lobby, an old man rummaged through his belongings for his identification. He tried to bypass the protocol, his eyes bleary from lack of sleep. Loren moved for the desk, his badge already in place.

"Loren," he said, jarring the officer's attention from the old man. "I was called."

Slowly the man moved for his notes. He appeared more lost than Loren, unsure of the question being asked. Loren sighed, tucking the badge away. It wasn't going to be his night.

The desk sergeant never had the chance to answer Loren, not that one was forthcoming. Instead, Loren was greeted by a man in a much-too-tight button-down with an undone collar and a loose tie. A button along his midsection threatened to give way, helped along by the man's extended hand. Both failed to distract from the deep blue bruise along the man's left cheek.

"Loren?"

Loren took the hand, shaking it once. "Yeah."

"Robert Standish," the man said, waving him toward the bullpen past the lobby. "I called you in."

Strike one then, Standish, Loren thought, following close to the overweight detective. The precinct was sparse with personnel, a departure from Central's constant flow of traffic in and out all day and night. The northern coves were considered the safer areas of the city. Lower crime rates. Less overall violence and break-ins. But this was not the sole reason for the skeleton crew. Balloons covered the corners, a large and colorful banner reading *HAPPY RETIREMENT, BURKE* hanging from the ceiling. A half-eaten cake sat on a staging table next to the coffee machine, melted ice cream dripping at a steady pace to the floor.

Looks like the party went somewhere else.

"We don't get many visits from Lucky Thirteen," Standish said, leading Loren down a hallway.

Lucky Thirteen. The Rath. Central Precinct carried with it many names and many stories. Most came at a cost. Instead of bringing the department together, instead of unifying them under the leadership of a central office, all it managed to do was alienate those not included in the so-called elite club. It created envy from the other precincts and their staff. Like the green eyes stabbing Loren's chest currently.

The status never meant anything to Loren. He started at the Eighth, never wanting anything more than to do the job his superiors tasked him. Then Ruiz called him up three years ago, well before he was ready for the big leagues of Central. If anyone could ever be ready for such things.

"You called, I came."

Standish stopped at the water cooler, a sneer on his lips. A plastic cup slipped free from the pile next to him and he filled it. Loren waited, impatiently, peering around the room. Evidence was kept in a locker on the northern wall. The bullpen stretched through the room, aisles of desks butted up close to fit more personnel. Two staircases descended from the main room, the sign over the one to the far left reading HOLDING.

"Don't mind the mess," Standish said, crumpling up the cup and tossing it in the trash.

"I've been in a few precincts, Standish."

"Yeah, well, doesn't compare to what you guys handle, right?" Standish moved through the clutter of the bullpen for the stairs on the far side of the room, Loren in tow. "I've been trying to get into Central for months. Friend of mine just made captain there. Mathers. Know him?"

"I've heard the name," Loren answered. Quite a bit, in fact, ever since the promotion of Rufus Mathers. Usually from his night shift counterpart, Ruiz. And never in a good light. Loren, so far, managed to remain off the new captain's radar but that wasn't sustainable. Not with Loren's mouth.

"He'll be running the place soon." Standish interrupted his thoughts, his smug grin spreading his plump cheeks out. "Smart guy. Pays to have smart friends, you know."

He did, though he didn't care for the implication. "Why don't you tell me what happened and why I'm here?"

Standish stopped at the top of the stairs, surprised at the sharp edge stuck to each of Loren's words. "We were out on patrol, my partner and me, when we saw the guy. Some drunk behind the wheel. Went off-roading on Plymouth until he didn't. Craziest driving I've seen this side of a redneck rodeo. Don't ask."

"I won't."

"Right," Standish said, clearing his throat. "Anyway, we cuff the guy. Hayes something or other, and are about to haul him here when this nut comes out of nowhere."

"Nut?"

Standish huffed, shuffling down the steps. His hand subconsciously grazed the bruise on his cheek. "Damn broads, right? Even the white ones are getting uppity these days. But the darkies? Off her rocker. Says she's trying to save him. Bogeyman nonsense."

Loren stopped on the stairs. *Bogeyman nonsense?* If he had known it was heading toward this, he would have turned off his cell phone. He should have. This was the last thing he needed. He had real work to do.

"And I'm here to…?"

"Look," Standish said, holding Loren back. Two fingers poked lightly against his much-too-thin jacket. Strike two was coming. Quickly. "This is my collar."

"You can have it," Loren replied, knocking the fingers away. "I take it I'm here to see the nut?"

"She asked for you. How do you know her?"

Loren dug his fingers into his eyes, squeezing the bridge of his nose. "I don't. Not well, anyway."

Standish nodded, pointing down the hall. "Don't get too close to her."

"I'll try to remember that."

Loren walked down the hall, part of him anxious to finish this night, the other to put Standish behind him. He knew cops like him. Hell, he knew too many people like him. Hateful, ignorant people only looking out for themselves. And people wondered why the world was going to hell.

Turning right at the junction at the end of the hall led Loren to the women's holding area. Six cells of emptiness. Only the closest held one occupant. She lay patiently on the lone bench in the cell, her legs stretched across the cool metal.

"I had a feeling," Loren muttered.

The woman with the dark skin and the leather jacket bolted upright at the sound of his voice. A smile grew on Soriya Greystone's lips and she leaned close.

"Pull up a chair, Loren. We've got some work to do."

CHAPTER TWO

The building would be the death of him. Owen Simms truly believed that, especially when he slipped into the lobby of the station house, the aggravation of his missing ID badge behind him for the moment. His watch chimed with the midnight hour, another night lost. Another chance at sleep wasted on his place of employment.

Fifty-seven and a decade away from retirement, if he was lucky, though Otis knew that ship had sailed long ago. His checking account was a pittance spent on groceries, rent, and the occasional film. His savings was non-existent. He had a laughable investment portfolio. A decade until retirement became a low-ball estimate, one he clung to with all the hope left to him. A dream of lazy days, of daytime television and a beer or two in the dim haze known as sunlight to the city of Portents.

Otis had no family. No loved ones. Nothing in his orbit except work and home. He thought about a cat but the hours he put in at the precinct made it impossible to care for one. Plus, he wasn't actually sure if he liked cats…or any other animal. It was one of those random thoughts that flitted between his ears during the lonely hours wandering the halls of the station, doing his best to prop up the building's failing mechanics.

Being put in charge of maintenance for the building, a relic from the early days of the city, had been a gift from his previous supervisor. Fourteen years working as an assistant earned him the right to take the top position. If he had known, if there was an inkling at the torment the promotion would offer him over the course of the last nine years, he would have told his old boss, long since passed from the world, where to shove it.

Brick and mortar was cracked and shattered along the edifice. The boiler in place remembered the Second World War intimately, while the components that stretched throughout the guts of the precinct were tweaked and retrofitted throughout the years in order to keep the place running. It was all Owen Simms could do. Keep the place running. Survive another day. Everything needed an overhaul, desperately, and his overlords knew his rants by heart on the subject. If he screamed loud enough, they would have to listen…wouldn't they?

Budget cuts were the answer every time. The scapegoat of the business world. Patches were approved sporadically and only in dire circumstances. But Owen was proficient in patches. Where he was forced to be an expert, despite the complaints from everyone around him.

The winter had been brutal, a lengthy display of chilling temperatures and nightly snowfalls that threatened to break the aging man. On top of that, the boiler was irregular at best, chugging along intermittently and never at full speed. He warned them all, every single person he could get to listen, and still there was surprise when the ancient mechanics failed to turn on.

No heat in a February chill? That was an Owen Simms problem all over. Even after putting in his eight hours. Even after the complaints lodged to his overlords. The building was his responsibility and would be until it killed him.

Tonight was as good a night as any.

"Thanks for coming in, Owen," Officer Shelly Kirk said, escorting the maintenance manager from the supply closet tucked at the end of the hall off the right side of the main floor of the station. The supply closet was a death trap in its own right. A reworked emergency exit, cut off from the outside world. The door bricked over and the room secured on all fronts. No access points other than the door. No vents. No air. Just a twitchy door threatening to lock someone in for the night whenever the need arose.

Shelly always walked with him during the late night hours when she could. Young, smart and beautiful but with too much baggage attached, and she was the first one to tell you about it. She was a talker and Owen let her.

She kept him from thinking about the damn building. He kept her from heading out into the cold for a few extra minutes.

Owen smiled, glad to have the company. "All part of the service, right?"

The pair walked down the narrow hall, Shelly cradling an empty coffee mug, a gift from her kids. She pulled right upon entering the main floor at the end of the hall for the waiting coffee machine.

"I don't know why they won't update the damn thing," she said. Her cup sat underneath the dispenser, finger slamming the faded button for what had long been assumed to be a fresh cup of coffee. No questions asked. The machine whirred but nothing dripped into the waiting mug.

Owen huffed, slipping a key into the side of the machine. The back compartment opened with a loud click, his hand deftly finding the plug even before he saw it. He shook the jam loose, tossing the crumpled filter aside before closing it back up. He pressed the button again, lighter than his companion but with as much anger. Dark liquid finally sputtered from its spout.

"You know exactly why," he finally answered.

She lifted the full cup. "Right." They shared a laugh before she slipped her gloves and hat into place. She looked at the half-eaten cake on the table next to the machine, tongue running along her top lip. Then she turned away quickly, throwing him a nod. "Good luck."

"Stay warm out there."

Owen watched her leave, grateful his life wasn't completely devoid of relationships. Shelly Kirk may not have been a loved one but a friend was as necessary in a pinch. There might not have even been that much between them, her need for a sounding board knowing no limit, but he appreciated that she turned to him more often than not.

With his only distraction out of the station, and more glares turning toward him due to the lowering temperature throughout the halls, Owen Simms moved for the boiler room down the stairs opposite the holding area. The only room at the bottom of the creaking steps, the doors to the boiler greeted him with a bright neon *AUTHORIZED PERSONNEL ONLY* sign.

The door wasn't locked; it never was. The sign deterred no one, particularly those trying to stay warm while feeding their nicotine fix.

The switch snapped loudly as the lights flicked on. After a burst of luminescence they faded, becoming dimmer and dimmer.

Another problem to fix. He had more pressing concerns, procedures to maintain. Owen went through his checklists for a solution to the heating issue. Quick would have been nice. Just once.

The condensers were fine. The air hoses showed no signs of a plug. None of the usual suspects came into play. That left the half-ton apparatus in the center of the room. Owen grunted, less than gracefully falling to his knees, then lay on the cold concrete.

"Talk to me, you lousy piece of…"

He stopped, looking up into the disabled burners. A soft glint of light caught his eye.

"Now what the hell is that?" Owen reached into the dark, his flashlight halfway across the room, always when he needed the damn thing. He was grateful the main switch had been his first stop. If the burners decided to function properly with his hand inside the device, he would be collecting disability quite a bit sooner than he hoped. His hand stretched into the dark of the machine, fingers spread wide for the light flitting across the space.

"Ow," he yelled, pulling his hand back. A small stream of blood ran from his fingertip. Not cut, though. Nothing sharp enough to inflict that pain. No, it wasn't cut at all from what he could see given the lack of light.

More like *bitten*.

Owen turned back to the darkness. Where one light had been present before, dozens opened up for him. Thin slits in the shadows of the boiler in the basement of the Second Precinct.

Eyes.

All moving for him.

"Wait," he yelled, unable to move. "WAIT!"

His screams filled the room.

No one heard them.

CHAPTER THREE

The interrogation room was a necessity. A hard fought one, no less. The holding area was too open with too many eyes and ears on the place. On Soriya. Loren needed her secured and alone. When it came to Soriya and the world she inhabited, both were better off put in the dark than left in the open.

That feeling increased over the last six months. Since their first meeting in the parking garage attached to Central. Since her help handling the Kindly Killings. They were connected from that meeting, like destiny and every fortune cookie he had. A number of cases that came through his office tied to her own work in the field.

Defining her work was another matter altogether. *Vigilantism* was too broad but pretty accurate. She saw the city in a unique light, one Loren fought to his core. Even after everything he had learned over the last few months. What was out there in the shadows of the city. *The true city.* He didn't want to see it, know it, or hear it.

And he sure as hell didn't want others to hear it either.

Standish eventually acquiesced to the interrogation room, even the one Loren suggested at the end of the hall. Only mild cursing followed the request. Giving the overweight officer free rein to escort the prisoner to the room helped appease him.

Loren stopped at the door, peering in the small window. Soriya pulled at the chains locking her to the table, eyes scanning the walls. He had noticed her need to be out in the open air as often as possible. Her dislike at confinement. Not a fear—the young woman, barely old enough to vote, didn't seem to have any of those. No nightmares keeping her up at night. Not like him.

She jumped to her feet upon his arrival, pulled back down by the cuffs attached to the table. "What the hell, Loren? We need to move quickly. I thought if you were here this would—"

"Stop."

Her nostrils flared, her eyes throwing daggers. "Dammit, Loren. You need to—"

He waved her down, pulling out his chair and taking to the far corner of the room. He stood on the cold metal seat, reaching for the small camera in place.

"What are you doing?"

Loren pulled the plug from the monitoring device and the small red indicator on the side blinked out. "The walls have ears. Or did."

She settled back into her seat, rattling the cuffs for effect. "No observation room."

"Why I asked for this one," Loren replied, joining her at the table.

"You didn't have to do that."

Loren tapped his fingers on the tabletop. He wanted to reach into his pocket for a cigarette. "Pretty sure I did. But we'll get there."

"Loren," she muttered.

"I said we'll get there. You dragged me here. We're going to do this my way."

"Wow," she said, leaning back slightly in her chair. "I figured after the last six months—"

"What?" Loren snapped. "What did you figure, lady? Trust? Friendship? Every time you show up, my life ends up in jeopardy."

"And I save it."

He ran his hands through his hair, settling back into his seat. "Not the point."

"Pretty sure it is." Soriya caught his frustration, leaning hard against the table between them. "You don't trust me?"

Loren stared at her. "I don't know you, Greystone."

"Soriya," she said, standing. "My name is Soriya. Not Greystone or lady or dollface."

Loren laughed. "Standish?"

She nodded, leaning on the table.

"Figured."

Her eyes softened. "You can trust me, Loren. After everything with—"

"Let's leave it, okay?"

Soriya sat slowly. "I don't think we should."

Loren nodded, checking his watch. No time for Ronnie Phillips. No time for Beth. "It's my night off, Soriya. I had plans."

"Some plans. Beth, right?"

Loren's eyes fell.

"Still hunting for her killer? That's the only work you do now, isn't it, Detective? Alone. How's that going for you?"

"Dammit." He slammed his hand against the table and stood, his chair falling back to the ground with a crash. He moved for the door, tired and frustrated, unsure why he answered the call.

"Loren, listen…" she called to him.

"No," he said, refusing to turn back. "It was stupid to come here. You can deal with Standish and whatever craziness is after you this time on your own."

The handle turned and a flood of light shot into the interrogation room. Standish's shadow loomed down the hall, pissed off no doubt at the camera feed being cut off.

"A life is at stake."

The words stopped him. They always did.

"Don't," he started, turning back to her. She sat, hands open, the truth trapped in her pleading eyes.

"That's why I'm here, Loren. He is too. He's in danger."

Loren stepped back inside and let the door close. "From what? You're in one of the most secure places in the city."

Soriya shook her head. "That won't matter when they come for him."

"Who?"

She hesitated to answer, her eyes dodging his glare. For six months Loren had been stuck with Soriya Greystone, forced to accept a world he did not understand. A world where asking *who* was the wrong question entirely. Loren rubbed his brow, fixed the chair, and sat back at the table.

"Oh, I'm going to regret asking this, aren't I?"

"Definitely."

"What are they, Soriya? What's coming?"

She caught his eyes with her own wide brown orbs, holding them in place. Her tongue ran the length of her bottom lip before she answered with a single word that opened up more doors in his mind than he could imagine.

"Gremlins."

CHAPTER FOUR

"Loren?"

The detective's head fell back, puffing out a long breath of exasperation. All hope at avoiding the fight faded. Loren only wanted a second to come up with an excuse, a failsafe reason for Soriya Greystone, his prisoner, without cuffs and gallivanting down the hall with a shit-eating grin across her face. He was good at the game, making up plausible reasons for actions that slapped the law in the face. Especially since meeting the young woman behind him. One should have been easy to come up with to appease the territorial detective at the end of the hall. Piece of cake.

Nothing came.

"Great." He stopped short, doing his best to avoid Standish's poking fingers.

"Detective?" Standish said, confused. "Just what the hell is this?"

Loren bit his tongue. He didn't need the grief. He didn't want it or this case thrown at him through an innocuous phone call. He had a plan for the night—Ronnie Phillips. Finding out why he killed Beth. A beautiful woman taken from the world much too soon. He didn't care about gremlins or Standish or even Soriya at the moment.

"Standish, listen—"

"Put the cuffs back on her. Right now."

Loren shook his head. "That's not going to happen."

"They're very constricting," Soriya said with a smile. Loren shot her a look and she backed away, her fists still balled up at her sides. Always ready for a fight, no matter the circumstances. Bold but naive—very naive.

"We're going to talk to Hayes. Find out what's going on."

"Both of you?" Standish balked. "I don't think so."

With cuffs in hand, Standish moved for the young woman. Loren stepped between them, grabbing the man's thick wrist.

"You're going to want to back off, Standish." Anger swelled in Standish's eyes, the bruise on his cheek pulsing. *The bruise.* Loren pointed to it, looking back at Soriya. "Your work, I presume?"

She shrugged. "Shouldn't have touched me."

Loren smiled, letting Standish go. "She's got a point, Standish. Step aside."

The overweight detective with the crooked collar held his position, puffing his chest out. Loren waited patiently, his companion less so. Soriya cracked her knuckles.

Standish grumbled, tucking close to the wall and ushering them ahead. "Fine."

"Thanks," Loren said without hesitation, heading for the stairs to the holding area. Loren snagged the key from the rack next to the stairwell, and Standish stopped him once more.

"This isn't over, Loren."

The guest to the Second Precinct nodded, happily accepting the consequences. Anything to move on from the night. He shuffled down the stairs, Soriya in tow.

Standish sneered. "Or you, you lousy—"

Soriya took a step toward the disgruntled man. Standish flinched, falling back on his heels. His head slammed hard against the wall and his curses trailed them down the hall, followed by the chuckles of neighboring colleagues. Loren offered a slight grin to the young woman before waving her to follow. She kept close, a smug look on her face.

The men's side of holding was packed compared to the women's. Seven cells stretched down the left-hand side, three of which held multiple individuals. A biker gang from the looks of them—leather jackets and tattoos, thick sunglasses even in the dead of night, thicker beards on their faces, all hooting and hollering at their new company. Loren would have felt flattered—it had been some time since he was a showstopper. Soriya ignored them completely, focused on the cell at the end of the block.

"That might not have been the best strategy," Loren whispered, flicking his thumb back toward the stairs and the humiliated Standish. "He seems like he holds a mean grudge."

Soriya shrugged. "You're the one who should be worried then."

She had a point. One call from Standish to his so-called friend, Mathers, could cause a heap of problems for Loren. His track record over the last few months was nothing short of abysmal, his work shoddy and uninspired. Ruiz covered for him and he knew it, almost dependent on his excuses. A necessary crutch. Until he had answers. Until Beth's killer was caught. Until he could move on.

Still worth it, he thought.

He turned to her. "I'm just glad I don't work with him."

The cell at the end of the hall contained only one occupant. A young man, barely out of his teenage years, lying with his back against the wall, eyes closed to the world. Shaggy hair but clean-cut face. His thick, hand-sewn hat acted as a pillow. Melted snow from his boots dripped rhythmically to the floor.

"This him?" Loren asked.

Soriya nodded. "Say hello to Franklin Hayes."

The cell door opened and the pair entered, approaching the sleeping kid slowly. Loren hovered over him a moment, then shook him.

"Wha...?" Franklin fell from the bench in a crumpled heap. "Ow."

He jumped up, rubbing his eyes. He looked puzzled at the detective but light blue orbs flared with recognition at the sight of the young woman by his side.

"Oh, no. Not again."

Loren glared at Soriya, who waved him off.

"He reeks," Loren said.

"Booze. Lots of booze," Soriya confirmed.

Franklin collapsed on the bench. "I'm right here, you know."

Loren waited, hovering over him. Soriya stepped back, keeping an eye on the hall from floor to ceiling.

Franklin sighed. "Can I help you with something?"

Soriya glared at him from the door. "Tell him."

"No," Franklin snapped. He shook his head rapidly, then moaned into his hands. "I'm safe here, you lunatic. I don't need any more harassment from you."

"Big fan," Loren said to his increasingly aggravated partner.

"He should be," Soriya replied. She rushed for the bench, Loren stepping between them. The ever-present mediator. "I saved you...what is it, twice now?"

Franklin stood. "You blew a hole in my kitchen. She blew a hole in my kitchen."

Soriya shrugged. "It was a small one."

"You wrecked my car," the kid bellowed, throwing his hands in the air.

"Don't even pin that on me."

Loren stepped away. Soriya crossed her arms once more. Her pout reminded him of her age. And why she shouldn't have been in the room.

"Kids, please."

Both of them grumbled at the word. Loren pushed through the groans, leaning on the closest wall.

"Detective Standish mentioned a car accident. Drunk driving."

"That guy was a detective?" Franklin rolled his eyes. "I was running away from her."

Soriya's eyes fell when he looked to her. "The kitchen thing, I guess."

"She came busting in—"

"Because—"

Loren's hand stopped her. "Soriya."

She huffed. "We can play this game all night, Loren. If we don't move this along, things are going to end very badly. We need to be quicker."

Fire filled her eyes and something more. *Concern.* Loren didn't need the push. He wanted his night back more than either of them. He started for the kid, helping him back to the bench. He sat at the other end.

"She's right, Franklin. I can't help if I don't know what's going on. Why don't you tell me?"

The kid hesitated, running sweaty palms along his jeans. "Fine."

"Good."

"My old man died," Franklin said to the floor.

"I'm sorry to hear that."

"Me too. He owned Hayes Auto on Evans."

Loren knew it, even without owning a car. "I've walked by it on the way to work. Big place. Very busy."

"It was," Franklin said, sadness creeping into his voice. "When he was alive, that is. He left the shop to me. Used to show me how to manage the place, how to take care of the cars and the customers, but I was never good at any of it. Never really wanted to be, I guess. Should have told him that but I never did. Then he was gone."

Loren listened but his concentration split. Soriya paced the length of the cell, her eyes flitting down the hall and up to the blinding fluorescents along the ceiling.

"What happened?"

"I lost my best mechanics. The only mechanics. I lost my best customers. Almost all of them. Couldn't do anything right. I kept the place going for my mom, for my sister and my brothers, but the writing was on the wall. I went in one morning to close it all up and…it happened."

"It?"

"The cars. They were all fixed. Better than fixed."

Loren shared a look with Soriya, whose patience had evaporated. She prodded him on.

"Overnight?"

Franklin nodded. "And the next and the next. Pretty soon the place was booming again."

"Sounds like a miracle," Loren muttered.

"Only it wasn't," Soriya said bitterly, fists balled up against her sides.

"What do you mean?"

"She's right," Franklin said. "It wasn't a miracle. Not in the least. But I let it become one of my own creation. When people asked, I took the credit. Magic hands, I said."

"Big mistake."

Franklin tried to stand, eyes flaring. Loren held him, forcing him back to the bench. "Easy, kid."

"How was I supposed to know? Tell me that!"

"Gee, I don't know. How about never take credit for work done by others? Isn't that taught in ethics class anymore?"

Loren smirked at her frustration. "Ethics class?"

She crossed her arms. "Isn't that a thing?"

"I take it you didn't attend public school?"

Soriya pointed at Franklin intently. "He screwed up, Loren. Took credit when all he had to do was admit the name of his benevolent saviors. No one would have believed him anyway. They never do."

Loren's brow furrowed. "Benevolent…? Wait. You're talking about…"

"Gremlins," Franklin whispered.

"You were serious about that?" Loren shook his head, knowing with her, anything was possible. Even rejects from a Joe Dante film. "Of course you were serious. But what the hell does that even mean? Soriya?"

She sighed. A soft cloud of mist formed before her lips. She shivered. "It's cold."

"Must be a problem with the heat," Loren said, curious at her startled look. They would be lucky to see the temperature reach above freezing by the end of the month let alone in the middle of the night in February. "So what?"

Her eyes filtered up to the lights and the ductwork running the length of the hall. "We're too late. They're already here."

CHAPTER FIVE

"I need the Greystone, Loren. Now."

Soriya cursed under her breath, the chill in the air surrounding her. She had been too slow to act. The request for Loren was meant to expedite matters but his lack of trust surprised her. Their limited time together offered her a rich connection. Something about him brought a smile to her face, a level of comfort she only shared with a short list of people in her life. Yet to him, she remained a complete stranger.

Another mistake? Possibly, and one with little time to rectify. The attempt was made, however, by letting Franklin Hayes share his story, but whatever lead time they had between the car accident and now was gone. Gremlins were in the building, trapping them inside.

"Loren?"

He continued to sit, waiting for more. "The stone? Why? Just tell me what the hell…?"

"Dammit, Loren," she spat, slamming her hand against the bars. The bikers adjacent to them shuffled away from the drama unfolding at the end of the holding area. Loren remained still. Refusal resided in his eyes, refusal to accept what she had alluded to in the interrogation room. What Franklin Hayes' story truly meant. What was coming for him and now them. All stemming from a lack of trust she never saw coming.

"He's being hunted," Soriya said, slowing her breath. Anger, impatience, would do little here. "You might think of it as a sleight, an impolite rube taking credit for someone else's work but to them it's worse than a slap to the face."

Loren shook his head. His hands clasped tight to his knees, squeezing with each mention of the threat. "But the stone? I've seen it do some bizarre things, sure, but it can't help here. We've got manpower on our side with whatever the hell you say is coming. Gremlins or fuzzy little puppets, it doesn't matter. I can have—"

"Won't matter. Whatever you think is coming, you're not prepared. You can't see them. You can't hear them until it's too late. And the numbers are very much against us."

"You're saying…"

"How big is your extended family, Loren?"

He sat up, surprised at the question. "No idea. Couple dozen. Why?"

"When gremlins take offense, they call everyone. Every single member of their family. This is personal to them all. And I'm not just talking brothers and sisters—cousins, second cousins, family friends…everyone. Hundreds upon hundreds. Already in the building."

"Gremlins," he sneered. "I've seen the movie."

"What movie?"

Franklin rolled his eyes. "Seriously?"

"This isn't a movie," Soriya snapped, ignoring the kid. She stepped close to Loren. "You know their history, Loren."

"Those old tales of pilots during World War II with engine trouble?" Loren asked. "Mechanical errors chalked up to little pests throwing a spanner in the works? Those are stories, Soriya."

"Facts, actually. They're everywhere and tinkering is all they know. It's all they do. They fix, they tweak, they build, they rebuild. Ever misplace a tool? Find a problem solved overnight and wonder why you couldn't figure it out after staring at it for hours the previous day?"

Loren stood, rubbing his neck hard. He paced the cell slowly then looked back. "Gremlins?"

"I didn't know," Franklin whispered.

"No excuse," Soriya replied, sharper than she meant. When this happened—and it did far too often in her eyes—not knowing was a fallback, a tried and true method of passing the buck. One that never played well with the threat. "Gremlins don't suffer the ignorant."

A hand fell on her shoulder. Loren crooked his head to the hall and Soriya stepped away. The question behind his tired eyes was clear. *How the hell could he know? How could anyone?*

"I should have told him the truth. My old man. It was never for me. It was his dream."

"Let's not throw in the towel yet." Loren extended his hand. The kid took it and stood with a groan. He patted down his creased pants and grabbed his fallen makeshift pillow, pulling the hat on his head tight.

Soriya smiled. "Good. Let's—"

"Hang on," Loren said. He pushed past her in the hall. "I'll go."

"We should—"

"When I said kid, I meant kids. You're not much older."

"Younger, in fact," Soriya said, hands on her hips. "Not the point here."

Loren shook his head. "It actually is."

Her eyes widened. First the lack of trust and now this? Maybe she didn't know Loren as well as she thought. Maybe the last six months meant nothing to him.

"Ageism doesn't look good on you, Loren."

Loren grinned, pulling at the ratty Superman T-shirt under his open jacket. "Little does. Now how do we stop them?"

Soriya sighed, unwilling to press the argument further. There was no more time. "Intense light. Or heat, but I think we can agree burning down the building is not an option."

Loren chuckled. "I thought this wasn't a movie?"

"We get one shot at this, Loren. We get them all or the whole thing starts all over again."

Loren shrugged, pointing to the ceiling. The blinding fluorescents showered down on them. "So we stay in a well-lit room until the sun comes up. Then we lure them outside and that's that."

Loren's smug smile vanished in an instant. So did everything else in the holding area, as the lights overhead blinked out, covering them in darkness.

"You were saying?"

"Please tell me there's a plan B," Franklin muttered.

"There is," Soriya said, pulling Loren close. "Isn't there, Detective?"

"Soriya…"

"You go, Loren. Be the adult. But I need the Greystone. Or we're all dead."

CHAPTER SIX

The emergency lighting dimmed and faded behind the onslaught of rushing feet. Loren wasn't moving fast enough, his sneakers squealing along the tile through the main floor of the precinct. His breathing was labored. Too many cigarettes over too few years. Too much investigating and not enough physical activity.

Excuses he didn't need at the moment.

The lights did what they could to keep him from running into furniture throughout the room. He didn't belong to the precinct. Every direction chosen was based on adrenaline and a mental picture taken two hours earlier when things were a little calmer.

Okay, much calmer.

Screams rang out behind him. From down the hall toward the lobby and back to holding where Soriya and Franklin Hayes waited for him. He needed to be faster. And he needed the damn Greystone.

The *why* of it all didn't matter anymore. From the excuses Soriya gave about gremlins and their behaviors to her belief that the stone held the answer to their predicament. He would have liked to know the why of it all, sure, but he was forced to accept that this was the right move. Against all his training, his experiences prior to meeting the dark-skinned teenager, he rushed for the stone kept within evidence lock up on the right side of the room.

Why? If only he had the answer to that one. Something about Soriya. Something that kept bringing them together. Trust? Loren wasn't sure if such a thing was possible. Not that he had time to wonder.

More screams filled the air. Loren turned back, his left foot catching the corner of a metal desk. He fell hard, his hands protecting his face at the last instant. Breath slipped away and he cradled his gut for a long moment. When he looked up he saw them: a black cloud hovering near the hallway opposite the holding area. A woman in full uniform pulled her gun on the growing mass. The shadows reached out, drawing her arms in before the rest of her joined the darkness.

Loren tried to cry out, his hand reaching before returning to his chest. The woman's screams echoed around him. Ringing in his ears. Never leaving him alone. Loren watched the cloud disappear into the ductwork above. The woman remained in a heap on the ground. Loren crawled, keeping low to the ground to avoid being seen.

When he was in reach of his destination, he kicked his legs underneath him to jolt him forward to the waiting evidence room. He slammed into the gate blocking the door. Loren pulled hard but it refused to move. Refused to let him inside. Locked. Desperate eyes scanned the floor for signs of life. Some sign of help.

"Come on," he grumbled, his hands slipping between the bars of the gate to shake it hard. Frustration built up, his head crashing against the metal, dulling the screams for a brief moment.

"What the hell are you doing?"

Loren turned quickly, hand at his holster. Robert Standish stood aghast. Not surprising to the detective, who fought for a deep breath. Sweat pooled along his thin strands of dirty blond hair, dripping down to his shoulders.

"Standish," Loren said. He kept his voice low, the screams loud but still distant. "You nearly scared the…. Listen."

Standish's eyes flared. "No, you listen. You show up and all of a sudden I've got cons walking around like they own the place, a busted furnace, and the lights are out. People are screaming, swearing they're seeing things in the dark. *Monsters*. Bullshit, I say."

"It's not," Loren replied. It was quick and sharp. Exactly what Standish didn't want to hear. The heavyset officer rushed him, pinning him to the gate.

"What the hell have you done, Loren?"

"You're right," Loren said with a smile. "I did it."

"Did what?"

"Broke the furnace. It's not something I'm proud of but I was playing with the thermostat in holding and…well, there you go."

Standish dropped Loren, pulled back and let his right hand loose, delivering a gut punch to the unprepared detective. Loren fell to his knees, nursing his ribs.

"I hate smart-asses."

Loren clenched his jaw, standing back up. "I hate dumb-asses, so we're even."

"Tell me what the hell is happening here?"

"I need the key to the evidence locker."

Standish balled up his fists. "Did you hear a word I just said?"

"Not really," Loren held out his hand. "Do you have the damn key or not?"

More screams. Standish turned away toward the holding area. Seconds ticked by—too many, too quickly.

"Yeah. I have the key."

"I need it."

Standish shook his head. "No."

"Are you kidding me? Standish…"

"Am I kidding you?" Standish bellowed. There was fear in his eyes. "I don't know how you play things at the Rath, but this is *my* house, asshole. This game you've got going with that bitch ends right now. I want her in lockup. I am going to process the hell out of her and there's not a damn thing you can do."

Standish's hand fell to his swollen cheek, the bruise yet another shadow in the growing darkness of the room. Loren's mouth fell open. The man before him was serious, completely withdrawn from the events around him. Standish was lost in his own fantasy of the situation.

"That's your focus now?"

Standish pulled out his cuffs, the keys glinting on his belt. "She assaulted an offi—"

The punch was immediate, a sharp right to the man's face. Standish fell, the cuffs clanking along the tile away from his crumpled form. He didn't get back up.

"Sorry I didn't let you finish," Loren said, crouching over the unconscious officer. The keys shook loose from Standish's belt, resting square in his palm. His knuckles flared but it was worth it. "I know saying sorry comes a little too late but there it is. Anyway, I'm sure you were about to bring up an excellent point about procedure and due process. All that stuff. Full disclosure? I just don't care."

The key slid into place and the gate fell open. Loren raced into the room, the light switch failing, of course. Emergency lighting was non-existent in the small alcove but the lost detective stumbled into his first bit of good luck on the night. A flashlight sat near the entrance. Clicking it on, Loren scanned the cramped room. Boxes of confiscated goods filled the shelves.

"Come on, come—"

The pouch and the ribbon belonging to Soriya sat near the bottom shelf in the back. He slipped the ribbon into his pocket then grabbed at the pouch, forcing it open. The small stone of grey rested upon his palm. It was the answer to all their problems—hopefully.

Loren flew from the room, quietly stepping over Standish, before breaking into a full run for holding. He turned back to the sleeping officer and sighed.

"This better work."

CHAPTER SEVEN

Too late. She was always too late. Soriya Greystone paced the small holding cell, fingers flexing into fists then stretching outward. Franklin Hayes muttered under his breath on the lone bench in the cell. Small curses upon his luck, his dead father, but most squarely against the woman trying to save his life.

She earned all of them.

There were ways to handle the situation. Ways that included a soft introduction, possibly a bite to eat before dropping the hammer on the whole gremlins-trying-to-kill-him deal. Hell, a simple knock at the door would have sufficed for the kid. Instead she waited for the threat to come forward; waited for the kid to be in danger before jumping into the fray. Smashing through the window of his kitchen, using the stone in such an enclosed space, both were the epitome of recklessness. Soriya's calling card, Mentor always said.

She scared Franklin with her actions. She still scared him, in fact, by jumping down his throat for every utterance. None of it was his fault, not really. Most fell on her. More lives were in danger now. The six gentlemen in the cells next to them. The dozen or so warm bodies upstairs milling about the station in the middle of the night, not to mention the dozens more out on their shift that could return at any time. She made the situation dire, unsure how to rectify her mistake.

She needed the stone. She was not kidding when she made the request. No, the stone remained their last hope. But it was too late.

Always too late.

Chittering sounds rattled above their heads. Small clacking against the metal of the vents running the length of the ceiling. Coming closer.

"Damn."

Franklin stood, joining her in the center of the cell. His eyes trailed her own to the ceiling, wide and fearful. "'Damn'? That's not what I want to hear right now."

"It's not something you ever want to hear." The sound stopped but her pulse quickened. Soriya grabbed the boy's hand and pulled him toward the hall. "Come on."

He hesitated. "Where? Do you even know?"

Loren. The only answer that came to mind, though she kept it to herself. She didn't have a plan, but together they might. She simply needed more time.

"Let's go," she repeated. He followed, running behind her.

They barely reached the first turn when the vent exploded. Hundreds of creatures escaped into the darkness, their slitted eyes searching for them. Screams rang out, far too feminine to match the burly bikers from the neighboring cells, but Soriya understood the fear. She understood the cries even from her companion.

"Holy...!"

The creatures turned at the sound, Soriya pulling the kid toward the stairs to the bullpen.

"Move it!" she yelled. The bikers were swept in the cloud of creatures rushing through them. Small specks of light flared at Soriya, forcing her to look away. The screams of the six men caught in their path followed her down the hall.

Franklin rushed ahead of her in a full run, taking the stairs two at a time. "I'm sorry, I'm sorry, I'm sorry..."

He tripped at the peak of the stairwell. She bent low, lifting him up. "Not helping, kid."

Emergency lighting failed around them, the skittering of tiny claws on tile moving closer with each passing second. The bullpen, abundant in shadows, seemed devoid of life. Vacant. Franklin tucked close, Soriya shifting between desks for some sign of Loren. Some form of a plan.

They stopped near the end of the first row. Low sobbing rose from beneath the metal desk. A younger officer tucked behind his chair, arms locked across his knees.

Soriya crouched low. "Sir? Are you...?"

"Shhh," the officer whispered. "They'll hear you."

Soriya shook her head. Movement shifted at the stairwell. "They don't need to hear us. They'll see us soon enough."

Franklin jabbed her side. She turned to let loose on him for the small act and he jumped back. Some things shouldn't be said.

"Hey," Loren said, rushing from the northern wall on the far side of the bullpen. Franklin jumped at his arrival, nearly landing in Soriya's arms.

"AHHH!" The scream didn't help either.

"Shut it," Soriya snapped over the shushing from the hiding officer.

"He scared me."

Soriya leaned in close. "*I'll* scare you."

"Really?" Loren said, rolling his eyes. She shrugged and her smile returned. The detective tucked his flashlight under his arm and retrieved a small pouch from his pocket. She took the pouch, snatching it away from Loren, and tied it along her belt. A deep breath escaped her at the warmth of the stone against her side. Loren waited, her ribbon sitting in his hand. She nodded, grateful for them both.

"Thanks."

"Now what?" Loren asked. His eyes were on the stairs.

"You don't have a plan?" Franklin snapped in astonishment.

Soriya ignored him. "I need the kid secured. Some place with no vents. No points of entry other than the door."

"I wouldn't even know where to look," Loren said, scanning the room.

"Are you kidding me?" The kid jumped in, hands running through his hair.

"It's not my precinct, Hayes."

"He's supposed to help us?" Franklin asked Soriya, then cowered at her silent reply.

"Hey," Loren snapped. "I'm not the one that put us in this situation."

No, Soriya thought. *That was me*. Her fault. From learning about the situation to the present, every choice she made was wrong. Now she was being asked to make another one. It would be the last stand for the life of a kid too dumb to know he screwed up.

"Service closet."

All three of them turned to the cowering officer beneath the desk.

"Excuse me?"

The chattering of the creatures reached a fever pitch. The shadows grew all around them. Another cop disappeared near the holding area stairs, pulled off the ground and out of sight by dozens of hands.

"There's a maintenance closet at the end of the hall," the scared man said, pointing from behind his chair.

"Where?"

The officer pointed again, stretching out to the far side of the room and the narrow hallway off the bullpen. "That way. Please. I hear them."

Soriya wasn't listening to the young man cowering in fear. In the distance, the shadows filled the outskirts of the room, the emergency lighting gone from view. In their brief moments of planning, what little time they had vanished with the light.

"Soriya?" Loren asked, his voice shaking.

"I see them," she said, pushing Franklin to the end of the row. "Go. *Go!*"

The three raced for the end of the row of desks, down the aisle leading to the far right of the bullpen. The screams returned and Soriya wondered which belonged to the man that had given them a chance. It was a small chance, but one they had not had before.

"Our Father who art—"

Soriya slapped Franklin on the back, almost toppling the kid over. "Too late for that."

The hall was narrow but long. They rushed for the end and the door waiting for them—the service closet. Loren reached it first. Soriya felt her heart stop when he grabbed the handle and pulled. The door opened, the flashlight illuminating the shelving units covering every wall within the confined space. He turned, nodding for them to head inside.

"Get in," Soriya screamed, pushing Franklin ahead. The kid hesitated for a moment before Loren took his arm and forced him inside.

"What about…?"

"Do it, Loren. Get in there."

Loren hesitated, hand on the door. "Soriya, I'm not just going to leave you out here."

"I'll be fine," she said, confidence in her words. The shadows swarmed the hall. The chittering sound of little feet and the thin slits of eyes surrounded them. Floor to ceiling. All heading toward them.

His hand grazed her arm. "You don't—"

Soriya stepped away from the door, Loren's hand slipping away. She took a deep breath then turned, her eyes steady.

"Trust me."

"I—"

"*Loren*. You have to trust me."

Slowly, Loren nodded. She waited, letting him slip inside the small closet and close the door behind him with a thundering finality. The lock clasped, cutting her loose.

Soriya Greystone turned to the creatures surrounding her and smiled. The stone slipped from the handwoven pouch into her palm and she held it before her. Surrounding her on all sides, the gremlins raced for her and their intended victim. They filled the hallway. The floor, the walls, the ceiling. All that remained was a pinhole in the darkness, the bullpen a world away.

She waited, letting them rush toward her, letting them scream and raise their weapons against her. She waited to see their sharp teeth, chomping at the air for a chance at her flesh. She waited until every eye was on her.

Then the stone erupted.

<

Light flew free from the Greystone, swallowing up every single shadow, every single gremlin in the narrow hallway of the Second Precinct.

CHAPTER EIGHT

Snow fell in steady flakes, blanketing the wide sidewalk down Evans Avenue. Dark clouds streamed north, heading for the metro area and beyond, an endless wall keeping the moon hidden.

Four days since his visit to the Second Precinct, Greg Loren still heard the screams in his ears. Still felt the cold, more chilling than the winter wind sweeping around his slow steps toward the Rath. Another shift was about to begin. Ronnie Phillips and the questions begging to be asked, the anger that welled inside him when he thought of each one, fell into memory. For now.

Much like his visit to the Second Precinct.

No fallout came from the affair. When the lights returned to the building, it appeared as if nothing had happened. The members of the precinct decided to keep it that way. Fear won out over the need to share any stories—fear that whatever happened might come back.

The screams were a distant memory. Even Standish remained quiet, surprising Loren, who was waiting for Mathers to show up at his office with a pink slip and a smile. Nothing came and nothing would. Standish tossed the charges on Franklin Hayes, giving the kid a warning, not that he needed one. Soriya was gone, vanished. All of it was better left forgotten. Focusing on the good, believing that there was something else going on in the station, made it easier for the men and women of the Second.

At least, Loren hoped as much.

He stopped, his feet crunching the accumulation on the sidewalk. Hayes Auto Shop sat across the street. The only thing visible was the sign across the plate glass window in the front of the customer area that read: FOR LEASE. *Out of business* would have been an admission but close to the truth. At least FOR

LEASE read better than *THE GREMLINS HAVE LEFT THE BUILDING*.

A light clicked on in the office and Loren saw Franklin Hayes wandering through the sparse lobby. He piled chairs into the corner, hesitating at the end. A long stare into the abyss, into the choice that had led him to this moment. A look that would stay with him for a long time.

Franklin, a mere boy of twenty-one, with scrawny arms and awkward legs, shuffled on his coat and exited the shop. He turned around, pulling the door twice to verify the lock clicked in place. Hot breath rose from his lips, clouding the window before him. He wiped the cloud away in long strokes, soaking his hand. His eyes, once the center of his youth, innocent and naive to the world, dimmed in the streetlight glow of the night.

He looked older. Much older than the night they had met.

"Closing up shop, Hayes?" Loren said, stopping out front. Franklin spun around, nearly slipping on the pavement in surprise. Older but still jumpy as hell.

"Detective Loren?"

Franklin steadied his feet, wiping his hands along his coat before tucking them into his pockets for warmth. He looked back to the bright yellow sign adorning the window.

"Yeah. Looks like I am. It was never for me. My old man tried. Lord, how he tried, but I never got it. I'm a simple grease monkey. Not a professional. He was the real mechanic. The real businessman."

Loren nodded but remained silent at the disappointment in the kid's words. The detective knew a thing or two about fathers and expectations. Especially how to disappoint them.

"What about your family?"

"My uncle owns a convenience store up north. He's agreed to give me a job while I figure things out. Even a place to stay for my family."

"Away from Portents."

Franklin nodded. "Oh yeah. Lived here all my life. Thought I knew the neighborhoods better than anyone. But—"

"Not so much."

"Or at all," the kid muttered. He looked into the night sky then down Evans Avenue toward the black tower at the heart of the city. "It's a little scarier than I'd like. A little darker."

Loren understood better than most. It almost made him glad to share the sentiment with someone. Almost.

Loren extended his hand. "Good luck, Hayes."

The kid shook it hard once. "Franklin."

"Franklin," Loren said with a smile.

The former mechanic, future convenience store clerk, started down the road for the subway and his waiting family. He refused to look back, stopping twice in the first block, before trotting into the dark of the city. Loren waited, the snow surrounding him, coating him. He reached into his coat for a cigarette remembering the last time he had one.

Beth.

Her name was enough to put the pack away again. He turned for the Rath and Heaven's Gate Park.

"It doesn't have to be scary," a voice called out of the darkness beside the auto shop. Loren stopped, a grin forming.

"I had a feeling you would be here. Keeping tabs on the kid?"

Soriya Greystone exited the shadows, a light jacket covering her arms and a hood over her head. "Just in case."

Loren nodded, leaning against the shop window. "You pull quite the disappearing act."

Soriya joined him, arms crossing her chest. "It's a gift."

"He's not wrong. About the city, I mean. It's darker than it used to be."

Soriya shook her head. "Turning on more streetlights won't help, Loren."

"What will?"

"Understanding? Acceptance? This is Portents. Always has been. Always will be."

She was right. When she turned on the soapbox speech she kept in her pocket, he could feel the words under his skin. The energy behind them. The truth behind them as well. But truth was harder to swallow than the fantasy they lived in during the daylight hours.

"I don't think you'll change his mind."

She turned to him, nudging his arm. "Not trying to change *his* mind."

"Right."

The same battle. The true city versus the fiction. The fiction he had known for years. Before Beth fell. Before Soriya and the Kindly Killer and the insanity that came with their partnership. *Partnership*—a strange term to define their relationship. But it was there, growing from that initial visit, that first favor earned, to their present situation. The two of them. Always the two of them.

"The precinct?" she asked, sensing his distance.

"Fine," he replied. "Some bumps and bruises mostly. A couple on leave. Maintenance guy too. Night terrors."

He tried to keep his eyes away, afraid of her seeing through his assessment. He would bury his nightmares from their time at the Second—eventually. He had to, with the job at hand. He needed the job, now more than ever. He needed to find out the truth about Beth, about everything hidden from him in the city. He needed the work and refused to let everything slip away.

"Good," she said.

Loren cleared his throat. "When I heard those screams, I thought.... Well, I thought the worst. You didn't. Somehow you knew."

"I hoped. That's all we can do when it gets dark, Loren." Soriya reached into her coat and handed him a small file.

"What's this?" He opened it and a photo of Ronnie Phillips fell to the snow. Crouching low, Loren retrieved the image of Ronnie boarding a bus uptown, wearing an apron from the restaurant he worked at...six months earlier. When Beth....

"Is this...?"

"From that night," Soriya said quietly. "He didn't do it, Loren."

"How did you...?"

She pushed off from the wall, starting for the shadows. A slice of pink ribbon slipped from her left sleeve, defining her form against the darkness.

"I never thanked you," he called out to her. "For saving my life."

She turned with a smile. "Thank you. For trusting me."

Warm breath slipped from his lips in a sigh. He turned to the sky above. "I'm trying, Grey...Soriya. But I don't know anything about you. Family? Friends? Home life? Hobbies. Nothing about the stone and nothing about—"

She was gone.

"...You," he finished, pushing away from the auto shop. He shook his head at the initial surprise when there should have been none.

With it came a new understanding. He knew her. On some level he always did. Like the disappearing act, he knew exactly where she was heading. To the next monster. The next shadow. Her next case.

Their new case.

It wasn't much. Not an address and a personnel file or her permanent record from school. Nor was it every secret listed out for him in a neat and understandable spreadsheet, but it was something. A connection and with it the knowledge that when she needed him next, for whatever reason—

"I'll be there."

VIEW FROM ABOVE

CHAPTER ONE

Soriya Greystone needed a fight. Something to punch. Someone to kick. A fury built in her body, one threatening any poor soul unlucky enough to cross her path.

It happened periodically. The buildup. The anger of her existence, tucked away in the darkness of the city instead of being the brash, loud and in charge soul that was her all over. Mentor's lectures didn't help—in fact, they only aided in her teeth-grinding, fist-clenching rage. Tonight was no different, the old man's condescension over her recent work in the city bitter and sharp. Questioning every decision made. A father figure unable to stop pulling apart perfection, though she was far from it in his eyes. She ran out without a word, racing into the night.

Thankfully, she had an outlet. A case. Or, more appropriately, a hunt.

Rumors began over the previous two weeks. A dozen incidents buried in the news, hidden away as best as possible, until they became too numerous to ignore. Thefts. Assaults. Home invasions. Most were left without a description of the perpetrator. Most.

Those that did come out—an older woman mugged after disembarking from the bus down the street from her home, in one case—spoke of a *creature* committing the crime. A tall, mangy hairball of a beast, growling and snarling for a wallet containing little more than forty dollars and a rewards card for the local grocery chain. Not exactly high profile in the eyes of the police, but the victim said the magic words to the dark-skinned protector of the city.

Creature. Beast. It piqued Soriya's interest.

And she needed the fight.

Inconsistencies in the thefts didn't sit right with her. Small embellishes that made her question her quarry. Of the dozen or so occurrences, only three pointed to evidence of the creature. The three eyewitnesses were cornered and terrorized, yet little was lost in these incidents. Almost like the description passed to the police and then the local news—not necessarily in that order depending on the victim—was the main goal of the act.

Terrorism by monster or something else? It didn't matter. Not to Soriya Greystone. Not tonight. She needed the fight and she would have it.

The northern coves of the city were nestled into a series of large sloping hills, homes, and streets etched into its surface in staggered steps. The different hills offered natural borders between districts. There was Venture Cove, the first of the city to be developed and the largest population center in Portents. To its right was Travelers Cove, its origins much like its namesake, home to no one yet filled with visitors to the great city. That changed over time, as residential neighborhoods filled out the area. The far left district was a great forest, originally called the Forest of the Veil, though recently the name had changed to the Rose Riley Forest—named for one of the pioneers of women's rights in the city. Acres and acres of woodlands covered in a deep fog, spreading deep beyond the natural border of Portents.

Separating the woods and the other districts stood Junction Cove, containing mostly apartment housing, two local universities, and a sprawling business district flowing directly into downtown toward the obsidian tower at its center. Business boomed in the area. Retail dominated every major corner but even mom and pop shops went toe to toe with big-time conglomerates. From diamonds to banking headquarters, Junction Cove carried them all and everyone made their way into the district over the course of a normal week.

Soriya tucked close to the shadows. The woodlands of the northwest border loomed, the city at her back. Ten blocks contained the events of the last two weeks. Ten blocks that served as a breeding ground to something dangerous.

She searched for hours starting at the first sign of darkness, her first chance to escape the lectures and the lessons. Where most in Portents learned quickly to head home with the fading of the sun, those in Junction skewed younger. *Dumber*, she thought, ducking down an alley off Carn, the heart of the cove and home to dozens of strip malls and plaza centers. Whatever was happening was happening here. The thefts, the assaults, the violence. Soriya felt it all in the wind, heard it in the slow, deliberate steps of the people filtering her streets.

The park behind her called first, however. A scream sent a chill along her skin. Soriya turned away from the city, unafraid, coming up short of the wooded hill.

Two children ran blindly in the dark. Both appeared slightly less than double digits in age, a boy and a girl, their matching brown hair and brown eyes a definite familial link. Soriya inched closer, tracking their movements as the pair flew deeper and deeper into the darkness of the wood.

"Do you see him?" the boy asked loudly over the sound of their stomping sneakers.

The girl shook her head, pulling ahead of the boy. "Don't look. Just run."

"I am running," he replied, his eyes forcing Soriya to keep low along the brush. "I can do both."

"Then do it before he—"

A shadow fell over the pair, leaping from the overgrowth beneath the tree line. Both screamed, falling back and sliding along the hilly incline. The beast stood at almost seven feet tall, dark brown hair covering its skin from head to toe. Its snout extended to a sharp end, its eyes yellow against the rising moonlight.

Wolfen.

Soriya knew the kind, had seen them in the past, though never so close. The kids were fixed in position, unable to move.

It was up to her.

Forgetting about subtlety or the shadows, Soriya leaped into the fray. Her hands grabbed a low-hanging branch, her body propelling forward with legs drawn out in front. They connected square with the side of the wolf. The blow knocked him aside, a low grunt escaping his lips.

Soriya blocked the beast from the kids, who were still stunned into silence. Sweat dotted her skin, excitement running down to her clenched fists and up to her widening grin.

"Get up," she commanded to the surprised creature. "I've been looking forward to this all night."

CHAPTER TWO

Vladimir Luchik couldn't find his shoes. Not that they would have done any good, not with his feet enlarged to twice their size and sporting fur the equivalent thickness of a shag rug. The shoes stood as a reminder of his human side, a side he ignored during his little fun. A human smile instead of a snarl from his fang-filled mouth might have gone a long way to appease his attacker.

Or as he decided to call her—the most beautifully violent woman he had ever seen.

"Now let's all…"

Calm down. He was going to say *calm down*. Instead, her fist connected with his snout, driving him back to the ground. He rolled down the incline, away from her and the two kids he had been chasing. The punch stung, even with the extra thickness the change added to his hide. She was strong. And angry.

Vlad needed help.

Unfortunately, the only assistance available sat stunned in the form of two frightened children. Robbie—definitely not Robert or Bobby—and Barbara—she preferred Babs—Corwell. They shared a simple plan. Homework then playtime, including a nighttime jaunt into the city for a raucous game of hide and seek. *Vlad style*, he called it.

What an idiot.

"A little theft? Some breaking and entering? I get those. But hassling kids? That's low. Even for a wolfen douche."

"How did you…?" he started.

The mystery woman didn't blink at him. She knew the truth about him. How was that possible? Vlad stood, rubbing his neck with an oversized paw. "Wait. Douche?"

Another punch slammed into his jaw. He rolled with it but the thrust threatened to pummel him back to the soft green of the hillside. *Great. She wants my head. Why am I such an idiot sometimes?*

That question frequently occupied his thoughts. Since he became something else—*wolfen*. He knew the term and the meaning held in most circles. Knowing and understanding parted companies at that point. He lived his own way, always had, and everyone else be damned. That edict cost him many lives, but he learned from the loss each and every time.

He didn't want to lose this one, not like this. Throwing his hands up in front of his face, Vlad retreated a step deeper into the woods. "Can we talk about this? Some talking would be nice, wouldn't it?"

"No."

The bluntness shook him. Her hands would do worse. If he let her.

"At least you're honest," he said. "Let's try this then."

He dropped to the ground, his leg kicking out and sweeping behind her knee. The mystery woman fell without a sound, not that he stopped to listen for one. Vlad was too busy running. Deeper into the woods, deeper into the shadows of the night, blocked by the overgrowth of trees along the hillside, Vlad fled from his attacker. He needed the space to think, to figure out a way to ditch the woman and circle back to the kids. If their dad found out what he had done, there would be no coming back.

Another life lost. One he enjoyed more than he cared to admit to anyone. Especially Babs. He would never hear the end of it.

"Running away? And here I was expecting a fight."

The woman's echoes surrounded him. She was still a distance away, his nose confirmed that. A filthy habit, smelling your way through the world, but it had its uses.

Fighting was never an option—not anymore. Once upon a time he would have loved it. The thrill and the adrenaline of a brawl, the sheer joy of pummeling someone to the ground. Until he looked for a reason behind the joy and found none. There were plenty of stupid reasons for sure. Women. More often than not, in fact. Pride was another one. Never anything substantial. No worthwhile cause. Now he tried to be better—to be different.

But the mystery woman wanted blood. *His* blood.

He raced deeper into the woods, branches swinging to and fro with the wind. The incline steepened but his legs were more than up to the challenge. Unfortunately, so were the jean-covered, lanky legs of his pursuer. *Very tight jeans.*

The distracting thought threw Vlad off. He dodged a low branch with ease without looking forward. Then Vlad's voluminous form propelled into a larger set of hanging limbs.

"Oh, crap."

He crashed through them, his footing lost completely. He fell hard to the ground, skidding and sliding to a halt in front of a large oak. Scrapes ran down his cheeks from the branches, friction burns running up his back. His pain did little to stir him. Not until he saw the woman over him did he struggle to stand. Her fists balled up, her brown eyes beaming in the darkness.

"Now, where were we?"

"Listen…"

She cracked her knuckles loudly.

"Hey," Vlad yelled and jumped to his feet. The change came naturally. It always did these days. None of the pain of the initial shock to his body. The growing and shrinking that came with his stature was as much a part of him as putting on a pair of baggy pants and an oversized undershirt. Pale skin replaced shaggy fur. Blue eyes replaced the yellow, the snout and fangs a memory.

"What are you doing?"

Vlad blinked hard, shaking his head. "Something incredibly stupid, probably, but that's me all over."

Her hesitation confused him. Then he realized she wasn't questioning the change. And she wasn't looking him in the eyes anymore. She was looking much lower.

"Oh," he muttered, covering up his naked body. "That."

"Change back," she demanded, her cheeks slightly flushed.

Vlad's hands shot down to cover up.

"Not until I explain," he said. "Not the naked thing. That's pretty obvious. And it's cold out. Cold-ish. You know what I mean."

"I don't."

Vlad shook his head. "Beside the point, anyway."

"So make one."

"I'm guessing huge misunderstanding?"

"I doubt it."

"Doubts are good," he said. He tried to smile—flashing a grin won him more battles than did his fists. "Doubts are great even. But…"

Her hand dropped to her right hip, pulling loose a small object from a pouch secured to her belt. A small stone. Vlad's jaw fell agape.

A Greystone, an actual Greystone. He heard stories about them but had never seen one. Never imagined he would, not with his low profile in the city. Not with the changes he had made since settling into Portents.

The woman clutched the small pebble tight and light grew upon its surface. Vlad closed his eyes, waiting for the end, when out of the bushes two figures rushed between them.

"Stop, lady!" Robbie Corwell shouted. His high pitch voice interrupted the woman's actions, ending the light show from the small stone clutched in her right hand. He carried a pair of shoes on top of a heap of clothes.

Babs followed, hands to her hips—a gift left by their deadbeat mother. "Leave Vlad alone."

The woman's hand lowered slowly, recognition coming in the form of a single name passed by the lips of his supposed victims.

"Vlad?" she asked. "You know him?"

"Of course we do," Babs replied sharply.

Her brother pushed ahead. "He's our babysitter!"

CHAPTER THREE

"Babysitter?"

It was the only question worth asking. Confusion was not her natural state, and it was one she tried her best to avoid. Especially in her city—her eternal playground.

No, the enigma invading her comfort zone was the man beside her. Now fully clothed, Vlad escorted the foursome away from the woodlands back into Junction Cove. They walked in silence for much of the journey, the question bouncing around her thoughts until they finally slipped off her tongue. It brought a gleam of satisfaction from the young man with the scraggly brown hair and sky blue eyes. The question also came with commentary from the peanut gallery.

"We're not babies," the girl named Babs snapped. She stayed close to Vlad, a dividing line between them. "Right, Vlad?"

Vlad patted her shoulders gently. "No, Babs. Not babies. She meant to say giant, mega-sized babies."

"Vlad!"

They stopped, the young man crouching low to face Babs. Soriya threw them a thin glare before she scanned the street. The night had been quiet so far, the stepped-up patrols throughout the business district of the cove keeping activity to a minimum. There was no reason to press their luck. The coves to the north might have been considered the safer side of Portents but even they held a dark element or two.

And deep shadows.

"All right," Vlad whispered, throwing both kids a disarming smile. "Quiet down."

"But—" Robbie started.

"Both of you." Vlad held tight to them until slowly they nodded their acceptance of the situation. Then the walk began once more, now a little quicker down the winding path to the suburban neighborhoods on the border of Junction and Venture.

Soriya walked with them. Why she hadn't bolted after her mistaken assault of the young man was another question she failed to answer. She remained even with the work ahead of her, the thief or thieves in their midst. Something about the young man confused her. She hated mysteries.

"Babysitter?"

Vlad nodded, letting the kids run ahead. "Their dad works swing shift. Construction. He helped me out awhile back. Place to stay for cheap. Free meals. I keep an eye out for the two troublemakers when I can."

"And he knows?" The question surprised her even after asking.

Vlad hesitated a moment, unsure what was meant, until her look washed over his once hairy form. "The hair in the shower gave me away," he said. Not even a chuckle. "Kidding, obviously. It's not something I like to advertise but I thought he should know. He trusted me. With his home and his kids. Thought I should return the favor. You?"

Soriya stopped. "What about me?"

Vlad stepped back, holding his hands up defensively. "Sorry. Not used to actually seeing a Greystone. That's what that thing is, right?"

She nodded.

"I've heard stories," he continued. "Like the bogeyman. *Be good or the Greystone will find you.*"

"Bogeyman?" The description never occurred to her. The other side of the equation. The perception of her role over those that did not fit the mold most labeled as *normal*. To her, the job was to protect both sides—to protect the innocent of both parties—but to think of the power behind the stone and the idea of a lone individual wielding it to decide the fate of others…of course fear played a part. It saddened her, nonetheless.

"Hey," Vlad said, reading her tone. "There are good ones too. Stories, that is. The protector. The guardian. I just never pictured someone so…well…"

"Hot," Robbie jumped in, both kids suddenly interested in the conversation.

Babs smacked her brother. "Robbie!"

"He wanted to say hot." Another slap upon his left arm made Robbie pull away, rubbing his wound. "Well, he did."

"She is not," Babs huffed, starting across Pike toward a two-story Cape Cod home in the center of the block. Robbie ran to catch up.

"Babs, are you out of your—?"

"Kids," Vlad grumbled, pulling them to the sidewalk. Their argument continued unabated, Soriya watching distantly. "Kids!"

Both stopped, turning. "What?"

Vlad towered over them. "Shut up."

"Look what you did now," Robbie snapped at his sister.

"Me?" Babs scoffed. "You're the one staring at her br—"

"I was not!"

Soriya joined them, the street clear for the moment. Not if this continued. "Always like this?"

Vlad smiled. "Only when they're awake."

The young man prodded the pair up the walkway to the front door of the Cape Cod, its bright green siding setting the cozy structure apart from the rest of the uniformly designed homes on the street. A key was unnecessary. The door opened to a dimly lit living room.

"In you go, you two."

Robbie stopped, grasping the doorframe. "But we were—"

"We never finished our game," his sister said.

"Oh, it's finished," Vlad replied, rubbing his ribs.

The fight slipped from her mind, her brutal assault on an innocent man. "Sorry."

"Not your fault. You didn't know." He kept his eyes on the kids, bending low. "All right, you two. Head inside and get ready for bed. Your dad's home so keep quiet and lights out in ten. Got it?"

"What about you?" Babs asked, pouting.

Robbie grinned. "He's going to ask her out."

"Is not."

"He's going to smooch her up."

"No way!"

Vlad rolled his eyes, pushing them inside. He closed the door behind them, their muffled argument fading as it hit the frame.

"Kids."

Soriya barely heard him. She stood at the sidewalk, waiting, for what she did not know. What was keeping her here?

Vlad's hand fell on her shoulder. "Hey."

"Hmm?"

He said nothing, pointing across the street. Pike stood as a dividing line, residential on one side and the other a series of four-story apartment buildings that fed into the business district.

He led and she followed, curiosity winning out over the job at hand. They stopped short of the nearest complex and the alley between buildings. Vlad pulled down the fire escape ladder and started to climb, leaving Soriya bewildered on the street.

"Well?" He turned back, hand extended. "Come on."

She did, the steps clanging under her sneakers. "Where are we—?"

Vlad stood at the edge of the rooftop, looking south at the city. Portents. Downtown stretched in all directions, the obsidian tower at its center soaring above them, piercing the shadows of the night.

"Whoa," she whispered.

Vlad grinned, sitting on the ledge. He patted the seat beside her and she joined him. "It's easier up here. Not sure why. It helps to see things more clearly, doesn't it?"

Soriya nodded. She had rarely been on rooftops before. Her work tended to stick to the streets or below. The shadows. The alleys. The darker places of the city. How had she been so unaware of this?

A small groan escaped Vlad's lips, his hand nursing the ribs where she had connected her first hit.

"About before—" she began.

He waved her off. "It's a game they like. A little more intense than hide and seek, I know. I'm just happy to be back in pants."

She laughed, and he blushed. "Me too."

"Sorry."

"You seem so—"

"Normal?"

She nodded. "One word for it."

"I'm not," he said confidently, leaning closer to the ledge. Below, few people lingered on the streets. "I mean, how could I be? But I make do. It's different for all of us—you included, I'm sure—but this family is more my family than any I've ever had."

"Even others of your own kind?"

The young man's look hardened, refusing to turn her way. "There aren't too many of my kind left anymore. Not that I mind. Who doesn't want to be unique, right?" His smile returned, weak and transparent. "You have any family?"

Thinking about family always made her edgy. There was Mentor, of course. He saved her from a life of solitude, though there were days when she felt alone in a city of millions. Her parents had been killed in a car accident—the same incident that ripped her previous life from her memory. Soriya Greystone was a false name, a false hope at something she no longer knew. A lost life, shrouded by her current one.

"It's complicated."

"Family always is," Vlad said. "Always pushing you. Making decisions for you and you get the consequences. The responsibility of not blowing it to make them proud or some other excuse that keeps you from living your own life and making your own choices."

Every word hit home. It sounded right. The pressure of her task, one thrust upon her by Mentor, along with his constant teachings and lessons, all bearing down on her. But there was joy as well. In the struggle—the hunt.

Balance was the key.

"Maybe," she finally said.

"Shouldn't be that way. Not all the time. Not for us."

Vlad stood, reaching for her hand. She offered it willingly, surprised at his human strength.

"What are you—?"

He held her close, smiling. "Tag. You're it."

Vlad raced for the edge of the rooftop, leaping to the adjacent building effortlessly. Soriya stood transfixed, lost once more in his actions.

"What?"

He stopped, hands thrown up in disbelief. "Haven't you ever played a game? Come on!"

She hadn't. Not the kind that didn't end in bruises and blood on the floor of the Bypass chamber—her home tucked beneath the center of the city. She didn't understand the rules of tag or what the game meant to the young man running faster and faster across the rooftops of the city.

But she was a fast learner.

They ran in the dark for what felt like hours—lost in their laughter, in the thrill of the warm summer wind against their skin, in their separation from everything and everyone below. Vlad never changed, never shifted, his physique keeping him just ahead of her—his body distracting.

The race continued for blocks, deeper into the business section of Junction Cove. No pause. A dance above the city. Just for them.

They stopped behind a billboard denoting a local law firm on top of a defunct plaza. The two fought for air, their grins refusing to diminish.

"I've never—"

Vlad nodded. "I figured."

Soriya stood, catching her breath. Moving to the edge of the plaza, she looked over Main Street. A clock chimed in the hour down the block—each clang bringing her back.

"There's that look again," Vlad said, joining her.

"This was fun, Vlad, but—"

He stopped her. "I don't even know your name. Mystery Girl isn't cutting it for me."

She laughed. "Soriya."

"It was nice to meet you, Soriya. Despite what my ribs tell me."

Soriya stepped back for the fire escape, unsure what to say. Personal relationships for her were few, and even those were difficult to maintain. The job came first.

"Hey," Vlad called and she turned back. "You're hunting something."

"Or someone."

He ran to meet her. "Let me help. Least I can do."

She shook her head. "I don't—"

The ocean in his wide eyes stopped her, drawing her in. "Come on. Why end the fun now?"

CHAPTER FOUR

It was a mistake. That much was clear to Soriya Greystone as she bounded between buildings. They had been searching less than thirty minutes, up and down the business district of the cove, but Soriya was lost in thought over her companion.

Vladimir Luchik whooped and hollered screams of pure elation with each step into the night. His cries of joy echoed in the alleys, causing windows to open and the grumblings of sleepy citizens to answer back. It brought others into play that didn't need to see the pair.

More than anything, it brought doubt. Soriya knew little about the young man, her curiosity winning out over common sense—a trait Mentor was quick to point out more often than not when it came to the work. Vlad was enthusiastic and charming, genuine through and through. But his presence unsettled her, rattled her down to her core, and those doubts needed to stay buried.

Especially tonight.

At Bleeker and Carn, she stopped. She leaned hard over the ledge of the corner office complex, staring out over the street below. No pedestrians and few vehicles traveled the road. Vlad pounced behind her, unable to remain still. His cries of joy continued until her glare cut through them.

"Quiet."

His smile faded. He joined her on the corner, keeping low and out of sight.

"Sorry. My blood is pumping. We're on the hunt." He stood, arms to his hips. The same idiotic pose she had seen on another partner—though she didn't think Loren even realized it when he pulled out his Superman routine. "Watch out, evildoers. Do you call them that?"

"Never."

He shrugged. "I'll work on the banter."

"Don't."

She paced the rooftop, leaving him behind. Her words stung, the flippant single-word answers too sharp to be taken as anything other than a rebuke of their time together, but she let them settle between them, though it bothered her more than it did her intended target. Settling on the opposite corner, she paused, pointing down the block.

"There."

Vlad slowly joined her, a gap left between them. "Really? Nothing ever happens in the cove, Soriya."

"Read a paper, Vlad. A dozen incidents in a ten-block radius but most centered down there." There were thoughts behind the extrapolation. Theories. Mostly from Mentor even if he never knew all the details. That was his gift over hers. He understood the information, any information, as it was delivered. She had to work for answers.

Lights distracted her, coming fast from the street. "Down."

Both ducked to let the patrol car pass. Vlad crept close, his breath on her back. Heat rose from his chest. He smiled and she pulled away, the pair finding their feet once the solitude returned.

Vlad cleared his throat. "Patrols have really stepped up."

"A headache we don't need."

"Why not let them handle it?" the young man asked. An obvious question, with the only answer she ever gave.

"I'm not sure they can."

"Because someone like me might be out there."

"Possibly," Soriya said. She recalled the description given to the police from a number of victims. The description was dead-on for the wolfen male beside her—albeit in his hairier form. The crimes themselves, though, *felt* wrong. Too small and too high profile, as if demanding attention. Or in her case, a distraction. "I don't know. Yet."

"I...." Vlad stopped, turning down the street. "You hear that?"

Soriya looked confused. "What?"

"Glass breaking."

She didn't, nor did she see anything anywhere down the block. "I didn't—"

Too late. Vlad leaped from the rooftop to the ground below, sliding his shirt off in the process. He was mid-change when he landed, his wolfen features taking over.

"Vlad," she called.

He turned, waving her on with wide yellow eyes. His enthusiasm returned. "Come on already."

She hesitated, watching him race down the block toward a sound only he could hear. "Great."

She caught up with him three blocks away, his discarded clothing in her hands. His massive chest heaved, yet he remained tucked close to the corner of the brick edifice housing an electronics store. Glass littered the front sidewalk and just inside the closed business. Vlad threw a fang-filled grin then ducked inside without a sound.

Her eyes rolled and she dropped the clothes to the ground. Quickly and without thought she flew down the alley adjacent to the building until she came to the rear entrance. Locked. She held tight to the handle, the cold metal sending chills up her arm. Then she twisted hard, refusing to relent until the satisfying snapping sound filled the air. It didn't take long. The door sagged open and she entered, every second counting against her.

She held back, tucked to the shadows. The back offered a break room for employees, a room for overstock and returns, and a small corner for a manager's desk. She paid them no mind, infiltrating the store proper.

Vlad's shadow loomed over the building—and the thief within, juggling a flat screen too large for his hands.

"Hey there," the wolf said.

The thief stumbled at the sight of the creature. "Holy—"

The wolf lunged forward, pouncing for the surprised criminal. Soriya cursed under her breath. "Dammit, Vlad. Don't."

She jumped between them, her shoulder jamming into Vlad's tender ribs. The wolf groaned from the impact, the pair crashing into a display of speakers. The thief, little more than a kid, took the moment and fled for the front of the store.

"What the hell?" Vlad cried out, pushing Soriya aside. He stood, oversized paw to his side. "What are you doing?"

"I—"

Vlad didn't care to listen, and instead rushed for the fleeing crook. Hearing the plodding footfalls of the beast, the thief dropped the television down the center aisle. Vlad jumped over the obstacle, hands extending for the kid.

Oblivious to the other thief in the store.

"Vlad, look—"

The warning went unheard. The accomplice, taking advantage of Vlad's vulnerability in mid-air, charged into the adjacent shelving unit. The unit moaned loudly, picking up speed during its descent, and landed on top of the unsuspecting wolf. Boxes of software and disc players crashed upon him, burying Vlad within the confines of the store.

Soriya closed her eyes, whispering, "Out."

The pair of crooks raced into the night, disappearing down an alley across the street. Soriya turned back to Vlad, whose groans filled the store. Pushing box after box off his hulking frame, he was soon free.

"What was that?"

She didn't answer, stepping out of the store and returning with his clothes. He took them, snapping them away from her in anger, then began to change back into his human form.

"Well? What the hell was that?"

"Listen—"

He snarled, his fangs still present. "I could have stopped them. We could have."

"There were only two. There might be—"

He stopped her, yellow eyes fading to blue. "You think there are more?"

She held no definitive answer. Everything she knew, every instinct she held from her years of training gave her pause about the crimes being committed.

"There could be. There probably are."

"How the hell would I know?"

"That isn't—" Her arms rested across her chest.

His look saddened. He nodded, finally understanding. "You don't want me here."

"I don't," she replied too quickly. "This was a mistake."

Vlad nodded, hand wiping away a string of saliva from the corner of his mouth. He pushed through her for the street. Sirens were approaching. Still, he stopped, turning back once more.

"You're not the only one who cares about this city. And I actually live in it. Not just hide in the shadows like you."

Each word hit home. The argument she always gave Mentor thrown right back at her. Her hands gripped tighter to her sides. "Doesn't matter. It's my job."

His eyes pleaded. "I can help, dammit."

"You can," she said quietly. Her words were cold, her look colder. "Stay out of my way."

CHAPTER FIVE

Stay out of my way.

Her words repeated on him, much like his lunch from her gut punch earlier that evening. The audacity of the words, the sheer condescension in them. They made Vladimir Luchik's blood boil.

He wanted to lash out, to break something—his angry youth returning full force. Instead, he walked furiously, leaving behind the businesses of Junction Cove for the quieter residential neighborhoods on the outskirts. Block after block, mile after mile, with Soriya's words beating a war drum between his ears.

He thought of going home—the only action that made sense. Vlad wasn't protector of the city or a guardian of the night or whatever other pretentious names people came up with for the Greystone bearer. Fun was the end goal for Vlad—had been his entire life. Showing off for a pretty girl, even one with a violent streak like Soriya, was standard operating procedure. Not hunting creatures, stalking the shadows for a fight.

What the hell did he know about any of that?

But her words stung. Her anger and his bitterness. The mistake that had been their little time together. *Mistake.* It summed up so much. His entire life. Before the Corwells. He tried to hold on to the image of Robbie and Babs but there was always the time before.

His family disowned him, the bite of the wolf ostracizing him forever. With that turn, Vlad found a new home in the darkness, surrounded by his own kind. A second family—a better one. It ended badly. He was never one of them. He didn't seek out violence. He looked for peace—a betrayal to their way of life.

Another family gone.

Alone, bitter and lost, Vlad found his way to Portents. He had nothing on him. No identification, no money of any kind. Just the clothes on his back, ripped and frayed from the transformations. From creature to human. Sometimes they became crossed. Confused.

Just like him.

Then the Corwells came along. An extended hand giving him a chance when no other would. He went to college—online courses. He put in some effort, not as much as he should but more than previous attempts. The kids helped. Everything about them helped. Things changed. He changed, forgetting the past and the pressure and the darkness. The fun returned.

But he remained alone, wolf among men, until she came. Part of him saw something greater in her. A nice thought, if only for a short time.

The shuffling of feet along the sidewalk interrupted him. Vlad ducked into the bushes running alongside one property, keeping low to the overgrown grass. His breathing slowed, caught in his throat, but his eyes turned yellow, cutting through the darkness down the street.

A lone figure passed. A little girl, no older than Babs, dressed in pigtails and a flower print skirt—running along the sidewalk with fear in her eyes. There was nothing behind her, nothing seen at least. She cut across several yards then stopped, beelining for the largest domicile on the street.

"Not strange at all," Vlad muttered. "Nope. Not at all."

Creeping quietly along the grass, Vlad watched the girl fiddle with the knob, her eyes scanning the block. Her teeth chattered despite the warmth of the summer night. The knob seemed unusually large in her hands, fighting her ingress to the home. Finally, the door opened, and the darkness within swallowed her whole.

Vlad wanted to walk away. It was not his problem, never should have been. He was a fool to still be out this late. He knew better. But the fear in the girl's eyes haunted him. Secure in his solitude on the block, Vlad rushed to the front door of the home.

Locked.

"Kid?" he whispered through the oak entrance. "You in there?"

Sobbing answered him, distant but audible. He could have changed, let the wolf take over, to rip the door off the hinges and save the girl. The mistakes of the night overshadowed that plan. He needed to be smarter. The girl inside needed that too.

Vlad jumped over the porch rail to the side of the house, looking for a way in—an open window, a back door, anything. The yard was open, no brush blocking the view from the street, so he ducked lower, moving faster along the outskirts of the home. An ajar window greeted his efforts. He slipped his hand in, gently pushing the sash up. The vinyl squealed loudly and he halted, catching his breath, his heart beating in his ears.

"Come on," Vlad said, stretching his fingers along the window. "Come…"

Light showered over him. A flashlight—and someone behind it. Someone holding a badge.

"Crap."

"That's how I feel about it too," the officer said. He kept the light on him, his sidearm replacing the badge. "Any idea the paperwork involved?"

Vlad raised his hands over his head, fingers open and disarming. "We could forget the whole thing?"

The plainclothes cop shook his head. "Get up. Slowly."

Vlad's head fell. "Or not."

The cop tucked the flashlight away, followed by the gun. Cuffs replaced them, quickly wrapping tight to Vlad's wrists. With the bright light out of his face, Vlad saw the cop clearly for the first time. Shorter than him, but not by much. Thin, almost too thin. Exhausted as well from the dour look on his face. The man reeked of alcohol. Vlad cursed his heightened senses but even a normal guy would have picked up the stench of booze. Alcohol, however, didn't hamper the cop's efficiency. He speedily led Vlad to the cruiser sitting at the curb.

The driver smiled. "Caught a shark, Loren?"

Vlad felt the cold metal of the vehicle pressed hard against his chest.

"More like a guppy," Loren replied.

"Any chance I—?"

"No." The cuffs tightened and Vlad figured out the score. Loren was not someone to mess with.

"You don't want to hear his innocence?" his partner asked, his jowls shaking with each word. "So jaded."

Loren slammed his fist on the roof. "Shut it, Standish. Listening to you puts me in a mood." He turned back to Vlad. "And so do lies about how you lost your keys and were trying not to disturb your lady friends inside."

"Lady friends?"

Loren turned Vlad back to the house in question, the one with the sobbing little girl that needed help. A large sign sat on the lawn with three large Greek letters painted in purple.

"Sorority house, dimbulb. You sure can pick 'em."

But he saw the girl. He heard her cries. Didn't he?

"Get in." The back door of the vehicle opened and Vlad was pushed inside. "And no talking."

Loren slammed the door shut then hopped into the passenger side. Standish started the engine, his ever-present sneer bearing down on his partner.

"Headache?"

"Yeah, Standish. You." Loren pointed down the road. "Now shut up and drive."

The patrol car shifted into traffic, Vlad's head sinking to his chest. Another idiot move. For what? He looked back to the house, hoping the girl was safe. Hoping she existed in the first place, or a whole new set of questions would come into play.

He froze at the sight of her—the little girl.

Her hand pressed tight to the picture window, the fear in her eyes gone. No terror at all. Joy, in fact. The young man slammed his hands against the door, his cries ignored by the pair in the front seat. All he could do was stare in horror as the little girl waved at the departing vehicle, her smile following Vlad for the rest of the night.

CHAPTER SIX

Soriya watched the scene unfold. The arrest, the humiliation of Vlad. All of it. Part of her was glad. With Vlad out of the way, her clarity of purpose returned.

Still, the other shoe dropped, a sadness at leaving him to his fate. Not only that, but her words, the coldness behind them, lingered. Not that she hadn't been right, but how it played out bothered her more than she liked. But the job remained.

Her job. And hers alone.

The arresting officer was a surprise. Greg Loren. Her partner more often than not. At least for the last three years, off and on. This was their off time. Two months without speaking, their last case ending poorly. Their last few had ended the same way, truthfully, and she had no reason not to be in the solitude of the night.

The drowning detective sought answers. Answers she held back during their cases. Questions turned to demands and demands ended in arguments. Her withholding slowed his progress, kept him from what he was actually seeking—his wife's killer, the case that refused to close. She could not help with that. Not with the constant comings and goings in the city. The past was forced to remain exactly that to a present full of monsters and murderers.

Loren needed more. He needed progress. He needed comfort that they were a team, and she held back. The truth obvious. She used Loren for resources, for his support, but the job remained hers alone.

There was more to it. Loren was drinking again. She could tell by his stance, by the staggered step into the cruiser after shoving Vlad into the back. Their casework tended to be a blessing in that regard. Work kept him busy, too busy to wallow in the loss of his wife, too focused on a case to worry about the demons waiting for him in the empty apartment he clung to harder than the bottleneck of his latest purchase. But the work could only be a balm at best, not a cure. And the past never remained buried.

Soriya Greystone crouched low to the rooftop of the building adjacent to Vlad's arrest. She noticed the young girl enter the sorority house as well. Refusing to make the same mistake twice, Soriya took the "wait and see" approach, keeping her distance. Vlad didn't. Lesson enough for her to try, even if patience was not her strong suit.

A minute after the departure of the patrol car, the little girl in pigtails stepped out into the darkness. A large, vindictive grin ran ear to ear and she skipped to the sidewalk and down the block, whistling with each hop.

Soriya followed her closely, sticking to the rooftops that sloped higher and higher with each step deeper into Junction Cove. The jovial child's skipping never slowed, the excitement carrying her further and further downtown. Something about the girl gave Soriya the chills.

A threat? Definitely. But what kind and why?

The child stopped at the corner before a dilapidated theater. The Royal. The worn-down theater had been closed for over a decade, the night life shifting to the east side, away from the generally quiet coves of the north. With the shift, all of the businesses on the block felt the pinch, the Royal hit fast and hard, especially with the opening of Garden Memorial downtown, an outdoor showcase for the arts. The Royal didn't stand a chance.

Hesitating for only a moment, with eyes shifting up and down the street, the little girl stepped inside the abandoned venue. The door closed noiselessly behind her, leaving Soriya with only the howl of the wind as company.

Three points of entry into the building were visible: a loading dock to the rear for set pieces, a door along the alley on the right for personnel and the occasional smoke break during performances, and the front door. The thought of sneaking around sickened Soriya.

Front door it is.

The lobby doors creaked under her hand. She softened her grip, slowing her pace. An announcement was unnecessary. The lobby stretched the length of the building with four double doors leading to the main stage. Unlit chandeliers dotted the ceiling. A gift shop stood to the right behind her, a coat check and bathrooms to the left. Stairs led to the balcony levels above.

Stepping deeper into the room, Soriya felt the ribbons along her left arm tighten. Her right hand slid instinctively to her hip—and her waiting Greystone. Not paranoia. Not fear.

Eyes.

And then more eyes.

A pair per hallway and more coming from each of the rooms behind her. Six sets of eyes, little specks in the darkness of the lobby, approached cautiously. With each followed a young man, no older than eighteen. Each carried a weapon; a bat for some, knives for others. They surrounded her, circling closer and closer.

All looking for a fight.

Soriya smiled, cracking her knuckles.

"It's about damn time."

CHAPTER SEVEN

A fist caught the last teen square in the gut and he dropped like a stone. The resounding thud and the low moans of pain matched that of his five companions scattered across the lobby.

Soriya Greystone exhaled slowly. Small drips of blood spattered the decayed carpet beneath her. Her knuckles were torn from the struggle but she remained in one piece—more than she could say for her assailants.

"This was fun," she muttered over their defeated and bleeding bodies. "Well, not really. Not for you anyway."

She stepped on the closest one and yelps of pain slipped from his lips, drawing a large smile from her. The others did their best to scatter from her footfalls and she let them—the lesson learned. There were bigger fish to fry. But then, there always were.

Four doors led to the main stage of the Royal Theater and Soriya took the one center right. The main stage looked small in the distance, overshadowed by the stadium seating stretching in all directions. Ornate candelabrum glistened along the ceiling, the moonlight filtering in through growing holes in the rooftop, causing splits in the artwork detailed along the peak of the room. Most of the seats remained in place, despite the age—a few sections ripped out and tossed among the wreckage of the room. The past forgotten, the history of Portents buried like so much waste.

Treasure littered the stage. Wads of cash mixed with jewels, sifted through the stolen goods of the last two weeks. Personal mementos and property of their victims. In the center of it all sat a makeshift throne, its base resting on a mound of empty beer cans, its seat a reconditioned wheelchair, the prize taken from a poor old woman forced to crawl for assistance.

The little girl sat on her throne, clapping at the arrival of Soriya. "Bravo," she cheered over the echo of her hands. "Bravo!"

Soriya felt her body stiffen, the ribbons of Kali clutched tight down her left arm. There was a blackness in the girl's eyes—thick like tar. Soriya's steps slowed as she inched closer to the stage.

The child's clapping ended, a look of disappointment on her innocent face. "No bow? No pride at smiting the great teenage threat? Come now, Greystone, have a little fun."

She knew. Of course she did. The visage of the girl was a tool—not the truth of the situation. Calling Soriya by her title was more than that, though. She held the cards and Soriya was still catching up—unsure the nature of the beast in the form of the girl.

At the orchestra pit, Soriya stopped. The girl eyed her expectantly, prepared for all. The woman reached up to the waiting stage, letting her body relax before launching into the air. The somersault carried her to the edge of the treasure, her feet slamming hard against the rotting wood. Soriya stood tall, balled-up fists at the ready.

"I plan to," she finally replied.

"Ah," the little girl said, hands folded on her lap. "The little girl routine is wasted."

She sighed. "I suppose it is."

The change came in an instant. The little girl with the pigtails and the flower print skirt was replaced by a full-grown woman, her long red hair running down to a tight black dress hugging every curve.

A shifter. Someone like Vlad but different. More involved. Something else. But what?

The woman's ruby lips pursed. "Better?"

"Not even close."

Thin fingers ran along her breasts. "My boys seemed to enjoy it enough. Such diligent workers once they saw who they were working for. For just a peek, a small touch of flesh, they would ravage this city for all its worth."

Soriya scoffed, arms spread to showcase the prized earnings from the last two weeks. "So you can sit and count your newfound wealth?"

The woman laughed, her deep voice filling the grand hall of the Royal Theater. "This? Worthless to me."

"Then why?"

More laughter, haughty and superior, causing Soriya's jaw to clench. The woman sat, hands outstretched on the armrests of her wheelchair throne, her right leg crossed over her left.

"You don't know? Dear, please." Black eyes stabbed at her. "The fun of it. Why else do we do anything?"

"I guess you have a point." The ribbons of Kali shuffled down her left side, whipping wildly about her. Where the teenage wasteland resting uncomfortably in the lobby failed to satiate her need, she hoped the woman before her would not disappoint.

"Right to it then."

"Why wait?" Soriya asked, inching closer.

The woman sighed. "I think I'll pass."

"I didn't see you as the surrendering type."

"Oh, I have no intention of throwing in the towel. Or raising a fist. Very unbecoming. Uncivilized."

"Those are the only options. So let me choose for you."

Soriya caught the crack of the woman's smirk before leaping into the air at her. Kicking out her leg, Soriya soared across the stage for the makeshift throne.

The woman was gone.

Surprised eyes whipped around the stage, throwing off the kick and sending her body spiraling into the wheelchair. The crash knocked the throne asunder and with it, Soriya fell among the treasures littering the stage. Fighting to her knees, Soriya searched for the woman, the cause of her night's journey and the pain of a dozen incidents throughout the cove. Only the woman was gone, the only other living thing standing on four legs on the far side of the stage.

A fox—red as the woman's hair had been, its black eyes harder yet unable to conceal the mischievous grin behind them. It stood tall and proud.

"I'll pick my own path, child," the fox said to a startled Soriya.

"Kitsune," she whispered, the name carried on the wind of the room.

The fox grinned, teeth bared. "Smart girl. For a Greystone."

Soriya knocked the wheelchair aside in anger, her free hand snatching the stone on her hip. She shook her head, her vision still unsettled from the impact. "It's over."

The creature backed down the length of the stage for the shadows, grinning wide.

"For now, perhaps," the fox said, swallowed up by the darkness of the theater. As it faded from view, its words filled the theater and the thoughts of the surprised Greystone bearer. "My fun has been spoiled. Don't make a habit out of it, child."

CHAPTER EIGHT

The night air never tasted sweeter. Six hours, forty-two minutes, and thirty-eight seconds in a jail cell and Vladimir Luchik never wanted to see another in his life. Most could say the same having been through the experience but Vlad's nose knew better. He couldn't stand the smell of the desperate men beside him, awaiting hearings and interrogations and who knew what other fun at the hands of domineering officers of the so-called law.

Never again, Vlad swore, stepping out into the city—the sweet fragrance of freedom filling his lungs. *I'd rather be dead.*

The sun remained tucked away, struggling to wake with the new day. The air was warm and humid, the threat of showers in the not so distant future. First, there would be sun.

It felt like days inside, even with his internal clock working as a constant distraction from the pacing men and growling alpha males surrounding him. They didn't bother him. He knew his innocence, even if the cops didn't.

They came around eventually.

The six men—boys really, though the twenty-year-old Vlad said little on the subject—had been escorted proudly through the precinct. A showcase by the officers looking for a win after so much bad press over the string of robberies in the area. The hoodlums held their heads low, bruises swelling along their cheeks, cuts lining their exposed arms and legs. There had been a fight, one that did not go their way, despite the numbers involved.

Word traveled swiftly about the arrest, even to the curmudgeon detective behind Vlad's incarceration. Loren had no choice but to cut Vlad loose, his story of the little girl echoed in the rants of the gang of six. Vlad had a feeling he owed someone thanks for the release, surprised that the angry detective shared his knowing stare.

It was time to go home. Nothing sounded sweeter to Vlad than twelve hours of sack time followed by another twelve for good measure. There would be interruptions, of course. Babs and Robbie would have their questions, appropriate or not. Their father might as well, but Vlad was hoping to avoid that as much as possible. He had a good life with the Corwell family. One he wanted to keep.

He stood in the center of the intersection outside the Second Precinct, letting the warm summer breeze whip through him. With the wind came a scent, subtle at first then drawn into him in long drags. Something familiar.

No, *someone* familiar.

Vlad sniffed the air, following the flow, his steps speeding up with each one. Across from the precinct sat a series of office buildings, eight stories tall, with a rattling and rusty fire escape clinging to the side of the closest. He climbed the metal ladder eagerly and unafraid, racing toward the roof.

Where Soriya Greystone stood, waiting.

"I thought I smelled you," Vlad said, his hand immediately slapping over his mouth. He shook his head. "Wow. That was the wrong thing to say."

"That's you all over, I've heard."

"True," he said, rubbing the back of his neck. He pointed to the precinct below, the sound of the morning traffic beginning to fill the streets of the cove, flowing deeper into the twisted paths of Portents. "I take it I owe you for the save?"

"I'm sure you would have been just fine," Soriya shrugged, joining him at the edge of the rooftop. He fought to keep her fragrance from overwhelming him, his body temperature rising in her presence.

"Doubtful."

Loren stepped out of the station, a slow stagger in his step. A cigarette dangled from his lips. He moved to light it, then paused. An unheard curse escaped and the frustrated detective snatched the nicotine-laden stick from his mouth and threw the cigarette in the trash on the corner.

"Angry cops in there."

She lowered her head, her eyes distant. "Sometimes."

It was the same stare on Loren when the six men were escorted through the precinct. A look of knowing. Of understanding.

And sadness.

"Soriya?" he asked, concerned. For the first time since their reunion, he saw her in the pale light of the new morning. Her tired eyes, the slump in her shoulders, and the small cuts and torn knuckles on both hands. "What happened?"

Her eyes softened and the smile returned. A friendly one that carried her away to the center of the rooftop. Away from the city surrounding her. Vlad listened as best as he could. He was never good at the role of student. Most of what she said sailed over him but the gist remained.

The story of the Kitsune, the Japanese word for fox, surprised him. The Kitsune were often described in folklore as possessing magical abilities that increased with their age and wisdom. They could serve as protectors or guardians but more to their nature than not, they often used their gifts as that of a trickster. Including their ability to transfigure.

Speaking of the creature at the heart of their night, Soriya sounded bitter—filled with unrequited anger. A case unresolved. For now.

Vlad, however, let the story settle over him for a long moment. Soriya had mistakenly hunted him over a description shared with authorities over the crook in their midst. The little girl lured him to a sorority house knowing the patrol car was coming. All for him.

"Great," Vlad muttered. "My very own nemesis."

"More like a target," Soriya said. "Kitsunes have a dislike for dogs. In all forms, it seems."

"So what's to stop her from doing it again?"

"Nothing. But she won't."

"Why?"

"This wasn't about you. Not completely. This was for the fun of it."

Vlad shook his head. "I am a fun-loving guy. As you well know."

Soriya tilted her head, her hair falling gently along her left shoulder. His heart quickened and his cheeks flushed. She moved closer, her hand extending. A card sat between her fingers.

"Here."

"What's this?"

"My number."

"Really?" His voice reminded him of Robbie instead of his own. He cleared his throat, slipping the card into his pocket. "I mean—cool."

Soriya laughed. "For the next case, Vlad."

"Oh," Vlad said, recalling their fight, now buried in the past. "Yeah. No, that sounds great. Crazy shape-shifting fox ladies come running around and we can—"

She kissed him, pulling him in close and holding him tight. His lips settled over hers, her scent—a mix of sweat, blood, and joy—filling him.

It ended as quickly as it began yet lingered between them. Her smile widened, his own a dumbfounded look of revelation. The overwhelmed man-child fell back on his heels, his body threatening to topple over from the exchange.

"Whoa."

"Tag," she said. "You're it."

She ran for the edge of the roof then turned back.

"Seriously?"

"Let's see what you've got, wolf boy."

The night was over for them. The pressure of the hunt, the weight of responsibility a memory. There was only the two of them now. Vlad raced after her, the city their playground. There would be more to come. More requirements. More expectations. But for now it was over.

The two of them danced through Portents, laughing like children.

EYES IN THE STORM

CHAPTER ONE

The storm was immediate—from out of nowhere, on none of the weather forecasts for the day let alone the week, yet everywhere at once. Rain in waves, pummeling the citizens of a Chicago barely out of its long winter's nap. To say it was dreary would be an understatement.

Especially for Detective Greg Loren.

He leaned hard against the side of the cruiser, a wet dog. Long, unkempt threads of dirty blond hair slapped the back of his neck. His jacket, a trap for water, collecting in all the wrong spots. He wouldn't be surprised if his sidearm jammed the next time he used it. But he remained out in the middle of the rain.

Something sat awkwardly in his gut. Not the buttered roll he tossed down with a side of Ginger Ale. (Someday he would learn to make a real meal for himself.) Maybe it was the weather. Or the call from Kendra Girard, a colleague from the precinct, asking for help.

Loren knew the truth. Three months and it still lingered in his brain. *Portents*. He spent ten years there. Found a life. Lost a life. Made mistakes and tried to figure out a way to rectify them. Relocation made sense. Head home, reconnect with the life he once held, with family and friends he never really cared for in the first place. A little harsh, but so was ignoring the fourth call that day from his sister, Meriweather. Another ploy to force a connection. Sitting around, joking about the decade spent away. Maybe reminisce about his dead wife over cocktails, or right before tucking his nephews into bed.

Great plan.

A cigarette dangled between his fingers. Soaked and useless, a testament to an addiction he swore he kicked years ago. He bummed it from one of the uniforms on the scene. The pack of matches sat in his pocket, drowning like the rest of him. Not that it mattered. The cigarette was a memory, just like Portents.

He was different now.

He tossed the smoke away, finding the pack of gum within the inside pocket of his coat. Blueberry. The flavor of the night. Satisfied with the chomping sound echoing in his ears, Loren sighed. He bent low to retrieve the cigarette then dropped it in a nearby receptacle.

The Field Museum had been closed for hours but one wouldn't know that as the clock struck midnight. Flashing lights from four patrol cars lit up the road. Every window of the complex showered the parking lot with light. Traffic concentrated toward the rear of the museum.

The Acquisitions Department.

"We doing this thing?"

Loren turned to the man waiting impatiently at the top of the stairs. Blake Eiseman. Loren's partner for the last eight weeks. Young and eager, sometimes a little too much so for the brass, but he made up for it with a tenaciousness for the work. He was younger than Loren would have liked, with a mind on the fairer sex more often than not, but he was a good fit for an out-of-towner like Loren.

Except for the constant talking. Queries about his past, about his time in Portents. Hell, small talk about his day, all of which amounted to a book or a movie and eight hours of sack time if he was lucky enough to finish the growing amount of paperwork from the previous night. He never did.

The constant need to communicate, to connect socially, made Loren miss the quiet of Portents. Even amid the murder and mayhem there were moments of sheer serenity working a case. And there was Soriya. After Beth there was always Soriya.

Loren grimaced, the blueberry-flavored gum popping under his tongue. "Coming."

Bounding up the steps to the waiting detective, Loren opened his jacket, dumping the flood that had settled in the folds. Eiseman held the door for him and the two entered the long hall leading to acquisitions. Loren slid the jacket off completely, tucking it in the corner of the room, before wiping his shoes judiciously on the wide, thick runner down the center of the room.

Eiseman watched with glee, his hair perfectly preserved. "Captain must really like you, Loren. Two months in and I've never been busier."

Loren nodded. Captain Roberts was an old friend and mentor from his time at the academy. She pulled quite a few strings to bring him back into the fold so quickly. He made it up to her in spades. Not that he minded. Hell, most of it was requested. A necessary distraction during his transition.

"Love what you do, Eiseman," Loren replied, leading the pair down the hall to the waiting security desk.

"Who wouldn't love this? The glory? The fame?"

"The corpses?"

Eiseman grinned. "Bingo."

A burly guard, his uniform stretched in all the wrong places, greeted them with solemn eyes. Their badges were out before the question could be asked.

"Detectives Loren and Eiseman," Loren said.

The guard blinked hard, focused on the badges before him. Then he nodded and started for the door leading to incoming exhibits.

"This way, please."

The guard shuffled down the lengthy hall. Once outside the security entrance, the hall expanded with large stalls on both sides for items. Exhibits no longer on display, some being prepped, some requiring further research by on-site staff, the rest on their way out for their next stop.

Eiseman remained fixed on the destination. A little high strung when it came to a case. Focusing on the minute details before expanding his vision. Losing the whole picture until it became necessary. It made Loren nostalgic.

He snapped his gum loudly, catching Eiseman's attention. *Filthy habit.* Damn, he missed smoking.

"This was Girard's call, by the way."

Eiseman stopped, surprised. "She has that much clout?"

Loren patted his shoulder, continuing toward the large crowd near the end of the acquisitions area. "I think she likes you."

"Me?" Eiseman shook his head, although there was hope in his eyes. "Don't see it. But the mysterious Greg Loren?"

Loren rolled his eyes. Ever since his arrival, internal probes circled him from every direction. Including his own partner.

Portents was a great mystery to the rest of the department. Loren knew better. Portents was a mystery to the world. And the world was the better for it.

Still, stories circulated. Gossip. Whispers about what truly happened within the strange city. What lay in the shadows. Loren refused to play the game, to corroborate the fantasies built in their minds.

For their sakes and his own.

"No mystery here," Loren said.

"Keep telling yourself that."

An empty stall greeted them at the end of the line. Forensics littered the scene, tape and markers positioned throughout for reference points later. In the center of the mess, Kendra Girard counseled a nearby tech for photos of the entrance.

The guard nodded, leaving them to their work. Loren thanked the man who shambled back down the hall. Eiseman worked the scene, or more to the point, the lead detective.

"Kendra."

"Detectives. Welcome." Kendra nodded, rushing to their side. She pulled them aside, stopping short of a series of management offices and research stations.

"We're already behind the eight ball on this one," she said, her voice deep and strong. It matched her physique. She remained a striking figure in a uniform, hers being a pair of khakis and green blouse. Her focus remained fixed on the scene, never greeting them personally.

Eiseman leaned close to Loren, nudging him lightly in the side. "Yeah. She's hot and bothered all right. Call yourself a detective."

Loren ignored him. "What are we looking at, Girard?"

Kendra huffed, hands falling to her hips. "New display transferred in and quickly transferred out by our perp. Mayan artifacts of some sort. I'm having a full inventory drawn up."

A female tech passed off a report to Kendra, who glanced at it for only a moment. Eiseman caught the tech with a compelling stare and a smirk. Loren cleared his throat.

"One guy?" he asked.

"From what I've seen so far," Kendra said, sighing. "Tracks from the rain leading away from the building."

Loren peered at the photo in her hand. "And this?"

She passed it over. "Some kind of protective cloth, preserving the piece underneath. An ax, I've been told."

It was old and worn but definitely a smaller piece of a larger cloth. The only remnant for the display left.

Eiseman rubbed his chin. "Sounds like you have this well in hand, Kendra."

"I usually do," she said without looking.

"I think what he meant was, why are we joining you this fine evening when we could be soaked to our ears chasing killers? We're still homicide, after all."

Kendra smiled, reminding Loren she was a woman, bold and bright. "No love for antiquities of lost cultures, Greg?"

"I prefer to deal with recent history," he answered.

"Figured as much."

She led them out of the hall and into the managerial office next door. Waving them to follow, Loren and Eiseman stuck close, curious about the destination. A quick turn to the research hub attached to the office brought the picture into focus for the pair.

The body of a security guard lay on the ground, his right cheek smashed against the tile. Two bullet wounds to the back, a pool of blood surrounding him, and a pair of eyes staring into nothingness.

"Meet Martin Sheppard," Kendra said. Loren and Eiseman stopped in their tracks. Kendra leaned close to Loren, patting his shoulder. "Recent enough for you, Greg?"

CHAPTER TWO

"...And flash flood warnings continue throughout the city. My advice to you? Stay in. It's going to be a bumpy one, folks."
More good news.
Loren placed the coffee pot back on the burner, sidestepping a pair of uniforms looking for their fix. They nodded a greeting, one he was more than happy to reciprocate. Little else entered into the exchange since his arrival. Names were a blur, making him grateful for the display of them on their uniforms. This was Loren's chance to make a real change—to be a better person. To start a new life, a new chapter, whatever the hell people called it when they tried to dump their memories off at the side of the road and peel out for greener pastures.

And there was lots of green in the forecast, it seemed.

The tired detective rubbed his eyes, shuffling for his desk in the middle of the floor. The precinct kept a bullpen-style floor plan with partners butted up against each other next to other divisions and departments. Offices surrounded them on all sides, as did conference rooms. Interrogation was down the hall, next to the restrooms and the elevators, ready to take anyone necessary to holding on the floor below.

Interviews with the staff of the Field Museum were extensive. Even with a skeleton crew working the night shift, it took Loren and Eiseman hours to get through them, looking for connections to Martin Sheppard, mapping everyone's route in and out of the building at all hours. Anything to help paint the picture of not only the robbery of priceless historical treasures but also that of the dead man no one seemed to know very well.

Those interviews led to a late start on Loren's sleep schedule. Four hours and a quick shower and he was back at the station, three cups of coffee in and a headache forming along his right temple.

"Anything?" Loren asked, finishing his latest cup and wishing it would actually help.

Eiseman refused to look up, his eyes bleary from the twin monitors on his desk. The overhead lights were staggered, never on completely, and the lack of light outside didn't help. Eiseman's desk lamp was a memory as well, a casualty of too many cases and not enough space.

"Tons," he replied. Loren offered him a cup of coffee but the junior detective shook his head, pointing to the Red Bull on his desk. A nastier habit than gum chewing, in Loren's book. "Literal tons from the museum. Security footage for weeks. Employee movements that we corroborated last night. Same with the time cards for entrances and exits. Yadda, yadda, and more yadda."

Loren sighed, collapsing in his chair. He put the mugs down on his desk and rolled the chair over to Eiseman's side of their small corner of the room. "Anything useful?"

"I assumed you might ask that," Eiseman said, clicking through the files taking over his computer desktop. "Check this out."

Loren watched the security feeds for the night in question. Nothing appeared out of the ordinary. Routine patrols throughout the museum as well as the offices in the back. Martin Sheppard stalked the halls of the acquisitions wing without alarm, the lone man in his area. A normal night for all involved.

At the turn of 11:00, every feed went dead. Eiseman caught Loren's surprise. He nodded and sped up the replay. Fifteen minutes passed in the blink of an eye. All static on the feeds. At quarter past the hour they came back as if nothing happened; only Martin Sheppard had disappeared from view and the stall containing the new Mayan display was empty.

"No other feeds?"

Eiseman shook his head. "Not a one."

"The storm?"

"That's what everyone in house thought. At least after the fact, when I questioned them on it. Thing is, the storm didn't start until after 11:00, according to the local station."

"Because they're always so accurate?"

"True," Eiseman said, holding back a laugh. "But take it off the table for a minute. Say it wasn't the storm. How would our thief cut the feeds from the outside?"

"You're saying he couldn't?" Loren leaned closer to Eiseman. He found a stick of peach mango gum in his pocket and jammed it in place, chewing loudly over the man's shoulder.

Eiseman shifted away from the sound, throwing Loren a look. "Not a chance. But someone inside?"

"Our perp wasn't an employee," Loren said quickly. He knew that much from the interviews. There was no intrinsic value in stealing artifacts from an exhibit. The trade value to a collector would set someone up for life, sure, but the heat brought on by that would dog the thief for months if not years.

"Our perp wasn't alone," Eiseman clarified. "Think about it. One guy? The feeds? The timing involved? And the getaway?"

Loren nodded, seeing the picture painted for him. "Inside job."

"Exactly," Eiseman replied. "Someone lied to us."

"Maybe."

"Maybe?"

Loren snapped the gum between his teeth. "We spoke to them."

"But not the people who weren't there or at least weren't supposed to be there." Eiseman stopped him, shuffling for the roster taken from the night before. "Look."

"I take it the circles mean—"

Eiseman snatched it back. "What do you prefer? Squares? Big giant arrows?"

Loren waited.

"Sorry," Eiseman said. It had been a long night for both of them. "Circles are for people that failed to show up to work for whatever reason. Vacation. Illness. Whatever. But the kicker is two of them showed up that night anyway."

"You find out why?" Loren asked, intrigued. Eiseman had been busy. What the hell had Loren been doing this entire time, other than drowning in caffeine and rain?

"About to—"

"What about calls? Something from whoever might have helped make this happen?"

Eiseman snapped his fingers. "There you go, detective. No calls. Not a damn blip. No e-mails even. Nothing on the outside feeds or the traffic cam before they went out during the fifteen-minute gap. Not even our dead guy."

"Martin."

"I know his name, Loren."

Loren shook his head. "It wasn't a test."

Eiseman nodded, standing to stretch. He lifted up the half can of Red Bull and downed it. Loren slid his chair closer to the terminals, clicking through the footage once more, this time focused on the movements of their victim.

Martin Sheppard walked the halls of the acquisitions wing alone for most of the evening, taking over the shift at 7:00 that night. He hummed a tune, snapped his fingers, and had a snack. Alone. He owned the wing.

Until it killed him.

"You see this a lot in Portents, Loren?"

Loren rolled his eyes, minimizing the window. The past was a closed book and he preferred to keep it that way. Permanently.

"Portents wasn't anything special, Eiseman. Just another beat." Loren moved back to his desk and his bonus cup of coffee. He let the gum slip from his lips to the trash before taking a sip. It was something that took several lessons to learn.

Eiseman grinned, hands on his hips. "Yeah, right, Loren. I've heard the stories. Bogeymen. Monsters. All crap, I'm sure, but still must make for an interesting time. Spill."

"Would if I could?" Loren said, refusing to look at his partner. "I must've been working too hard to notice." Eiseman's stare locked on, demanding more. Finally, Loren relented, taking a deep breath. "Look. Portents is a place that currently has my wardrobe and some dusty old books I keep telling myself to read. That's all."

Eiseman threw his hands up in surrender. "All right, all right. You play the mysterious loner with the shadowy past card well, my friend, but I will hear it all. I promise you that."

"You can try, Eiseman," Loren said before finishing his coffee. "You'd have better luck stopping the rain."

Both men laughed, but their bond was broken by the sound of a throat clearing behind them. They turned to see an older black man, rain dripping from his thick glasses.

"I don't think anyone can stop the rain," the man said. "And I think it's my fault."

CHAPTER THREE

Eiseman was the lucky one. The young detective shot out of the squad room, eager to begin the slog of interviews with staffers and missing personnel from the Field Museum for their whereabouts and other information about the deceased. Not a crucial track, but something needed to be done while phone records were procured. Most likely the day would prove to be pointless but it freed him from Loren's waiting guest.

Doctor Carson Wells.

Loren was able to glean his name through manic breaths involving rain spirits and the anger of the gods, watchwords for the in-department psych staff, though none came to relieve Loren. Instead, it fell to the detective to handle.

At least he wasn't stuck in the rain.

He left Wells in the conference room at the end of the hall. The lean professor sat facing the window, watching the deluge. His mutterings went unheard but those waiting for the room quietly looked for another venue rather than interrupt the man rocking back and forth in his chair.

Loren hesitated to enter as well. In his few minutes of preparation, most of which he spent trying to get Girard to come in early to take over, Loren found little on the man other than his photo and a small bio on the Field Museum website. A doctor of archeology, Carson Wells toiled away researching dead civilizations in the hopes of finding links to the present. Treasures long buried to revitalize. Past lives to influence a world too involved in the present to care.

At least from Loren's perspective. He had spent enough time in the past. It wasn't worth his time and he was afraid Carson Wells, rants and all, matched that feeling.

He entered slowly, offering coffee to the seated doctor, a danish set before him on the table forcing him away from the window.

"Thank you," Wells said, shifting back to the table.

"Thought it might help," Loren said, joining him. Wells was definitely calmer since his arrival. That made things easier.

"I apologize about before, Detective...?"

"Loren. Greg is fine."

"Yes. I was looking for a Miss Girard, I believe?"

Loren nodded, wishing she would answer the damn phone. "She's not in at the moment, but I'm handling the case as well. Just from a different angle."

Wells looked away. "Martin."

"Unfortunately." Loren nodded. "Did you know him well?"

"Somewhat. I mean, I worked in his vicinity for years but never really...never made it past hello."

"I understand." It was a simple enough concept. Taking those around you for granted. The work comes first. Or family. Or life. Yours over someone else's. And the Martin Sheppards of the world faded into the background. Lost.

"He was good at his job. I mean, from what I gleaned during our encounters," Wells continued, his words clinging to a connection that didn't exist.

"I see."

"I'm sorry I can't be more helpful, detective."

"Greg. And it's all right." He took a deep breath, letting Wells' comfort grow in the room. He needed him comfortable. "I would like to talk about before."

"Before?"

"When you came in. About the rain?"

Wells' eyes flared. "Oh."

"You said it was your fault."

The doctor shook his head. "I...no. Well, I did but—"

"Doctor."

"Carson, please."

Loren nodded. "Carson."

Wells ignored him, reaching into his coat. He came back with a single piece of paper. "I was told to bring a list. Of the items stolen."

Loren took the note, browsing it quickly. He didn't care about the stolen items. Not really. Relics from the past meant little to him. He was after a killer, not a thief. "Yes. Thank you."

"A surprising find to be sure," Wells said. He finished his coffee, a thin stream escaping the corner of his lip. "Especially after the Nix-tun-Ch'ich dig of 2014. To find a second community so close, probably the same at an earlier juncture but to be so close and surprisingly preserved—"

"Meaning more valuable?" Loren asked, trying to find the relevance in the history lesson.

"We're not talking about jewels or gold," Wells replied, wiping his chin. "No inherent street value. But to the right collector? A priceless find. Too bad no one saw it on display."

Loren recalled Girard mentioning the same thing. "What do you mean?"

"The exhibit was set to debut next week. Honestly, it only arrived three days ago. I barely had time to catalog everything after—"

Loren stopped him. Timing was everything in this. The arrival and quick departure of the display before its debut solidified the inside man theory. Someone knew how to make this happen.

"Did anyone else have access to the stall where the items were kept?"

Wells shook his head. "I was the only one with access. Besides security, I mean. I'm afraid I am very territorial that way."

"Caution is a virtue with some things, I imagine. Did you notice anything strange over the last few days with the exhibit? Someone around that shouldn't have been? Something about the items in question?"

"Well..."

"Carson, please," Loren said. Wells was sweating, refusing to make eye contact. Loren pushed harder. "Everything helps. For Martin."

Wells took a deep breath. "The items were preserved particularly well, even those exposed, but one was wrapped." Wells removed a small piece of cloth from his pocket, tucked in a small storage bag. Loren had seen another piece of it in the stall the night before. "It tore during my examination."

"And again during the theft."

His eyes went wide. "That's right."

"What is so important?"

"The cloth covered an ax. Wait...." Wells held up a finger, bending low toward his bag. "I have a photo here. The only one I was able to take before—"

A small file fell on the table. He opened it and slipped the photo in front of Loren. The detective looked at the item curiously. The ax stood at about a foot in length, thick and ornate. A stone blade and handle, the latter carved in the shape of a snake, the reptile coiled tightly around the piece with its mouth open, hissing, at the apex.

"What is it?"

"The ax represents the power of Chaac, the Mayan god of the rains and storms. A well-worshiped deity for his role in the harvest of maize."

Loren pointed outside. "The crops would be drowning here."

Wells' head fell low. "It's getting worse now."

"Is this what you meant? About the rains being your fault? Carson—"

"It started three days ago," Wells muttered, his words low. "I was examining the ax. I took the cloth off to examine it, pulling this small piece away for a closer look. Someone came rushing past the door, a fellow doctor. Soaked. It had been sunny all day. She just laughed. The sky had opened up. Out of nowhere. I covered the ax up immediately. And you can't tell me—"

"I won't," Loren said, stopping him. He had seen too much over the years. But the ax didn't matter. The rain didn't matter. A man was dead. "You mentioned the exhibit just arrived?"

"Did you hear what I said, detective?" Wells stood in anger. "This is—"

"Not your fault. Now, please, Doctor Wells. Where did the display come from? Your thief may have followed it."

The frazzled doctor paused. "Oh. I didn't even think of that."

"Not your job."

Wells nodded. "The dig was only a few months ago. Not even publicized. We were waiting until the opening. It only came through one city, just passing through for a quick look by an enthusiast and one of the main backers of the dig."

"Where?"

"An out of the way place, really," Wells replied, lost in the rain outside. "Have you ever heard of the city of Portents?"

CHAPTER FOUR

Loren needed a car. The Blue Line did its best, dropping the weary detective three blocks from his apartment on West Jackson Boulevard. The rain coated him like a blanket, soaking through the thin jacket into his very bones. Carson Wells took much of his shift, the rants and ravings bringing back too many memories for the recently transplanted Loren.

Portents was everywhere.

He needed the break. After Wells dropped off the list, Loren took the opportunity to stop home. A quick shower and a bowl of soup. Maybe a refresher on his empty pack of gum.

Eiseman was more than happy for the reprieve as well. His shift took him through every employee off the clock at the Field Museum. Questions about the place of employment and Martin Sheppard gave him a distinct view, one filled with little answers. The deceased may have been a longtime employee of the Field Museum but you wouldn't have known it by talking to any of his colleagues.

Doris Sheppard waited for them. The widow of the deceased. A last hope to find out more about a dead man and to learn who could have provided such detail in committing the robbery at the museum so soon after the exhibit's arrival to the city.

She could wait. Loren needed the time.

A ground floor apartment on West Jackson was not ideal. Crime was heavy, heavier than most of the city. Violence plagued the streets, an unsettled feeling resting on the majority of the populace though little attempts were made to appease the masses. Loren kept his badge tucked away. He preferred to keep quiet about much of his life, both past and present. The apartment was used for sleep and eating. In the three months since his arrival, he hadn't even purchased a television. A book from the library down the street every week kept him busy. It kept his mind off Portents—off the anger and the mistakes of the past.

Loren took the steps two at a time, his legs heavy from the rain. Keys dangled from his fingers, then slipped at the sound of his name.

"Greg."

Stooping low to retrieve the keys, Loren turned back to his visitor. A large blue umbrella kept her covered from the weather. Her free hand kept the coat wrapped against her skin to retain some warmth.

It didn't stop Meriweather Loren-Burch from visiting her older brother.

"Meri?" Loren asked, surprised. He shouldn't have been. Three months in the city was plenty of time for his sister to track him down. She stood four inches shorter and thin—too thin for a mother of three. She was older than he remembered. Ten years between visits had that effect.

"I thought it was you," Meri said. The morning light fell dim, slipping through the cloud-covered skies, but her smile glowed.

Loren ducked close to her, sharing the umbrella. He pushed his shaggy blond hair out of his face, and the wet dog look gave her pause. Meri looked him over quickly, a motherly gaze. She poked at the Superman shirt peeking through his open jacket, hole-ridden with the collar stretched beyond repair.

"Still haven't thrown that shirt out?"

Loren smiled. "Don't mess with the S. How did you—"

"Wasn't hard."

"Once you put your mind to it. I remember."

"Then you probably remember my frequent messages."

Loren led her up the stoop to the overhang of the roof for some cover. There had been messages. Too many to count over the last few months. Ever since he let her know he was back. He had waited three weeks before telling her, not sure what his arrival meant or what he actually needed by coming back to Chicago. Part of him realized family was necessary. Some form of comfort to break away from Portents and the mistakes made. But part of him feared his time away had changed him too completely. That the past would never be forgotten.

"I do," he admitted. "I do. I was.... Would you take work for an appropriate response?"

"Greg."

Loren sighed. "I've been busy, Meri. That's all."

"It isn't, though. Almost three months and no visit? We're family. We're still family. Even after...well, whatever we used to be."

"Still family," Loren replied, looking away. Even through the screaming and the fighting. The beatings and the berating. Through the struggle to find their own piece of happiness in the life handed them by a pair of unprepared parents, by an abusive father ashamed of his own actions.

Still family.

Meri's hand rested on his arm. "You left, Greg. A long time ago. Things changed. In the end, before Dad died, it did get better. And it's better now."

A year since his father's death. A year without acknowledging the fact, lost in his own misery. Loren regretted his actions and the pain that came with them, the sins of the father passed on to the son. The anger and the mistakes.

"I'm glad," he said, leaning hard against the frame of the front door to his apartment. "I am, Mer. I'll try to stop over...."

"Sunday."

"Sunday?"

"Dinner," Meri continued. "A family meal. You need one."

Loren turned away. "Meri."

She pulled him back. "I never met her. Beth. I wish I had. She made you happy. I could tell on our calls. She made you better."

He felt the scruff on his chin. The overgrown rug of hair on his head. The tired eyes. They never existed before Beth's murder.

"She certainly did."

"But you came back, Greg. Home." Meri looked around the neighborhood. The Loren family once lived less than a mile away. A small apartment sandwiched between other families, struggling to find room for four in such tight quarters. Loren and his sister used to run the streets, night and day, doing anything they could to stay away from home. It always made things worse in the end but they were the best times of their lives. "Our home. That means something."

"Cozy, right?" Loren said, mockingly.

"There are plenty of places—"

"I'm fine, Meri. Really."

She let it drop, rain dripping in thick streams from the umbrella with each step down the stairs. "We can help. I can help. You have to let us try, Greg."

"I don't...." He stopped, unsure of what to say. How to say it.

"Dinner is at six."

"Mom doesn't want—"

Meri shook her head. "She does. You do. You're both too stubborn to admit it."

"But—"

"Wear a different shirt. Please."

"Meri, I'm not sure I can."

"You will." Her soft voice was almost lost in the wind. She smiled. "You hate disappointing people. Especially your favorite sister."

"I'll try," he said. "Try, Mer."

The rains were worse, unending. And according to local weather reports, they were spreading. Loren worried what that meant.

For everyone.

"Do you need me to...?"

She laughed, her hand running along his arm lovingly. "I know my way around town."

"Of course you do."

Loren watched her depart, her slow steps carrying her toward the Blue Line. He knew the truth. He was the one that was lost, stuck between two lives—and two cities.

Only that wasn't quite true. The rains saw to that. Carson Wells did as well. Only one city claimed him heart and soul at the moment.

Portents.

Even after three months of running and avoiding the past, he was still caught in its web. Greg Loren was still in Portents and always would be.

CHAPTER FIVE

"We're sorry for your loss, Mrs. Sheppard."

Loren practiced the words before arriving to make sure they sounded genuine. They were, of course, but after years working homicide he feared his objectiveness toward the work, for the sake of the work, might come off as callous and apathetic to those left behind from such tragedies.

Mrs. Sheppard nodded, ushering the pair of detectives into her home. Eiseman shambled ahead, both men stripping off their soaked jackets. The rain was getting heavier, the weatherman unsure when it would end and how much of the country would be affected before it faded.

Loren did his best to wipe his sneakers clean, wishing he had a better pair. His socks were soaked beneath, giving him little in the way of options upon entering the small home on the upper east side of Chicago. He kept the shoes on, wiping them vigorously before catching up with Eiseman and their host.

"Yes," Eiseman said, following the large woman's staggered gait across the living room. "Thank you for seeing us so soon after—"

"It's all right," Mrs. Sheppard replied, waving him to the couch. "And it's Doris."

"Doris," Eiseman said. She took his hand, holding it tight, and shook it. Repeatedly. Loren did his best to ignore the exchange or the awkward grin pasted to Eiseman's face. Instead, Loren collapsed on the couch, feeling his still-sopped sneakers squish on the very dated shag running the length of the living room.

The house was quaint, well maintained, but little more than a two-floor box tucked in the middle of an overpopulated residential district in the city. It was home for Doris though, the myriad collection of photos lining the walls denoting copious memories.

Eiseman pulled his hand away slowly, gently joining Loren on the well-worn couch. His pale cheeks were now flush from the exchange. Doris' smile spread with each glimpse at the young detective. Eiseman refused to look at his grinning partner.

"We were hoping for more information on your husband. His friends, family, anyone that might want to hurt him."

Doris, staggered by the comment, sat back in the recliner across from them. "I thought he was shot during a burglary?"

"Yes, that's right."

Eiseman leaned closer. "Like I mentioned on the phone, this is just a follow-up."

The smile returned to the middle-aged woman with the swollen cheeks. She nodded in agreement with the young detective, as if every word out of his mouth was gospel sent from the Lord above.

Loren rolled his eyes, standing to look around the room. "Did Martin usually work alone at the museum?"

"I think so. He mentioned other people sometimes but never much about them."

Loren eyed the images on the wall. All of Doris, some with friends and possibly family, but none of Martin.

"Martin didn't have friends, did he?"

Small tears dotted her cheeks. Her eyes reddened. Eiseman reached for a tissue and held it out for her.

"Thank you," she replied. She wiped her face, never looking away from her knight in blue. "Just me. He loved me. So much. Always tried to give me the world. A true saint of a man."

There's no denying that, Loren thought. The photos in the house, the decorations lining the walls, tucked on shelves, even crowding the windowsills, appeared to be from all over the world. The photos corroborated much of his thinking. Doris in Mexico for the Day of the Dead. At the Vatican. Disney World. Skiing in Switzerland—though that one may have been doctored. Doris Sheppard didn't appear to have the body for that much physical activity.

"I'm sure he was," Eiseman finally said, another tissue in hand.

While she dabbed her cheeks, the young detective shrugged to his senior. Loren shook his head, unsure how to help the kid. He did know what would help the case, however.

"Blake," Loren started, his voice soft. "Weren't you about to ask Doris here for a cup of coffee?"

"Was I?" Eiseman asked, eyes flaring. Both saw Doris stand, the tears shut off like a switch. Loren nodded to his partner.

"I believe you were."

Eiseman sighed then stood. "I was. Yes. If it's not too much trouble?"

"Not at all," Doris answered. Her arm slid into his own, pulling him toward the kitchen on the far side of the home. Halfway, she stopped, turning back to Loren. "Anything for you?"

"No, thank you. Just point me to the bathroom, please?"

"Of course," the enthused woman replied, gripping tighter to Eiseman's arm. "Down the hall on the right."

"Thank you."

The pair slipped into the kitchen without another glance, leaving Loren with free rein in the home. The bathroom was a concern, or so his multiple cups of coffee demanded, but it remained second on his list of priorities.

Martin Sheppard topped the list. His death and any insight into the theft that led to his murder.

Loren shuffled down the hall, his heels squishing irritatingly. He headed for the office straight ahead. Inside, there were no photos on the walls. Martin's sanctuary.

A simple desk in the corner with twin, four drawer filing cabinets beside it. The monitor was old, hooked up to a smaller desktop system—something more Loren's speed than the current technology offered. There was nothing elaborate about the office. A simple escape or another responsibility for the man of the house. Monthly bills. Internet surfing. Trip planning, for sure.

Not Loren's problem.

Loren ignored the computer completely, moving for the files. Bills took up the majority of the cabinet's space. Minimum payments stretched across a dozen accounts. The Sheppards' jet-setting ways may have enticed Doris to stay with her less-than-exciting husband but it did little for their bank accounts.

The identity of the inside man became even clearer in the second drawer of the cabinet, tucked behind the files littering it. Loren gripped it tightly, struggling to pry it free from the small cubbyhole.

A cell phone.

There was a reason no calls could be traced to the museum personnel, incoming or outgoing. No clue as to who could have organized and communicated with the thief. Martin Sheppard was smart about it. A burner phone tucked away, used for only one number. Nothing else connecting him to the crime, especially with his death.

Loren let the phone boot up, listening to the sound of laughter, half forced, from the kitchen on the far side of the home. Quickly, the detective flipped to the contacts listed in the phone.

Martin was definitely smart enough to pull off the job from the inside, but he needed help. And help came with a name. A name Martin didn't believe needed hiding.

Owen Chase.

Loren smiled. "Well, hello there."

CHAPTER SIX

Loren desperately needed a car, some mode of transportation that didn't put him in the passenger seat of the rusted-out Ford Blake Eiseman deemed a *classic*. Candy wrappers crunched under his feet, paperwork piled high along the dash. The back seat slipped into memory, boxes covering each side, waiting for a quick turn to crash to the floor.

There had been times in Portents where stakeouts were downright enjoyable. With Soriya. With the work they did after the loss of Beth. The craziness of the world, the things rushing through the shadows, thrilled Loren as much as they scared him. One of them possibly took his wife from him and he would not rest until the case was closed. That thought carried him for so long...and now?

Now there was the rain and Owen Chase.

Eiseman did his best to make the situation tolerable. He kept the distractions to a minimum, the music turned off. Both sets of eyes were focused on the road through the thin strip of glass cleared by the high-speed wipers.

The storefront across the street was recently purchased through a hastily created shell company with ties to Owen Chase, all funneled through accounts seized earlier that evening by the Chicago Police Department. The deli that had occupied the space went belly up with the rest of the block as most people shifted their needs away from the area. Chase bought the property months ago yet it remained empty.

The man himself, younger than Loren had imagined, paced nervously inside. Concerned, but not enough to block the large display window at the front of the building. Or to hold his business in a more secluded spot. Some people refused to accept their vulnerabilities.

"He's not much to look at, is he?" Eiseman said, catching Loren's look. Eiseman might have been a little too involved in Loren's personal life but it didn't make him any less keen on what the senior detective was thinking.

Loren cleared his throat, sitting back. Rain fell in rhythmic sheets all around them. He ran his fingers along his swollen eyes, fighting back the long day he'd endured and the longer night ahead. "What were you expecting?"

"I don't know," Eiseman replied between gulps of soda. The alley beside them wouldn't notice the frequent pit stops with all the rain. "Not this guy, though. How about some chick in leather? A real femme fatale?"

"Move to Gotham then."

Loren checked his watch. Girard was late. The weather, unrelenting and worrisome even to the professionals on air, made traffic in the city worse than usual. Still, Girard wanted to be there for the arrest. It remained her case, after all.

It was his own fault. He could have called the moment Owen Chase's name fell into place. Once the puzzle had been solved from the burner phone tucked in Martin Sheppard's home. He hesitated, though. Maybe it was Portents sneaking back into things. The ax mentioned by Carson Wells and the rain surrounding them. A connection Ruiz would have called paranoia and Soriya would have seen as enlightened. Two worlds he could never reconcile.

Even now.

Loren inched to the edge of his seat, hand securing his Glock in place. "Owen Chase might not look capable, but he is. Ask Martin Sheppard."

"Point taken," Eiseman said, nodding. "Think that's the take?"

A large bag sat on the counter. It lay opened but turned away from the window. Chase circled it with each lap around the shop, waiting for something. Or someone.

"Seems to be," Loren said. "He's moving quicker than I would have thought."

"Murder's involved. Chicago's not a good place for him to be right now."

"True."

Headlights flared and both men slid low in their seats. A black sedan inched down the avenue, parking next to the former deli. An expensive car for the neighborhood. Out of place. Like the man within.

Tall, thin, and *confident* were the first triggers in Loren's mind. The occupant of the vehicle wore a nicely pressed suit, his umbrella blocking the torrent of rain above.

"Is that…?" Eiseman asked, eyes wide.

"Who?"

Eiseman shot him an incredulous look. "You don't know?"

It frustrated Loren, who quietly cursed his lack of knowledge of the city. Even after three months, he had been unable to catch up on the ten years he spent away.

"Not up on the nightlife around here, remember?"

Eiseman nodded, watching the man enter the deli. "Noah Somerton. Guy has more antiquities than the entire state of Illinois, including our illustrious Field Museum. And he likes to tell people that as often as possible."

"Looks like he's expanding his Mayan collection."

"Probably be a damn press release about it a couple years from now linking it to one of his own digs," Eiseman said, checking his sidearm. He gripped it tight, reaching for the door handle. "This guy."

Loren sighed, preparing for the rain and the struggle ahead. "Shall we?"

"Please."

The pair shuffled through the rain, Loren wishing for a hat or something to keep a clear field of vision. Luckily they remained out of sight from the display window of the deli, using the row of parked cars for cover before making the final jaunt behind Somerton's own sedan.

Outside the front door to the defunct business they paused. Eiseman sidled up to the edge of the window for a closer look. Loren held tight to his sidearm, taking deep breaths. Situations like this were always messy. Unpredictable.

"It's happening," Eiseman whispered.

Loren nodded, head tilted for the door. Eiseman took up position, weapon steady in both hands. He took a deep breath then kicked the door open. Loren rushed in, knocking the flailing metal out of their way.

"Police!" Loren yelled to the startled Somerton and Chase. Eiseman had his six o'clock, scanning the angles, so Loren remained fixed on the two men in the center of the room.

"No one move!" Eiseman shouted.

Somerton's hesitance faded, survival mode kicking into high gear. "Chase, you idiot!"

Both men bolted, Somerton heading deeper into the deli for a back exit. Chase grabbed the goods from the counter, slinging them over his shoulder before finding a nearby stairwell.

"Somerton," Eiseman said, starting for the rear exit.

Loren held his partner back. "Leave him."

Eiseman looked incredulous, pulling away from Loren. "What? Greg, what the hell?"

Loren shook his head, starting for the stairs. "Trust me. Somerton won't stick. But we have Chase. For this and the murder. Take the win."

The young detective knew the truth better than most. Convictions were tricky in most situations, but Somerton had the clout to fight an arrest. Besides, he wasn't the case. He didn't steal the goods, though he may have backed the plan, and he didn't commission the murder of Martin Sheppard.

Owen Chase was the one they needed.

Eiseman nodded slowly, falling in line behind Loren up the steps. The second floor was converted office space for an Internet startup that fell flat before opening their doors, if they ever had doors to open. It was out of Loren's wheelhouse. Catching fleeing perps, though? Much more in line with the thirty-six-year-old's skill set.

The defunct space was wide and open, a large room that would have been proud to hold a cubicle nightmare for twenty-somethings sipping $6 coffees and wearing Bluetooth headsets all day. Instead there was little in the way of furniture. A couple old couches, some ratty old metal desks, and some standing lamps.

Owen Chase sprinted through the area, rushing for the emergency exit to the rear of the building. He turned at the sound of their approach, a mistake that cost him his footing. He tripped on a small area rug tucked under one of the couches and fell. The bag of artifacts slipped from his shoulder, crashing with him in a heap. The backpack was unzipped and some of the goods spilled loose, scattering across the floor…including the ax of Chaac. The protective cloth around it caught on the floor, exposing the tool for the first time. A snake adorned the handle. The blade, as sharp as the day it was forged.

"It's over, Chase," Loren called out, approaching with caution. Eiseman kept to his rear, eyes on the stairs behind them for unexpected company. There would be none. Chase was a lone operator. He used Sheppard for his own purposes, preying on the man's financial woes, then killed him for services rendered. No one was coming to help Owen Chase.

Struggling to find his feet, Chase launched deeper into the open suite, landing near the exposed weapon. He lifted it, clutching tight to the handle as if his life depended on it.

Then he screamed—a visceral growl that stopped Loren and Eiseman in their tracks. Chase's bellow echoed, his body contorting in all manner before collapsing.

"What the…?" Eiseman tried to ask. Loren stopped him, suddenly afraid.

Outside, the storm intensified. Lightning shattered the skyline in all directions. Thunder rumbled deep from within thickening clouds. The rain pounded the windows. There was no question where it was coming from, how it was occurring when everything said the storm was impossible in the first place.

The damn ax.

"Greg?" Eiseman asked.

Owen Chase turned to them. Anger seethed from his lips, his nostrils flaring wide. He no longer featured soft blue eyes, eyes used to con Martin Sheppard into throwing his life away. Instead, white orbs remained. Blank.

The young thief stood, tall and confident, the ax held tight in front of him. A slow breeze surrounded them, picking up speed with each pass. It swirled like a twister, deep and powerful. The wind threatened to bowl them over, grabbing at their waterlogged clothes. Where it failed with them, the increasing gale succeeded with the remnants of furniture through the room, lifting the couches and desks like paperweights and flinging them through the office space.

Loren turned to Eiseman, a couch heading their way. "Blake, look—"

Too late. The arm of the couch clipped Loren hard on the shoulder, knocking him to the floor before continuing for the unprepared officer. Eiseman fell back hard, pinned against the wall by the piece of furniture, then both crumpled to the floor.

Loren grabbed his sidearm and tucked it away. The oppressive wind pounded at him but he found his feet, his shoulder aching. He stayed low to the ground as the wind continued to swirl. Shuffling beside his partner, Loren checked Eiseman's vitals.

"Still breathing."

Owen Chase, no longer a simple thief, towered over Loren. He was something else now, visible even in his stance, confident and assured. In his blank stare, glowing in the dim light of the room. He was *someone* else now. Chaac. God of the rains and storms, looking mighty pissed at the only other person in the room.

Loren stood, patting his unconscious partner's back lightly.

"Lucky you."

CHAPTER SEVEN

Chaac had arrived.
Carson Wells was right to be concerned. Everything about the storm raging throughout Illinois and beyond pointed to the object clutched in the crook's right hand. If Wells had been with him, standing beside a confused and overwhelmed Loren, he might know what to say—how to act when dealing with a Mayan god clearly upset over his current condition, and the conditions outside the windows.

"What have you done?" the great god of the storms screamed over the rushing wind.

Loren tucked low, inching toward the center of the storm and the blank eyes within.

"This place? This city? I feel no connection to the earth. To my people."

Loren tried to find the words, but his lungs immediately filled with wind. He fought through it, edging into the storm, hoping to make a difference—a positive one, preferably.

Chaac waited but a moment for a response, unable to see the struggle of the detective cowering low to the ground. Loren attempted to wave him down, to get a second to breathe, but to no avail. The winds slammed harder against him and he fell to the ground, tucking tight to the wood floor. Tables and chairs soared over his head, crashing to pieces against the far wall.

"Answer me!" Chaac yelled. Lightning snapped around the building. Thunder shook the sky.

"They're…" Loren fought to speak. Chaac saw the strain on the mortal man's face and for a brief moment the wind slowed to a dull roar. Loren stood, brushing off his jacket, before stepping into the center of the storm. "They're gone. It's been…well, it's been a long time."

"How long?" the god asked.

Loren rubbed his neck deeply, his other hand inching closer to his sidearm. "Centuries."

Chaac laughed, his blank eyes wide. "Centuries?"

Lightning crashed harder, the wind surrounding Loren in a wave, but never pushing at him. No, Chaac needed him for the moment. He needed to know.

"You destroyed paradise in such a short time."

"We—"

Chaac stopped him, forcing Loren back against the floor with the brush of his hand. "No more."

Loren slammed to the floor, his chest on fire. "Wait."

"No." The ax rose and with it the man that was once Owen Chase. The sky darkened in all directions, spreading faster and faster. "The world begs for this. A cleansing. Purifying her people. The old ways held strength. They brought the world together. You'll see once I have drowned away all the sickness and decay you have wrought."

The cloth, the covering keeping the ancient tool intact, lay before Loren and he snatched it up before standing. He held the cloth like a flag in his left hand. In his right was his sidearm, pointing directly at the floating figure.

"Why is it always the same with you guys?"

Chaac paused, curious. "Your paltry weapon means nothing to me."

"Tell that to your paltry human host."

Loren shifted, his weapon no longer square with the chest of Owen Chase, but with his right hand. And the ax in it. Blank eyes blinked and Loren realized that even gods felt fear.

He fired once. Once was all that was needed. The bullet pierced Owen's hand, forcing his fingers to snap open. The ax dropped, and with it, the hovering form of Chaac. Outside, the storm continued. Loren held tight to the cloth in his hand.

It wasn't over.

"What the hell?" Owen screamed, watching in horror at the blood streaming down his hand to the ground. His blue eyes were wide with anger at the approaching detective. "My hand! You son of a—"

Loren's fist crashed into the man's right cheek. Chase fell hard to the ground and did not get back up. Loren cringed at the pain shooting up his arm, then put the thought aside, the sound of the winds rushing through his ears. He raced over to the ax, making sure to keep the cloth as a barrier. He didn't need to experience what Owen Chase had. Not ever. The cloth slid around the snake-decorated handle, covering it and the sharp blade completely.

The storm silenced. The clouds began to fade, dissipating from the horizon in all directions. The rain slowed to a drip.

Loren fell to the ground, his head between his knees to catch his breath. Weary eyes looked over the unconscious form of Owen Chase and the large welt forming on his right cheek. Loren slipped his hand into his pocket and retrieved a piece of gum.

"You're welcome, kid."

CHAPTER EIGHT

Birds chirped. Kids cheered. The final remnants of the storm faded with the morning sun. Greg Loren watched everything from the sidewalk. Children blitzed by him, screaming incoherently. Old couples walked slowly hand in hand. After days of dreariness, the storm had passed. No explanations came with the local weather report. Just glad tidings that it had ended.

Forgotten.

Loren had tucked the ax away before seeing to Eiseman. Questions were asked—lots of them, in fact—but Loren kept him distracted. So did Girard's arrival, and with it, the attention Eiseman had hoped for. Owen Chase was arrested for the death of Martin Sheppard and the theft of the Mayan artifacts. He stayed quiet about any accomplices. Because of that, charges failed to stick with Noah Somerton. The wealthy philanthropist pleaded ignorant to the fact that the artifacts being sold to him were stolen. *Because most people buy Mayan artifacts in empty storefronts in the middle of the night. Right.*

That was the job.

Loren understood all of that. He knew it, inside and out. Even the pieces left off the reports. Chaac. The ax he buried in a landfill the following night, offering the museum little in the way of answers for its disappearance. What Loren failed to grasp, what eluded him at all turns was everything else—life.

Especially across the street.

His sister's home sat along a pristine stretch along Jefferson Park. Good schools. Good neighbors. Perfect families. His mother laughed, the three kids squirming in their chairs around the dining room table. Meri's husband, Michael, brought out dinner.

Loren wanted to join them. More than anything he wanted to feel that connection, the one he hadn't felt since Beth's passing. He wanted to play the part of the dutiful son, the big brother and the fun-loving uncle, the way it was meant to be.

But he couldn't.

Not yet. It plagued him all week. The pull, the divide. Not just with the case, not just Martin Sheppard's empty life mirroring his own, but with Meri's requests. Everything brought him back to Portents. To Beth. To Soriya and the work they had done. The things left undone.

Loren dialed quickly, listening to the ringing of the phone. Across the street, Meri stopped serving dinner, passing excuses to the family before leaving the dining room. Loren waited for an answer, but was instead greeted by her voicemail.

"Meri," Loren said, drawing out her name with his excuse. "It's me. Listen…ah, I hate messages. Something came up. I can't make it. Next time."

Ending the call, Loren slipped the phone into his pocket. She would understand. She had to on some level. On every level, when it came to him. Part of him was lost with Beth, a part he was trying to reclaim with his relocation home, but it had only been three months.

He needed more time. Didn't he?

Turning away, Loren started for the subway, cursing his lack of a car. Meri waited for him at the corner.

Loren smirked, his eyes cast downward at his own cowardice. "Hey."

"You really came all the way here just to walk away?" she asked, her frustration clear.

"Looks like."

"Greg," she pleaded. She reached for him but he pulled back. "Come on. Try a little—"

"I am," he snapped. "Christ, Meri. I am trying. But your life, your family, isn't mine anymore. The things I've seen, the things I've done…what I've lost…."

Meri's hand fell away. "Beth."

Loren nodded. "I'm not the same. But I am trying."

"You don't have to do this alone."

"I'm not," Loren said, his hand taking hers. "I know that much."

She hugged him tight, like they used to as kids—the big brother protecting his younger sister. Now, it was the opposite.

When they parted, both turned toward the brick home across the street. Meri's arm wrapped around Loren's waist, keeping him close for as long as possible.

"It's a nice place," Loren said.

"It is. Even nicer inside."

Loren nodded, pulling away. "You should…"

"You should too."

Loren sighed, the silence giving his final answer.

Meri shook her head, starting across the street. "Take care of yourself, Greg."

"Mer," Loren called, stopping her. She turned, hopeful. "I'm…I'm heading back to Portents."

Her eyes fell. "I figured."

Shaking his head, Loren caught up with her, walking with her across the street. "No. Not like that. To pick up my things. To close some doors. When I come back…." He paused, looking over the city, seeing the life returning to it after so much darkness. "When I come back I'll try harder. Be better. Maybe be a family."

"I'd like that, Greg," she replied. Her hand grazed his cheek, her eyes capturing every line of his face. Then she pulled away, moving for the front door. "If you come back."

Loren fought to reply, searching for a way to prove his intentions to her. The front door closed behind her, leaving him alone, silent as ever. Then, he knew, deep within himself.

There was no escape from the past. Especially from Portents.

THE CONSULTANT

CHAPTER ONE

Seth Groves didn't move fast enough. Carrying two large, black trash bags—the collective crap from an entire week in his two-bedroom apartment—Seth failed to close the gap before the metal door to the complex firmly slapped him along the backside. The bags dropped and with them every curse in the forty-three-year-old's vocabulary.

Taking a deep breath, the overweight and overtired manager of a less-than-lucrative electronics store struggled to gather his belongings. He threw a deep glare at the heavy door, still leaning against his ass, pushing him deeper into the wet blanket that was Portents.

To say it was raining would have been an overstatement. It came in little specks, practically spitting from the heavens upon the street. The storm came unexpectedly and the fact that it had remained consistent for three straight days kept the city locked in a cloudy gloom of gray.

"Now why would the trash be taken out before I got home?" Seth muttered. Twelve-hour shifts devoured his week, while his wife devoured what little remained in their budget. There were mounting bills, growing debts, and a rash that refused to abate on the man's chest. Not that he was one to complain. Complaints came at him. From employees. From his darling wife of twenty years—married much too young. No, Seth left the complaints to others. Except when alone.

"It's not like I work all day, every day," Seth continued, shambling down the wide alley dividing the four buildings in the complex. He ducked beneath the window leading to his kitchen, noticing the wide shadow of the woman he had wed. His grumbling quieted as he quickened his step toward the waiting dumpsters.

"Always plenty of time for me to do this," he said, rain pelting his eyes and the thin strands of hair that made up his comb over.

The trash clanged loudly in the dumpster. His shoulder ached from the toss. He needed more exercise. He needed to stretch more. Work less. Plenty of things that would never occur. Not when there was always more garbage to handle, more hours to work.

"Not like I ever have better things to do," Seth grumbled, completing his task—satisfied to move away from the stench that seemed to infect the entire alley. Not even the rain helped wash it away. He turned back home, his steps slowing even with the pelting rain driving him forward. "Better things to—"

He stopped at the sight of the building across the alley. The windows lay open, the occupant within not caring about the smell. *The occupant.* It was funny to think about her that way. But thinking about her had become more than a hobby for the middle-aged man. Obsessing was the wrong word. It cheapened his feelings toward her.

Twenty feet away and he had never seen her, not in the three months since her arrival. Just the shadow of her against the curtains. An outline to be filled in by pure imagination. Except for her voice.

Her singing.

Melodic and soothing, she sang every night, the sound drifting into his apartment, even with the windows closed. *Thin walls.* Not that he minded. The sound was blissful, drowning out the world for the overtired man. The sound carried him to sleep. He never slept better. Even his wife felt the effects of her voice, relaxing even in the midst of a tirade about Seth's ineffectiveness as a man and a husband.

A word of thanks was the least he could offer for that small favor.

The open windows dared him. A quick peek, nothing more. A quick confirmation that the sweet voice was just a precursor to a beautiful woman with curves he hadn't seen in a decade. To put a face to her, one he could carry into his nightly dreams.

Seth Groves danced, dodging the growing puddles in the alley. The joy of his mission, the fact that he had something to look forward to amid the trash, the inventory at work, the monthly bills, and everything else. To solve the mystery before him snapped him from the gray surrounding the city. It brightened the darkness.

"Just walking by," Seth muttered, calming his giddy steps. The smell grew with each step toward her open window. "Nothing creepy about it. A simple stroll on my way—"

The wind blew the curtain away from the window, allowing him to see the entire living room. Giving him a perfect view of the woman within.

And the true origin of the smell dominating the alley.

Seth Groves tried to find the words, tried to scream at the sight of the dead woman in the apartment, broken and twisted in ways he could never imagine.

But he would imagine it. Splashing through the puddles for his home, Seth Groves would imagine her broken and decayed body for the rest of his days. His screams echoed after him, his overweight frame racing home—rushing back to his tired little life and his complaints.

He wondered if he would ever sleep soundly again.

CHAPTER TWO

Rain trickled along the railings of the fire escape. It tingled along her hands, black as the night, before pausing at the tips of her fingers in an attempt to stop from hitting the pavement below. The steady drip was background noise, filtered out by the woman lost to the shadows of the alley.

Soriya Greystone was working.

The placement on the fire escape just above the first-floor apartment perfectly shadowed from any onlooker or random glance, the lights minimal throughout the alley. A pause in the rain would have been nice. The spitting precipitation clouded her eyes at times.

Officers worked efficiently inside the young woman's apartment. Eurydice Baros. *Doesn't get more Greek than that.* She noted it on the mail near the open window, soaked from the exposure to the rain, though no one took care to notice. They were busy with the scene in the living room.

The dead woman at the center of it all.

There was a time Soriya would have been in the room with Loren, piecing together the final moments of the young woman who had met her end so violently. Jokes and playful banter between them, for sure, but the work first.

Unfortunately, Loren was gone—the job proving too much for him, something Soriya never understood. Would never understand. The image of his dead wife swallowed him up, refusing to let him move on. Until he did.

Without Loren, the police were less than an ally. The truth of the situation, the new reality she had found herself in over the last three months since Loren's abrupt departure, was that the men and women in blue would be just as likely to arrest her rather than allow her to assist in their investigations.

Her investigations.

Eurydice Baros.

The woman, if she could even be called that anymore, was little more than a mass of flesh and tissue, blood and guts. A mess of a corpse spread across an area rug, limbs torn and shredded by deep claws. Blood ran the length of the rug, spreading in all directions around the room.

Forensics worked carefully to leave the scene undisturbed. Most kept their gaze on the evidence and not on the body. Flashbulbs went off, capturing the end of the woman's life. Most of the men and women in the room would forego their next meal, probably their next few, until the images of Eurydice Baros faded from memory.

There was a word bandied about between the crew in low mutters. A word to characterize the scene. To glorify it in a way, making her death more, making their job more.

Monstrous.

Soriya knew better. The claw marks. The rage in the kill. The destruction of the victim. It was more than monstrous. More than the work of a man. In Soriya's work, it meant the work of a true and terrible *monster*.

The young woman in shadow shifted her weight, quiet against the slick metal of the fire escape, and closer to the wall of the building. Out of sight from Portents' head coroner Hady Ronne. The short, rotund woman with the stringy black hair kept her clipboard close to review her notes. She did not hesitate to view the body, or what remained of one. She did not blink. Did not gasp. There were no surprises from the dead for her.

Orders flew and forensics worked quickly to execute them. It was time to transport the body. Time for Soriya to make her move.

Deftly, she swung over the side of the fire escape, holding tight with her right hand to the railing to arc toward the bedroom window of the apartment. She landed gracefully, her sneakers silent along the room's carpet.

Down the hall, officers left the scene, grateful for the reprieve. Soriya would only have minutes before they returned. If not them, then it would be Hady Ronne's staff, or as Loren would say right to the coroner's face, her pets.

Keeping an eye on the clock, the soaked woman took in the room quickly. A single bedroom apartment meant not a lot of unused space. The bed was tucked close to the entrance, a small desk and nightstand accompanying it. Books. Photos with friends. A journal tucked near the pillow.

Normal.

Questions about what had happened in the other room permeated her thoughts. The depravity of the act. Soriya saw no such thing. Not anymore. She had seen too many in her all-too-short twenty-two years. Seen too much since the loss of her former life at the age of four. Since finding the stone at the scene of the car wreck that claimed the lives of her parents.

The Greystone.

It ushered her into a new world, with the help of her mentor. A wider world, more open to possibilities than any could understand. But it was a darker one at times as well. Darker than the night outside. As dark as the depths of the killer out on the streets of Portents.

Soriya grazed the journal at the edge of the bed. Her work kept things from her. The normal things of life. The work and Mentor. Her job was focused: protect the city, keep the Bypass safe in its chamber hidden under the center of Portents. There could be no distractions.

Sometimes she hated that.

Quickly and without a sound, Soriya skirted down the long hall for the living room. She didn't need much time. Just an inkling, a hint of what might be running loose in her city. And why Eurydice Baros, tucked away in her cozy little one-bedroom apartment, might have earned its wrath. Even if Soriya needed more time, she wouldn't dare take it. Not with Hady Ronne on sight. Something about the stumpy woman with the cavernous bags under her eyes made even the stalwart protector of Portents uneasy.

The dead woman no longer had a face. Nothing remained of her eyes. *Mutilation* barely covered the viciousness of the assault on her delicate frame. Soriya had no time for it. She surveyed the body, trying not to look directly at the larger picture. Only the details mattered. The cuts along the woman's abdomen were lost to the blood and exposed organs. The amount of blood was too great to hope these cuts came after death. One thing was clear: Eurydice Baros suffered in the end.

Only one cut remained clearly defined to Soriya. A long gash across her neck, right through her vocal cords. The initial strike to cut off her cries for help among a crowded apartment complex? Or something more personal? A sign for why she among all others in the city was targeted?

The room was in disarray but nowhere near what should have been. Tables and chairs had been shifted. The couch was pushed back against the far wall. But there was no real damage to the collectibles lining the bookshelves. The door remained intact. A scuffmark near the entrance in the shape of a shoe indicated the killer's entry into the apartment, but the lack of force used meant the victim allowed the killer inside.

Someone she knew? A delivery man? A neighbor? Someone trusted?

The police would handle these questions among the complex. It was her job to find out what could have done this and why.

Steps approached, forcing Soriya to race back down the hall for the bedroom. She snagged the journal from the corner of the bed. She stopped short of the window, a sliver of light illuminating the sill.

Claw marks. Three distinct, long and thick. One barely visible in the wood. But the fifth clinched it for her.

A fingerprint.

Chatter increased. Her time was up. Leaping through the open window, Soriya caught hold of the fire escape with her free hand, arcing back to the second floor landing of the fire escape above. Without pause, she flew up the stairs two at a time for the rooftop.

She needed answers. Needed to know more about Eurydice and what could have ended her life. Too many questions that kept her from noticing the large figure on the rooftop near the stairwell.

"Whoa," Soriya said, sliding to a halt before the hulking frame of a man in a blue suit jacket. "Where did you come from?"

He smiled, unfazed by her arrival. "Stairs. You?"

"Fire escape," she answered without thinking. She backed up to the edge of the building. "If you'll excuse…"

The man wasn't looking at her movements. He was busy staring at the journal in her hands.

"Wait," he called, stopping her. He reached into his pocket and pulled out his badge. "It looks like we're working the same case. Care to share notes?"

CHAPTER THREE

The man before Soriya Greystone was tall, blocking the light from the adjacent building and throwing her into darkness. Yet she saw him clearly. Young—younger than she expected from his physicality—but refined. His suit tastefully formed to his body, accentuating areas she tried to ignore, but his grin proved otherwise.

"You're not a cop," Soriya said, standing away from the ledge of the building. Her confidence returned with the chill breeze of the night, driving the rain against her back. A slow drizzle but a consistent pest nonetheless.

His smile grew. "I find that statement amusing, coming from you. Or are you hiding your badge somewhere in that outfit?"

She let him get a good look. Tight jeans, torn at the knees. Sneakers faded from age, stained from use. A dark shirt tucked behind a thin jacket. Her hair was contained in a ponytail that ran down to her shoulder.

When he realized an answer was not forthcoming, the towering man tossed his badge to her. She caught it deftly, moving closer to him to block the rain. She eyed the badge. It did not have a gold shield, as typical of the officers of the department. No, this one listed the man as a psychologist.

"Russell Kerr?"

"Russell is fine," he replied.

"A shrink?"

He laughed. She handed him the badge, which quickly made its way back into his breast pocket. "I've been consulting on a number of cases over the last couple months down at the Central Precinct. Can we get back to who you are?"

"Concerned citizen," she answered, arms crossing her chest. The movement pulled her jacket up slightly, ruffling over her hips. And the Greystone resting on her right side.

Russell's eyes flared at the sight of the stone, his lumbering frame staggering back a step. A slight shift, a discomfort at its presence. One she noticed immediately but let fall away like the rain around them.

"Crime scene is downstairs, Kerr. Why are you up here?"

He cleared his throat, moving for the edge of the rooftop. He stared out over the alley below, then against the skyline of Portents in the distance. "Taking in the view."

Soriya understood that better than most. She loved the view from above. The quiet over the roar of the streets. *A way to see more clearly*, a friend once said. Loren hated the rooftops, hated heights in general, due to the loss of his wife in a tragic fall. Russell Kerr was much different from her old partner.

He fascinated her more than she wanted to admit.

"Sounds like slacking on the job to me," she finally said, moving beside him.

"Yes, well…." He reached into his left pocket and pulled out a small sandwich bag. "I was also sneaking a snack. Long day."

She sniffed the air. "Honey?"

"Good nose," Russell replied, impressed.

"Donut?" she asked. "Pretty cliché."

He laughed, opening the bag. He held one of the small pastries out to her. "Cookie, actually. Weakness of mine, it seems."

Soriya stopped at the admission, curious at the man's distant stare at the snack like a memory was running before his eyes. They were bonding, more than she had with anyone since Loren's departure. It felt good. Too good.

"Listen," she started, moving back to the fire escape. "This has been fun but—"

"There was another victim," he called out without looking. He took a small bite of the cookie and put the rest away for later, satisfaction filling his face. "That's why I'm here. On this case."

"Profiling?"

"Trying to, if such a thing is possible," he admitted, ushering her back to the stairwell. "Your interest disturbs me, though. Most would run screaming from a scene so vicious."

"I'm not most people," she replied defiantly, the words of a child slipping out and she regretted the tone. She was a woman, dammit. "Or so I'm told anyway. Repeatedly."

"Touchy subject?"

Soriya turned away. "The victim?"

"A baker. Good stuff too," Russell said, his hand patting his pocket and the cookie within—his eyes distant once more. Russell Kerr had more on his mind than the case. Something personal.

"Another animal attack?" Soriya asked.

"Big time," Russell said. "Grisly, really. I'm working up a full profile for the detective bureau and Captain Ruiz to work from but…some things are just too strange."

Soriya shook her head. "Not in Portents."

"I'd be happy to share the file with you but I left it at the office and—"

"Yeah," she said. "I'm not dressed for that party."

"No, you are not," Russell said with a smirk. "There is something about this victim and—"

"Eurydice," Soriya said over the rain.

"I'm sorry?"

"Her name was Eurydice."

Russell flinched. "Of course."

"I should…."

He nodded, stepping for the door. "Be sneaky and all that. Right. Listen—"

"Here it comes," Soriya said, head lowering.

"What?"

She turned to greet him, finger flat out in front of her. "I don't need the warning."

"Oh?" Russell threw his hands up. "Oh!" He shook his head profusely. "No. I mean, I would, but I don't see the point. You're going looking for this guy, aren't you?"

"You don't have a problem with that?" she asked.

"I'll be honest with you," he said, rubbing his neck. "I've read some of Detective Loren's case files. They don't do you justice."

"You've read…?"

"On my own time," Russell confessed. "Crazy crap and I don't really get most of it, but the way that man described you? Dead on."

"I feel like I should take a bow."

"I just…." He stopped. "I said I wouldn't but, this might be dangerous."

She sighed. "That's the job. Rain or shine. Murder by man or beast."

Russell fell silent. Soriya waited for the questions to begin. Questions about the creature that may have committed the act within the apartment below. About the city and what really existed beyond what everyone else realized.

Curious or not about the consultant, he wasn't necessary to the task at hand—a task that was slipping away with each moment. She had the journal. She had the faintest of leads on the creature, having seen the transformation in the claw marks littering the windowsill. She didn't need anything more from Russell Kerr.

"I have a lead." His voice thundered over the rain.

She kept walking. "Follow it."

"Hey," he shouted.

She turned back, fist clenched.

"Listen. This isn't…it's not exactly above board. The journal in your hand—the baker had one as well. Same make. I bet there's a message inside."

Soriya lifted the journal slowly, opening to the inside front cover. The message read:

A gift for the survivors.

It was signed with just a letter.

H.

"What does it mean?" she asked.

Russell shrugged. "No idea."

"Great."

"Wait," Russell shouted. "I may not know what it means but I know where they both bought the journal."

"Where?"

"The Maple. A shop called Locales. Know it?"

She smirked. Of course she did.

"They should have a database, something to track down who H is and where we can find him," Russell continued.

"Bring it to Ruiz. He'll—"

"He's not my biggest fan and with what I think we'll find—"

"You think H is the next victim?"

Russell nodded. "I do."

Soriya hesitated, letting the journal fall back to her side. "You want to use H as bait."

"Little bit of bait," Russell answered, cringing at the admission.

"I can see Ruiz's problem with that."

"But not yours?" he asked, a light in his eyes. "Back me up." Soriya turned back to the city. Her city. Her job.

"Three hours," Russell said. "Be there or don't. I'm not letting this guy kill again."

She gripped the journal tighter. Her lead. Her connection to Eurydice, the dead woman below. She deserved justice. And Soriya deserved to close this case—without help. But the murderer was still out there, the only true lead brought to her by the towering shrink behind her.

Slowly she turned, nodding. "I'll be there."

Without another word she stepped over the ledge of the building, falling into the night. The ribbon down her left arm caught the fire escape, acting as a bungee, dropping her silently into the alley of the apartment complex. She tipped an unseen cap to the man, who watched her with wide eyes from the ledge, then raced into the darkness of the city. A long night still ahead for her. And too many questions demanding answers.

Especially about a young man named Russell Kerr.

CHAPTER FOUR

Soriya Greystone sat on the second-floor ledge, looking over the roundabout that surrounded William Rath's memorial statue. The city's founder stood at fifteen feet tall looking out toward Evans Avenue and Heaven's Gate Park. Behind the imposing figure, the Central Precinct, or "Lucky Thirteen" as it was known to its occupants, loomed. Six floors, most of which were made up of higher level offices including the commissioner and his staff. The building, one of the oldest structures within city limits, featured large gargoyles along wide cornices, their gaze stretching in all directions as guardians in the dark.

Like the woman hiding among them.

The window clicked open under her delicate fingers, the locks old and worn. This skill was something she learned over the years sneaking into Loren's office just to mess with him. The small space was dark, perfect for her needs. After their rooftop rendezvous, Soriya needed to know more about Russell Kerr, and with his impending deadline and the life at stake, time was an issue.

Eurydice's journal did little to help. Flowery language, lyrics to songs never to be sung again. They were not the musings of a young woman, something she recognized in herself but never jotted on paper for fear of Mentor's prying. No, the language used, the subjects gleaned in the scant moments Soriya was able to dedicate to the former life of Eurydice Baros, proved that the woman was wise beyond her years.

What it failed to produce was a logical extension of Russell Kerr's lead. The so-called H inscribed on the front cover was the only connection between the two victims thus far. Soriya needed more—more on Russell Kerr. Some way to trust him completely, the connection she had been missing since Loren's departure three months earlier.

All to catch a killer.

The office remained clean, a rarity when it came to the workload heaped upon the members of the Central Precinct, especially those on the night shift under Captain Ruiz's care. There were no mementos, no glimpses into the life of Russell Kerr. No personal story to be gleaned from his trophies. Only a plaque with his name engraved and a single file at the center of the desk.

Aeneas Petrou. The previous victim. A baker, as noted by the consultant. His body matched the young woman in the one-bedroom apartment. There would be no open casket for either. The furniture in the room followed suit as well. The killer was welcomed into the home, at least on some level.

There was more, however, than in Eurydice's apartment. The killer focused its anger, all its violence, on the young woman herself. With Aeneas, something else ended up destroyed.

His kitchen. Cabinets. Dishes. Appliances.

All shredded and upturned. Dented and clawed.

Not from the struggle. Aeneas was found in a hallway, apparently fleeing from his attacker without success. This was personal, just like the strike against the woman's vocal cords. This meant something, to which Soriya had yet to understand.

Nor did she have the time. The door to the office cracked open, a lean figure against the glass. Soriya ducked out the window, standing precariously on the thick ledge beside one of the gargoyles, its tongue threatening to lick her face. She tucked close, kneeling low to avoid any eyes from the street below. The figure at the door continued into the room, clicking the light.

"Anyone get a preliminary yet?" Captain Alejo Ruiz screamed.

Garbles greeted the question, lost to the dripping rain outside.

Ruiz stepped deeper into the office, shaking his head. "I don't need excuses, Pratchett. I need the report."

"I think Ronne is..." John Pratchett muttered in the doorway. Ruiz spun around, hand tight to the door.

"Then tell her to move her damn ass!"

The door slammed shut, leaving Ruiz in the empty office. Soriya crouched lower, away from view, but she could see inside. Ruiz looked tired. True, the man pushing the half-century mark always appeared worn to some degree—in his eyes, in the way his sleeves were rolled up and his stained tie lay over his chest. Now it was more. His stance, his slouch, his every step spoke volumes to the exhaustion creeping into his bones.

Part of her thought of jumping back into the office. Getting her questions answered about Russell Kerr. Maybe even ask about Ruiz, his family, something to make their transition from Loren easier. Ruiz, however, distrusted her more than anyone, since most knew nothing about her role in the city. Although Ruiz's eyes were open, he chose to keep them shut tight, hating her and the world she represented. More than ever since her world had swallowed up Loren in the end.

So Soriya waited.

Ruiz paused at the desk. "Where is this guy? Two months and what the hell has he done? Glorified paper pusher."

He snatched the file from the center of the desk and flipped through it. A knock at the door startled him.

"Captain?" Pratchett asked through the glass, his hand wavering near the knob.

"What?" Ruiz shouted. He stopped, took a deep breath, and leaned hard against the desk. "What is it, Pratchett?"

The door creaked open slightly and the lanky figure peeked around the frame. "Your wife."

"Of course it is."

"I could—"

Ruiz stopped him with a wave. "Put it through here."

Pratchett nodded and departed. The phone rang moments later, Ruiz running his hand through his salt and pepper hair. His wristwatch caught his attention and his bloodshot eyes reddened further. "Of course that's the time too."

Ruiz sat down at Russell Kerr's desk and lifted the receiver, slowly placing it to his ear.

"Michelle, before you start—"

Soriya tried not to listen from outside the window, hearing everything she needed about Russell Kerr. Still, she remained, watching the man's shadow fall further with each word spoken as well as those left unsaid.

"I do know," he muttered. "I do. There was…"

Ruiz paused, which didn't surprise Soriya. He always paused when it came to his family. The line he had placed between them.

Knowing the true city and trying to keep it from them. To save them from the darkness that surrounded Portents.

"Work," he finished. "Yeah. Like always. I'll be home soon." His head lowered, the lie hanging between them. "I said I will. I...."

He pulled the phone away, a dial tone on the other end. The receiver clanged loudly into place on the desk.

"...Love you."

Ruiz stood, file in hand. He marched to the door, stopping short to fix his tie and arch his back. He took a deep breath then returned to the noise and chaos of the detective bureau.

"Will someone get me Ronne on the phone? I've got two eviscerated bodies and no patience!"

Soriya dropped from her perch to the street below. Holding tight to the wall of the precinct, Soriya clung to the shadows like a shield, watching the entrance and the man approaching.

Russell Kerr.

His gait staggered then paused at the approach of another. Hady Ronne waddled toward the building. Russell let her pass, eyeing her every step for the door. His teeth gritted, shining in the darkness. Even through the rain, Soriya could hear them grinding, almost snarling at the woman.

A shift in the wind pulled at her, alerting her to soft steps approaching from behind. Her hand shot out to greet her visitor. Slender fingers snatched the pale arm of the person sneaking up on her. She let it drop, not bothering to look.

"You should know better than to sneak up on me," Soriya said, a wide grin on her face. She turned to see a man step out of the shadows behind her, his hair as pale as his skin, his beard close cut along his cheeks. His right leg slowed his step and though a scar ran from his left eye to his ear, she knew he saw more clearly than most.

Mentor reminded her of that fact whenever he could.

"And you should know better than to work with outsiders."

CHAPTER FIVE

"I thought I would find you here."

Soriya had grown accustomed to the tone after so many years together. When Mentor first saved her from a life of obscurity and ridicule at Saint Helena's Orphanage, Soriya believed she found a family. He offered her a new beginning, a new life. In a way, that was true, though Mentor kept the title to be more of a teacher than a parent to her. Their titles gave them strength as well as purpose. More than a name. Names were for normal people.

For Soriya, however, her title brought with it lectures. Lessons drilled into her, even at the age of five. Most children went through it, of course: brush your teeth, comb your hair, go to bed. Where Soriya's education differed was in the job laid at her feet upon turning seventeen.

At becoming the Greystone, the protector of the city of Portents.

Where others learned social skills by playing with their contemporaries, Soriya received lessons on the nuances of the King James Bible and the extended family of the Greek Pantheon. Preparing for the job ahead. The job she wanted more than anything. To please her teacher. To make him proud. A child looking for affection, for that connection she lost at the age of four.

She was still waiting.

"I'm working," Soriya said, her voice sharper than intended. She hated his presence when working of late—the pressure that came with it. Turning back to the front of the precinct, she realized Russell Kerr was already gone. Lost in the shadows of the night, most likely heading to their rendezvous at the Maple. To hunt a killer.

Her job.

"With others again." Mentor reached for her and she pulled back, pacing deeper into the alley. "Soriya…"

"I've heard the lecture before," she snapped. Her fists balled up against her sides.

"Not a lecture," Mentor replied. "A warning."

It meant the same to the woman of twenty-two. They were lessons and edicts handed to a child—pounded into her being. It kept choice out of the mix. It was Mentor's way with no deviation. No alternatives. But Soriya wanted one—she wanted more.

No longer the child dutifully serving her teacher to the best of her ability, Soriya was the Greystone. She had her role and she thrived on it over the last five years, earning the title, yet Mentor saw only her youth. The rashness. The mistakes.

"Loren…." Soriya stopped. Bringing up her former partner, the detective, was always a sore subject with Mentor. Loren helped with many cases over the last four years, before leaving town for a new life in Chicago. He gave her so much during their time together. Friendship. Partnership. New eyes to see the city in a fresh and unique way. Above all, trust.

A trust Mentor had difficulty with when it came to their relationship.

"Loren is gone," Mentor replied. "He left. The work we do, the cause we serve, is not one taken lightly or easily understood by others."

She waved him off. "Outsiders. I get it. I do."

Mentor sighed, pointing to the street. "Who is he?"

"A shrink," Soriya said quietly. "Working for the precinct on these animal attacks."

"Not an animal." Mentor shook his head. "Not completely."

There was no assumption, no doubt behind his words. Just knowledge. For Mentor, everything came down to knowing. Somehow, without having to hear anything about the case, the details at the scene of Eurydice's murder, the state of her body, Mentor knew what was out there. Soriya bit her lower lip, frustrated to no end at how much harder she had to work for the answers.

"I figured as much," Soriya said, unwilling to ask for the answer Mentor held. *Answers came to those who found the right questions. To those who saw the world more clearly.*

"Do you trust him?" Mentor asked.

"I don't know," Soriya replied. She turned to him with soft eyes. "I don't distrust him."

Mentor smirked. "Caution is a sign of wisdom."

"A compliment?"

Mentor turned away. "An appreciation. Do you want my…?"

"I've got it," she said quickly. It was in his face, in the way his hand grazed his right leg, an old injury from an old friend. The exhaustion. The pain. The reason she worked alone. A reason why her teacher spent more time in books, buried deep in their underground domicile, and less on the street actively chasing the monsters in the city. A reason neither wanted to admit to the other. She patted the pouch to her hip containing the Greystone. "Thanks. I can handle it."

Before she slipped into the night for her rendezvous, Mentor stopped her. "Soriya…"

She sighed, realizing the first lecture would not be the last one on the evening. "Outsider lecture was enough, Mentor."

"Your reliance on the stone of late—"

"Saves lives," she finished, her body tense.

"No," Mentor said. "*You* save lives."

His thin, gray eyes caught hers in the dark, holding her there. She understood the lesson. She always understood them on some level. It was in the listening aspect of their relationship where she faltered.

She nodded slowly.

"You know where to find me," Mentor said, dropping his hand away. He moved for the shadows of the alley, letting them slowly envelop his wiry frame.

Soriya looked to the street before them. The bustling traffic dwindled due to the late hour. The young, the brash, surviving in the shadows of Portents. The city thrived around them.

"You should trust them more. It's their city too."

Soriya turned to face the darkness in the alley, knowing Mentor was already gone.

CHAPTER SIX

Commerce under the gleaming black spire of Evans Tower in the heart of the city came in many forms. There was the industrial complex on Burroughs and the warehouse district along the eastern border of Portents. There was also the Cobblestone, an old world market on Allure, offering goods and services in a more traditional sense. Bartering. Camaraderie. Business thrived in the downtown district.

None more so than the Maple.

Stretching the length of three city blocks with suspended walkways bridging the connecting streets, the Maple stood as a hub for the people of Portents. During the day, thousands of shoppers entered the mall's waiting arms for commercial and personal pleasure of all kinds. A gym occupied the interior of an entire block. Cafes ran along the ground level exterior for the casual passerby. Hundreds of shops littered the confines of the space, allowing a thorough distraction for all.

During the day, anyway.

Night told a different story, the same story the people of Portents understood on a subconscious level. The shops closed with the fading sun, the doors locked, and the people were gone until the morning for another round.

The city wasn't safe at night.

Soriya Greystone understood that more than most, sticking to the shadows outside the Maple complex. She found an unlocked platform door, rolling underneath it to the loading zone for the mall's shipments. It took her little time to exit the area through hallways that supported mall operations until finally locating the main employee entrance. No security presented itself, no opposition noted.

Was she in the right place? No, that was the wrong question. Was she doing the right thing? That was closer to addressing the doubts in her mind. The doubts Mentor gave her with each lecture. She didn't know Russell Kerr. There was no reason to place her faith in his tip. Still, she came. Why?

Instead of an answer, the sound of muffled breath, of clicking heels along tile echoed in the hall. Soriya tucked close to the wall, waiting for the approaching target. Her hand slipped to her hip, untying the pouch containing the small stone she carried.

A shadow stepped around the corner, and she instinctively grabbed the figure's arm. She threw the tall shadow against the far wall.

"Hey," Russell cried out, his face scrunched against the wall. "It's me!"

Soriya let the arm drop and stepped back.

Russell nursed his arm. "You're late."

"Not even close," Soriya replied. "Get a watch."

Russell put a finger to his lips then led them down the long hall. Soriya stuck close, letting her new consultant lead. Her right hand remained close to her hip and the weapon attached to it. She felt the ribbons down her left side tighten against her skin.

Outsiders are a risk. Outsiders cannot be trusted.

"It's down here," Russell said, leading her through the back of the mall. Doors ran the length of the right-hand wall, each to a different storefront on the first level of the three-block mall. He paused for a moment, peering into the small window of the nearest door. "I think it's down here, anyway."

Soriya sighed. "How exactly are we getting inside?"

Russell dug into his pocket. When his calloused fingers returned, a key was dangling between them. "Found this."

"You found it?"

"At a security desk," he replied, shrugging. "I'll put it back."

"A rule breaker?"

"When I have to be," Russell said. "Come on."

They took the stairs to the second level, heading quickly through the overpass between blocks. Another hall stretched before them. And more doors.

A security station sat empty in the center of the corridor. Offices split off behind it, the operation's center for this part of the complex.

"Where is security?" Soriya asked.

"Few needed with the amount of surveillance throughout the place. Welcome to the future and all that."

"Probably keeps the psychiatric community flush with paranoid patients," Soriya chided.

"I do all right," Russell smirked, moving for the station. He stopped short of the console, eyes on the ground. "Better than these guys, it seems."

Soriya joined him. Two large men lay on the ground in a crumpled heap. She crouched low, checking for vitals. "Unconscious."

"Looks like we were both late," Russell said. He stepped over the bodies for the console. The monitors were blacked out, the cameras down for the night.

"I wasn't...." Soriya stopped at the sound of footsteps down the hall. "Is that the place?"

Russell nodded. "I'll call for backup."

"Not necessary," Soriya replied with a smirk.

"Soriya," Russell started and she waved him off.

"Right. Shrink."

Russell sighed. "We don't typically like that term."

"You want to argue that point now?"

"Let me call it in," Russell said again.

Soriya shook her head, starting down the hall. "No time."

"Hey," Russell called. "These are vicious killers. Don't be stupid."

She smiled at his concern. "I won't. Also won't risk someone's life playing it safe. I've got this, Kerr."

Russell tossed her the key, then pulled out his cell phone. "I'll be right behind you."

Flying down the hall, Soriya's grin remained undiminished, the trust shown by her new colleague filling her with confidence.

She stepped inside the shop called Locales—small and packed, an antique shop with various odds and ends. The counter sat to the left with a clear view of all traffic in and out of the shop. The walls were crammed with scenic displays of European destinations, the shelves packed with souvenirs from each venue.

Cautiously, Soriya removed the Greystone, clutching it tight to her side. Her steps slowed, matching her breathing. She listened intently, scanning the aisles lining the store, unaware of the door closing behind her until it slammed shut with a resounding echo. She spun around, reaching for the handle.

Locked. She tried the key but the door refused to open.

"Great."

As she turned back to the room, two men waited for her. From out of the shadows littering the space, the lighting above offering little more than a child's night-light would, they lumbered toward her. Big ones, tall and built. It seemed to be a thing with her and men lately.

"Hello boys," she called out.

The pale one to her right grinned. "Finally."

"Some fun," his dark-skinned colleague said.

Soriya watched them closely. "Hey now. That's my line."

"Shouldn't have gotten involved, lady," the pale one continued, cracking his knuckles.

"Nothing personal," his colleague said.

Soriya nodded, fists clenched. "Agreed."

She waited for the attack, anticipating the battle cries and the blood to start flowing. It was a rhythmic dance she yearned for more than she cared to admit. Instead, she watched the two men stand before her, both carrying wide grins.

Then the change started.

Low and guttural cries of pain escaped their lips. Their bodies became mangled, their faces twisted from the handsome killer look to something out of a horror film. Noses turned to snouts, ears enlarging and teeth sharpening into fangs. Hair erupted, long and ragged, dark on one, white as a sheet on the other. Where once two men stood now there were a pair of rabid dogs.

Very large dogs.

"And I thought you were ugly before."

They pounced, and Soriya dove under their assault. A claw seared her left arm but she made no sound, letting her momentum carry her across the room, and then immediately bouncing back to her feet. The ribbons, a gift from Kali, worked quickly to bind the wound before stretching out to greet the dog to her left.

It wrapped quickly around his arm, the searing pain doubled back upon him in the form of heat and flame. The beast yelped in pain, swiping at the ribbon to no effect. It snapped back into place, retracting through the air in a dance before their eyes.

Soriya gave them no quarter, no time for repose, and leapt back into the fray despite the remnants of pain down her left side. She kicked out hard, connecting with the pale-haired mutt to her right. His head snapped back from the impact, and he sailed through a Mediterranean display.

As she attempted to press her assault on the fallen beast, Soriya was greeted by the claws of his companion. She dodged them, sliding back deeper into the room. There were no exits. No way out except through the two men that had managed to trap her in this space.

Why? Who were they? What were they after? Too many questions filled the room, a room that required absolute silence to focus on the dance before her. She gripped the Greystone tightly in her right hand. Nothing would give her greater pleasure than ending the threat but the questions remained.

Mentor would know. Instinctively, without effort. He would see the creatures for what they were.

The beasts snarled and growled at her, two animals without reason. Without cause.

There would be no answers coming.

Soriya slipped under the assault of the dark-haired dog, kicking out at the knee of his companion. The pale dog fell once more in a heap, mowing down shelves of purses. Soriya caught the second's arm between her hands. Using his strength to lift herself up, she drove another kick against his left cheek.

Both struggled to rise. She couldn't let them, sensing the tightness on her left arm, the sweat covering her like a film. They would offer no answers and she would not ask.

Survival won out.

She held the stone before her, finding its coldness soothing. Light surrounded her, the face of the stone shifting, and the energy of the rune forming on its surface taking hold.

ᚦ

Soriya focused every ounce of will into the stone, the Thurisaz casting causing the beasts before her to howl in pain. They thrashed along the ground, feeling the effects of the purging forced upon them by the stone in the grip of the young woman. Hair receded, facial features reformed. Their bodies, gnarled and mashed by the transformation, returned to their human state.

Dazed from the change, both struggled to find their feet. Soriya refused to let that happen. After tucking the stone away, its job completed, she met each of them with a solid right hook. First one and then the other.

Breathing hard, Soriya scanned the room. No potential victims in sight. No clear threat to anyone other than her. There was also no sound of sirens approaching.

No backup called.

These are vicious killers.

It hit her harder than her attackers could. *Killers*. Plural.

He knew.

Russell Kerr, his name suddenly making a sick kind of sense to the adrenaline-soaked Soriya at the sight of the two men at her feet. Even the number of them spoke to her.

He set her up.

CHAPTER SEVEN

Monitors beeped, lines constricting and contracting to the beat of Soriya Greystone's heart. She hated waiting—the sense that she was missing something when it was all laid out before her. The answers she had spent the night gathering. From Eurydice's body to her journal, from Russell Kerr to his two unconscious buddies.

It was all about the man in the bedroom behind her. The final piece handed to her not by a database in a shop but by the lessons pounded into her by Mentor, the stories and history learned, pointing her to the final victim and the killer that had led her along all night.

Russell Kerr.

The sound of the window opening kickstarted her adrenaline. Her heart pounded in her ears, her body tense with anticipation. The sound could have been anything, really. She knew the truth, though. Ten stories up in the penthouse apartment of the Parthenon uptown, the sound of a window opening from outside meant the party was about to start.

It meant the killer had finally arrived.

He dropped without a sound in the large, open living space connected to the bedroom. His eyes were ravenous with excitement, the thrill of the hunt leading him so far in such a short time.

Two months since taking his position with the Portents Police Department. All for this moment. Soriya couldn't help but smile at being the one to dash his dreams.

"I wondered how long it would take you," she said, her words cutting through the darkness of the suite.

Russell Kerr jumped to his feet, the excitement turned to curiosity. "How did you…?"

Soriya cracked her knuckles. "I'm sure you figured your boys were all set with little ol' me downtown so you had the rest of the night for this. No rush. Not with this one. Not with your precious H."

"I don't know…." His words betrayed his stance. He had the words of a psychologist, but the body of a cold-blooded killer.

"You don't know much. About me, anyway." Soriya slipped out of her jacket, placing it gently on the couch behind her. Her arm ached but she ignored it, letting the thin ribbon race down her left side, dancing in the stale air of the penthouse. "You saw me as a threat. And, boy, I sure am one now."

Russell's chest heaved. Sweat trickled down his cheeks. "This wasn't meant to involve you. Or anyone. What he did —"

"Was a lifetime ago. Many of them, in fact. What took you so long?"

"He was hidden, kept safe by shadows. You know nothing of this, Greystone."

Soriya smiled. "Oh. You think I don't? The honey cookies? Eurydice, the woman with the melodic voice? And this guy? How could I not?"

Soriya failed to mention the rest. While waiting in the darkened penthouse, she cracked open Eurydice's journal once more. This time later in the book. The lyrical prose turned to fear. She felt eyes on her, heard the barking of dogs chasing after her in her nightmares.

"Then you understand this is personal. Get out of my way."

"No," Soriya said, slipping the Greystone from the pouch on her hip.

"Don't make me—"

"You'll have to. Go on. Show me."

Russell Kerr hesitated for a moment, her confidence staggering him. Then he heard the coughing of the man in the bedroom, unaware of his unwanted visitors. Russell's eyes flared, the anger and determination in them obvious before the transformation began.

Dark brown hair erupted from open pores. His eyes widened, his nose turning to the snout of the beast. The great dog snarled at her in its rage.

"There you are," Soriya said. "The third head of Cerberus. And damn are you ugly."

"He's mine," Russell growled through enlarging fangs, his control over the beast inside greater than that of his brethren. "For what he has done, his death belongs to me."

"Not tonight."

Russell lunged for her, claws swiping at the air. Soriya danced around, the ribbons of Kali spinning around her like a shield. The Greystone rested tight in her grasp yet she hesitated to use it. Mentor's words refused to abate, the lessons unceasing in her thoughts.

It didn't matter to her in that moment. The heat of the exchange drove her—exhilarated her greater than sex, yet centered her. Her peace of mind dodged the beast's anger—futile attempts to dismember her lost to the thin wind blowing through the apartment from the open window.

Russell remained determined, cutting the air over her. She dropped to her knees, the blow missing by inches. The ribbons down her left side shot out, ensnaring the great dog's limbs and wrapping tight. The smell of burning fur filled her senses and she grinned, listening to the screams of Russell Kerr above her.

Satisfied, her leg shot out, colliding with his knee, driving him toward the balcony. The wounded beast staggered, trying to catch his breath. The ribbons retracted, allowing Soriya the freedom to follow through on her assault, continuing to force him back.

Russell snapped his teeth, hoping for a moment's breath. He was met with another blow, this time by her fist.

The French doors to the balcony shattered from his weight, and wind whipped around her. She jumped toward the flailing beast, catching hold of long strands of fur on his chest to keep the creature from falling.

"It's over!" Soriya shouted over the rain.

Through gritted fangs, Russell spat blood at her. Even in this form, she could see his grin. "You think there are only three? You're wrong. More will come for him."

She pulled him close. "Then I'll be here. Now be a good boy and play dead."

Soriya dropped him on the balcony, letting the rain wash over his wounds. He was defeated. There was no reason to continue.

Russell Kerr failed to see it that way. Seething from his loss, the great guard dog of Hell lunged once more at her, looking for the kill.

The stone lit before he even left the ground. She held the Greystone before her. The rune was already glowing and the wind, once whipping into the penthouse, turned back onto Russell Kerr.

ᚺ

It slammed into his assault, his towering frame suspended in mid-air for a moment, before the second rush of wind struck him like a hurricane. His body soared into the night air, over the edge of the balcony, and down ten stories to the street below.

Soriya peered over the railing, knowing what would be there. Russell Kerr, naked and broken. His final task incomplete.

She turned back to the penthouse. The French doors refused to close properly but she did her best to keep them from slamming against the frame.

Nothing remained from the struggle. The noise of it all. The blood-pumping thrill from it. All that was gone, lost behind the sound of the machines beeping and air struggling to escape the lungs of the man in the bedroom.

Quietly, she opened the door, slipping inside. The man was old, wasted away from lifetimes of struggles. A withered husk, not long for the world. His eyes opened, piercing the dark and seeing her.

H. The man the world once knew as Heracles. Gatekeeper of Olympus and a hated enemy of Cerberus. One of many as the body count of the night indicated. Aeneas and Eurydice taken before they knew of the threat. Before they could act.

Her finger pressed tight to her lips. Soothing. She approached, her hand reaching for his. "You're safe. He won't—"

"Safe. From him." The old man coughed but nothing came up. He steadied, patting lightly upon her cold hand.

"Yes. I took care of him."

"So proud of this." He tried to smile. "I remember the feeling. Pride at my work, my trials—all twelve passed beyond measure. But nothing prepares you for the last. The final trial at the end of things."

His hand slipped away, his eyes closing from the exertion. In the darkness, Soriya Greystone nodded. She understood. He didn't need saving. He certainly didn't need killing.

The world took care of that.

Her steps toward the door were slow, her thoughts heavy from the events of the night, refusing to listen to the sound of the machines falling silent.

CHAPTER EIGHT

Dawn approached and signified the end of a long night for Soriya Greystone. Her limbs ached, blood caked to her ebony skin like a badge of honor. She stood on the rooftop of the Parthenon Luxury Suites, staring out over the city. The rushing sound of the morning traffic. The ebony tower at the center, guiding the citizens of Portents through the streets of the city.

Her city.

Mentor had been right. He always was, in his own terminally curmudgeonly way. His lessons echoed in her thoughts, knowing they would be repeated over the course of the next few days. He would know the truth even if she never mentioned the events of the evening. He always knew.

Outsiders could not be trusted. Russell Kerr proved it to be true. Outsiders were a risk, one that almost ended Soriya's short stint as protector of the city. Most of the time it was due to their inability to understand the truth of the city around them. This time, however, came from her own ignorance to the situation. To the world around her.

Cerberus.

A real threat, one possibly larger than she could handle on her own. But it was hers to handle, and would always be hers. Russell Kerr would not take that away from her.

Nor would he stop her trust of the city, even against Mentor's wishes. She needed the connection. It made her whole. Not only that but the fact that her trust in Kerr, no matter how thin or tenuous it was, gave her the ability to save a life. That initial trust showed her the true face of Kerr and his brethren. The slightest trust ended the threat.

Even Mentor would not deny that. She did her job.

Doubt lingered within her. Loren would have been able to make sense of them, while also congratulating her on a job well done. He would have helped her.

Loren.

Even after three months, everything came back to him. To their relationship. Their partnership. The trust between them. Everything was simpler with him. Even in the darker times.

Dawn approached, the sun fighting behind the cloud cover. Remnants from the previous week's unexpected storm had finally faded. The day brought a new beginning for the city and an end for Soriya. Sleep was in the cards, as were more lectures from Mentor, of course. There was no avoiding them, though she would do her best. But after that, there would be rest.

Soriya inched to the edge of the rooftop, shuffling slowly along the ledge toward the fire escape. Her hip vibrated, the phone opposite the small stone pulsing against her. Curious, she lifted it despite the pain running down her arm.

Vlad. Another outsider. Another trusted friend. His text filled the screen.

It was about a new case.

Four women were missing. All of them connected to a downtown bar called the Night Owls. All mundane police work until the last bit of information passed on the screen.

POSSIBLE GOD INVOLVED. GOT SOME TIME?

Soriya Greystone tucked the phone away. She smiled coyly against the dim light of the dawn. Her pain was gone. The aches subsided. She raced for the edge of the building, soaring out into the sky.

Ready for more fun.

ABOUT THE AUTHOR

Lou Paduano is the author of the Greystone series of novels including *Signs of Portents* and *Tales from Portents*. He lives in Buffalo, New York with his wife and two daughters. Sign up for his e-mail list for free content as well as updates on future releases at www.loupaduano.com.

AVAILABLE NOW

Portents is a city like no other—and one that Detective Greg Loren can't wait to escape. Since his wife's death years earlier, Loren has looked forward to the moment he can leave the city of Portents for good—and never look back.

But fate has another plan for Loren. Called back to duty, Loren finds himself embroiled in a series of murders that has shaken the city. Together with Soriya Greystone, a young woman with unearthly powers, Loren must work quickly to find the otherworldly being that is killing citizens of Portents one at a time. Loren is tasked with deciphering the mysterious signs left at each of the crime scenes…even if it means traveling to worlds not his own to do so.

COMING SEPTEMBER 2017

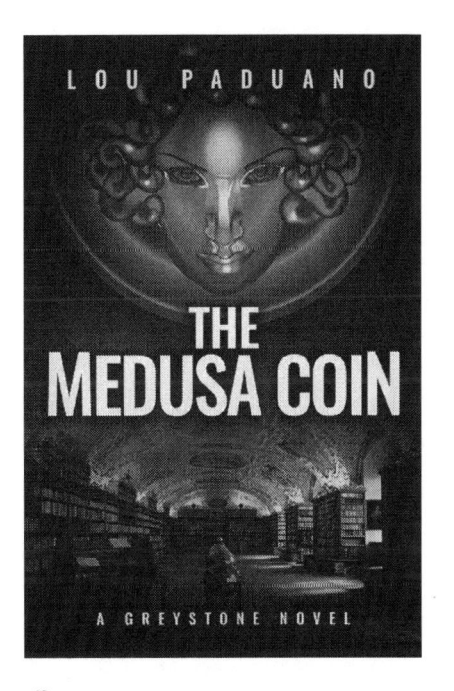

Death has come to Portents.

Three months after the Night of the Lights the city has changed. Detective Greg Loren struggles to find his place in the city, while his partner, Soriya finds her confidence shattered in an instant.

Something is wrong with the Greystone. There isn't time to worry about it, however. A new menace stalks the streets, slaughtering innocents mercilessly. Who is controlling it? Who has found access to the mysterious Medusa Coin? And what does it mean for the city?

Faced with an insurmountable challenge will Loren and Soriya be able to overcome this new threat or will they fall with the rest of Portents?

Made in the USA
Columbia, SC
16 May 2018